Night Noise

Night Noise

by

Lynn Romaine

Enjoy the book —
Lynn Romaine

Turquoise Morning Press
Turquoise Morning, LLC
www.turquoisemorningpress.com

Turquoise Morning, LLC
P.O. Box 43958
Louisville, KY 40253-0958

Night Noise
Copyright © 2011, Lynn Romaine
Trade Paperback ISBN: 9781937389024
Digital ISBN: 9781937389031

Editor, Karen Block
Cover Art Design by Kim Jacobs

Trade Paperback release, July 2011
Digital Release, June 2011

Turquoise Morning Press
www.turquoisemorningpress.com

Dedication

...to the memory of my niece, Emily Wilkes, and my close friend, Randy Martin, both of whom left before I wanted them to leave this life.

And acknowledgements to:

~Joy Andreakis, who has been a faithful friend through the ups and downs of my writing years

~Rudi Romaine, my daughter, who keeps being amazing and living a created life

~Katie Shake, my young housemate, who is a master editor and keeps me on track with my writing

~Debbi Wilkes, my sister, who is my PR/best sales person

Praise for Lynn Romaine's Suspense Novels

Leave No Trace

"...I dare anyone to figure out who-done-it before the author allows it..."

~Long and Short Reviews

"...an excellent whodunit! Lynn Romaine has created an intense plot driven romantic thriller not to be missed. I was left on the edge of my seat."

~Joyfully Reviewed

Long Run Home

"...one of the best mixes of opening qualities you'll find in a novel. It starts as a paragon of suspense, plot tension, and characters who stand out for being fresh and intriguing."

~Long and Short Reviews

Night Noise

Murder can ruin a spring morning. And destroy everything Miller Abel has loved and trusted. Her family murdered, Miller is living in the dead zone and planning revenge, when FBI antiterrorist agent, Robert Matisse, knocks on her door. Grabbing at the opportunity to work with him and unravel a connection between the murders and his ecoterrorism case, she throws herself into the path of a killer and there's no way Matisse can stop her.

With ricin in the Chicago water supply and secrets from her childhood lurking in the night, Miller Abel will stop at nothing to find a killer and get revenge....

Prologue

The stench of blood can ruin a spring morning

Saturday, May 28th

Miller snapped off the ignition and sagged against the seat. Only six in the morning and already exhausted. Blown generators were a bitch.

She pulled down the visor, checked herself in the mirror, and ran grubby fingers through matted hair. Hard hats were bitches, too. She sniffed at her scorched carbon overalls and studied the smudges on her face. Thirty-two years old today. Even with the dirt, she didn't look half bad for a dame who'd spent most of the night on her knees servicing a twelve-hundred-degree blast furnace. With a new condo, a new car, and a Bahamas vacation in her future, life felt sweet.

She glanced over at her parents' house across the street, the property indistinguishable from the next and the next and the next. Any moment now her dad would pop out the front door, cursing as he hunted about in the shrubs for the morning paper.

The sun broke through oak trees casting a leafy-fingered pattern on the pavement. Time to get the celebration rolling.

Grabbing her box of crullers, she scrambled out of the Audi and strode up the front walk. Her kid brother's beat-up El Camino sat at a crazy angle in the driveway. Jacob parked his car like he did everything in life, as if time were too short.

She automatically wiped her work boots on the welcome mat and reached for the screen door, unable to suppress a smile at the squeaky hinges. Some things never changed.

It took only one step inside for the foul smell to reach her.

She took two more lurching steps and stopped. "Mom? Dad? Where is everybody?" The seconds stretched out as taut as a stretched rubber band.

Still clutching the greasy white box under her arm, she pressed a hand over her nose and stumbled toward the back of the house. Her mind revolted against whatever lay beyond.

The smell grew stronger now, an invisible wall of coppery stench that clutched at her throat.

She made it to the kitchen and hesitated. The room looked normal enough, the morning sunlight reflecting off her mother's hanging pots, a cake sitting on the counter ready to be iced. The screen door stood open, letting in the sounds of May. Somewhere down the street a neighbor started his mower.

Thin shafts of light bounced off grotesque russet splotches on the walls and floor.

Blood.

With drunken steps, she lurched around the center island.

Her mother spread out prone on the floor, bare legs twisted under her like a rag doll, her head turned towards the island as if taking a last look at the birthday cake. Less than a foot away lay her father, his right hand flung out, reaching for his wife. A single pool of blood encircled both heads like a halo. The smell of death hung in the air, as thick as black fog.

Miller stumbled back, tangling with a chair in her path. She made it three steps before she saw Jacob. Like the others, he lay sprawled out, the soles of his worn

Nikes exposed. A thin stream of blood ran from his head toward her, stopping inches from her boot.

"Jacob!"

She pressed back a sob with shaking fingers, turned, and ran back down the hallway. Reaching the front door, she struggled with the doorknob before flinging open the door and falling over the threshold onto her knees.

The cry of a wounded animal ripped into her. Then she realized the sound came out of her own mouth.

A film of gray settled about her, a partial eclipse of pain, turning the world a dull gray. She took a blind step, falling into the boxwood shrubs bordering the sidewalk.

Sobbing, she clawed her way out of the tangle of branches. Moving in slow motion, she staggered across the driveway separating the neighbor's house from her family's home and up the front steps. Still clutching her donuts between numb fingers, she pounded on the door.

"Help! Help me!"

The screen opened and Mr. Kowalski stepped out, yanking at his red suspenders. No suit coat. The thought fluttered by. She'd never seen him without one on.

"Miller! What is it?"

She gestured at the other house with wild fingers. "My mother! My dad!" The words came out garbled and she tried again.

"Stay here!"

He limped across the conjoined driveway, through the dew-covered grass, and up the steps. As he disappeared inside the house, she fell to her knees and vomited into his manicured shrubbery. Clawing at the wet dirt, she retched again. She swiped at her mouth with the back of her hand only to gag on the taste of mud.

Slowly, she raised her head and stared about her. It was still Saturday and still sunny.

Chapter One

Revenge and despair keep good company

Friday night, July 8th

Miller hugged her too-thin body, shivering in the ninety-degree room. Even in this mid-July heat, the cold stayed with her. Freezing in July might seem crazy enough, but her bigger worry was how the hell would she deal with minus twenty degree wind chills roaring off Lake Michigan in December.

She leaned out the window, swiping at damp hair sticking to her forehead and watched the bobbing lights in the distance. Maybe a cargo ship was moving up the lake heading for the St. Lawrence, the Atlantic, and on to freedom. Or less appealing, the dancing yellow spots could be the swaying lampposts at the steel mill parking lot, protecting the night shift. A train whistled goodbye in the distance in harmony with a baby crying in the next building. And as always, the lake continued its rhythmic slapping of the rocks. The night noises brought relief to her from the harsh noises of day.

The old house cried out around her at the assault of wind off the lake, protesting each gust with a creak or a groan. Ten straight days of ninety-degree heat left even the leaves on the trees belly-up, begging for water. Tonight's storm brought the first real rain in two weeks yet had no effect on the heat. The apartment pulsated with it, struggling to breathe.

She pulled at the faded T-shirt, in good company with her worn cutoffs dragged off a donation pile at the

Goodwill. Here she stood, a ghost of her former self, glued to the same spot every night like a displaced child. Waiting.

A thick fishy smell saturated the air, a reminder that Lake Michigan lay out there in the dark less than a thousand yards away. Just over the horizon and a world away, shone the lights of Chicago. This was Whiting, Indiana. It might sit with Lake Michigan at its back door, but summer people didn't crowd the streets. This was a steel town struggling to keep the last mill going, where everyone worked hard, especially Miller, an enigma with her engineering job in the middle of mill town good ole boys.

No one would question her right to behave erratically. What no one could predict was that two days after the funerals she'd toss out every physical reminder of her former life. The hundred dollar shoes, the white designer furniture, her new blue Audi, all gone. Even the two thousand dollar a month condo she'd signed a lease for two months before the murders and never inhabited. They were all gone, along with the belief that money protected and preserved happiness. With everyone who mattered dead, she had no fear and nothing to lose. She purposefully shed all the dead weight of her former life, except the high paying engineer job that gave her ready cash. Within a week of the murders, she'd signed a lease on a bare apartment in the worst part of town. And here she stood at her window each night, waiting for some word on the killer.

Most of her friends would shrug their shoulders, explain her erratic behavior away as shock, and predict all that would pass with time. Then three weeks ago her world got worse. She woke up one morning and instead of thinking about getting back her life, a chilling rage replaced the numbness. It crept into her body overnight and settled there like an uninvited dinner guest, destroying the last of her dreams for any future. The hunger for revenge burned deep, growing inside of her, taking over until nothing else mattered except finding a killer and destroying him.

The duplex she lived in, and two others, faced the lake, their backs turned to the rest of Whiting. This gave the residents a clear view of the steel mill where they spent the majority of their days or nights. Sixty years of abuse by the wind left the buildings barely inhabitable until ten years ago when some clever developer saved the whole lot from the wrecking ball with a minimal refurb and some white paint.

Her building was in the middle of the threesome. In her former life, Miller would have ignored the neighborhood. Why would anyone making the kind of money she pulled in as head engineer at the mill give this place a second glance? Now she called it home. So far she'd kept clear of the other tenants, most of them laborers, too exhausted to make trouble, too busy trying to survive.

Rickety wooden stairs led up to her door that opened directly into a plain kitchen, the white walls flanked by enameled cupboards. Faded floral linoleum covered the floor. Two eight-paned windows on either side of the door flooded the kitchen with sunlight and heat. She'd rented the place because of its expansive view of nothing but water and the austereness of the rooms with their startling lack of comfort that fit her mood. The few items in the duplex were someone else's throwaways, perfect companions to someone else's clothes. None of that mattered.

The rain began again, a soft curtain that turned her weed-infested yard mysterious. The narrow dirt path below led from the foot of her steps to the alley where a gate hung ajar, pathetic in its attempt to guard her apartment. She always parked her Honda up against the wire fence separating yard and road. The car was painted gold, an ironic color for such a shabby vehicle. Fifty feet beyond her car the mud flats stretched out to the lake.

While on clear nights the view at sunset took the breath way, this was a waste of prime property, since this was the Region, northwest Indiana rust belt country. No one cared much for views here when putting food on the table came first.

Miller turned to the table, shoving a chair out of her way. A stack of sympathy cards waited for her attention and every night she ignored them. They were from friends who'd approached her at the funeral with carefully composed faces, horrified when their composure failed them.

In turn, she'd kept her control, been gracious, pretending she wasn't the sole survivor of a massacre. As soon as the limo made its last lap around the cemetery drive, she'd fallen back against the plush seat with a final, lingering look at the gravesite and her friends.

Paring down her life had proven easy enough. It took one week to get rid of the new furniture and fancy clothes, keeping only the two-drawer oak chest passed down from her grandmother, the one piece of furniture her dad had loved. It had been easy enough to create a new life. All she had to do was buy a few pieces of used clothing, exchange the Audi for a fifteen-year-old car, and find somewhere basic to live.

Purging friends proved a little harder. She got the knack of it soon enough. For a month she'd turned down the dwindling invitations to eat at their houses, made excuses to avoid them, ignored the ringing phone, until all attempts to comfort her stopped. Only a few friends persisted, impervious to her rejection.

The rain stopped again, leaving the small room feeling as though it was underwater, thick and hushed. Miller pushed the window up further and propped herself on the ledge facing the table. A maroon and gold embossed

'Stages of Grief' card topped the stack, mocking her. Someone had thoughtfully included it in a sympathy card, and she'd tossed it on the table two weeks ago. There it lay.

Denial was the first stage. She'd gotten through that fast enough, maybe even in the first hour. Or it may have taken the entire first day, refusing to think about the blood-soaked bodies. Or was denial the numbness?

Next came *anger*. There was no doubt she'd hit that stage. And stuck there even though it didn't feel exactly like anger. More like restlessness. The anger of a caged lioness, looking for a way out. She definitely had that stage down pat. She could write a small book on sleepless nights, roaming from room to room, staring out into the darkness. Maybe she should make her own list. *Restlessness with a purpose.* She felt as focused as hell, the insomnia from a mind too busy planning and formulating to rest. Not anger, this stage of grief should be called *Deadly Purpose.*

She turned back to her window and watched two small dots of yellow creeping down her alley in the dark. The headlights disappeared, reappeared, then disappeared again. A faint humming grew louder. A car.

She leaned out her window, waiting, ignoring the rain sliding off her slate roof, trickling down her neck, like she ignored most things these days.

The purr of an engine grew louder and the twin lights bounced off the building next door.

The rain came on harder now, soaking through her thin cotton shirt, plastering the material to her skin. She squinted down at the alley where the darkness was solid except for very dim street lamps illuminating either end where dirt alley met street pavement.

The car crept steadily along, a large dark thing that made her shudder.

Then the lights disappeared and she held her breath waiting for them to reappear. She saw nothing in the night.

When a sharp gust of wind slashed rain across her face, she pulled in her head and slammed the window.

It was a Friday night and she expected no one.

She stood without moving, letting out her breath slowly at the uninterrupted sounds of the growing storm.

Then she heard it, a soft crunching on the gravel, growing louder. Someone was coming up the path.

Whoever it was had reached her stairs now, the sound of footsteps growing louder and coming fast up the steps towards her.

Three short raps sounded on the door.

Her heart hammering, she moved to the window and peered out. No one had ever bothered to install a landing light and she could see no one.

Knock, knock, knock. They came louder, more persistent.

She glanced automatically at her backpack hanging by the door. Inside it she kept her revolver. She reached for the pack, the solid metal in her cold fingers reassuring. "Who is it?"

"FBI. I'd like a word with Miller Abel." The low voice sounded reassuring rather than threatening.

"About what?"

"I'll need to speak directly with Miller Abel."

"Slip some ID under the door."

A flash of lightning lit up her kitchen, the crash of thunder that followed shaking the walls. She could hear him curse softly, then shuffling noises, followed by a small brown case inching under her door.

She reached for it. "Agent Robert Matisse, Federal Bureau of Investigation," embossed in gold letters, ran along one side. His badge pressed against the plastic window opposite.

Miller slid the chain off and opened the door. A gust of wind shoved her back and Robert Matisse fell inside.

"Hell."

"Hell is right." She used the weight of her body to force the door shut.

He looked like he might be in his mid forties with gray-streaked, close-cropped hair. An interesting face for an FBI agent, the kind of man one wouldn't hesitate to go up and ask for directions from, if lost. But he also looked tired, as though his kindness was wearing thin tonight.

"Sorry to bother you this late. I've got to get hold of Miller Abel, tonight, if possible. This is the only address I have for him."

"I'm Miller Abel."

The scowl came and went on his blunt features. "The Miller Abel who works at North American Steel?"

"That's me." She jumped as a flash of lighting back-lit him. "You thought I was a man?"

"Sorry. An assumption on my part." He flexed rain-soaked shoulders, as if shrugging off the thought.

"Look, it's late, Agent Matisse. What's so urgent it can't wait until daytime?"

He looked as if he didn't have an answer. Or if he did, he didn't want to give it to her. "I'm sorry about dropping by this late. I just got into town and I need to get a few questions answered tonight."

"All right." She pointed to one of her two chairs. "Sit down."

He eased his raincoat off. "You have somewhere I can you hang this up?

She took the coat from him and hung it on the hook next to her backpack.

The seat he took at her small table faced the window, leaving her the only other one facing him. She took the seat, not speaking, forcing him to take the lead.

He refused to be hurried. Instead his eyes strayed to her desk, a makeshift affair with stacks of newspapers and books huddled beside her computer. Atop the pile in clear view was Capote's "In Cold Blood." He turned his gaze back to her and she saw him shift into cop mode, a little less kind, a little more wary. His starched shirt looked pristine even at this hour, his suit meticulous and out of place in her shabby apartment.

"I'm with the FBI Counter-Terrorist Division out of Chicago. The Hammond police called me in on a possible connection between a case of mine and your father's murder." He didn't flinch at successive flashes of lightning that cast the room in bizarre light, followed by the staccato rattling of her windows. "I need a few things cleared up tonight before I meet with the Hammond Police in the morning."

What the hell? There was no way he'd showed up here with a few questions this late. The FBI kept business hours, not cop schedules. And they for sure didn't need to run around getting their suits ruined in the rain. And for damned sure any self-respecting federal agent would get his facts straight and know she was female. Whatever his agenda might be, he wasn't letting her in on it

For six weeks she'd badgered the local police daily, throwing questions at them and getting no answers. Now they'd pulled in the FBI?

"I don't get it. What kind of connection can an FBI case have to my family? And what could I possibly know that would help?"

She got no answer, just a passive stare. She abruptly stood up. Two could play that game. "Want a beer?"

"No, thanks."

"How about coffee?" The question came from her former life, a hundred years ago.

"I'll take a coffee."

She turned her back on him and fumbled with mugs, conscious of his eyes following her movements. "Cream or sugar?"

"Black's fine."

The rain pounded on the roof as she ground the coffee and heated water. Her thoughts raced over every possible reason for his visit. She refused to speak as she made the coffee and he waited patiently, apparently in no hurry himself.

At last, she filled a mug and passed it over to him with fumbling fingers. His were as steady as a heart surgeon's.

"I'm with the Counter-Terrorist Division out of Chicago. So here's what I can tell you. Yesterday I got a call from the Hammond police. They were investigating a multiple homicide." He stopped and waited as she pulled out a chair, her own coffee cup left on the counter. "They contacted us because of some information they turned up that may or may not be pertinent to the case I'm working on."

"What kind of information?" she asked.

"A hard copy of an email from a local environmental group turned up in your father's files. The email hinted at some irregularities at the water department."

"What irregularities?"

"I can't be more specific. The police notify the FBI automatically when an investigation of their own crosses one of ours. They're searching for a killer. I'm searching for a terrorist." He shrugged. "The two cases probably have nothing to do with each other. I'm here to make sure."

He spoke succinctly, giving her the facts without making them pretty. No one, not even the police, had done that. Not yet. It landed on her like relief, not more unreasonable weight.

"What possible connection could a terrorist plot have to do with my dad?"

"That's what I'm here to find out. Like I said, it may go nowhere. It's my job to look into every lead, however small."

"So what do you want from me?"

"Right now, some answers"

"All right. What are the questions?"

"Do you recall your father mentioning any threats or warnings he'd received relating to work in the past year?"

At last a lead, however unlikely, to the murders. And someone actually dared to tell her. She searched her mind for some answers, anything to keep him talking. "No threats, although I do remember he was upset about the local environmental group barricading the entrance to one of the water treatment plants earlier this year."

"Do you remember when that was?"

"Sometime this past winter. March, maybe. You'd have an easy time tracking the information down, since it made the local papers. Nothing came of it."

His eyes were unwavering. The piercing blue seemed at odds with his calm voice. "Do you remember if he mentioned any names?"

She pulled up a mental picture, unwanted in its familiarity right now, of her dad sitting at his kitchen table sipping coffee, looking at a story in the paper. Life had been so normal–and seemed so permanent. "The group called themselves The Lake Coalition."

"Did he say anything else? Mention any meetings with them?"

She avoided his eyes and weighed his questions. Six weeks of nothing until tonight. Now the FBI had turned up at her door, willing to toss her a lifeline of information, a way out of this waiting game. She couldn't suppress the small sense of hope this man represented, sitting at her kitchen table on this stormy night. "If you'd give me more information about the email, maybe I could map it onto something more he might have said."

"The police found a hard copy of it in a safety deposit box of your dad's."

"A safety deposit box?" She frowned. "That doesn't seem likely. Why would he put something related to his work in a safety deposit box? There'd be no point." She stood up abruptly and retrieved her mug from the counter. She sipped at the coffee. It was cold. "And why the hell did the Hammond police not mention the safety deposit box to me? I'm executor of my dad's estate."

"Someone cleaned out his work desk last week and found a key inside an empty file folder."

"Was there anything else inside the safety deposit box?"

"Sorry. I can't give you that information." He paused, looking as if he was about to add something. He didn't go on.

The storm had moved on now, the silence settling about them in the kitchen, punctuated by the quiet drip-drip of rain off the roof. Miller exhaled softly. Matisse's reluctance didn't surprise her. She tried another tactic. "Can I get you more coffee?"

"No. Thanks. I'm good."

She dumped her cold coffee into the sink and poured herself another cup. It was never too late for caffeine when the alternative was sleep filled with nightmares. She stood at the counter as she drank. "So that's it? All you wanted? To ask me if I knew anything about my dad's email?"

"Yes." His hesitation lasted too long and she caught something else behind his bland expression. Obviously, he wanted something more from her.

"What is it?" she asked.

"You work at North American Steel."

She nodded. "I'm an engineer in production management."

"What do you know about the plant's water use? Its waste disposal capabilities?"

"Basic stuff." She shrugged. "We have an environmental specialist who works directly with those issues. Like all steel manufacturing facilities, we use large amounts of water in production, a lot of it from our recirculation system. As for waste disposal, the plant follows strict EPA regulations for that."

"I see." He stood up, pushed in his chair, and reached for his wet coat. "Thanks for your time."

"That's it? Just thanks? No explanation?"

He opened the door, letting in a thin breeze that whipped up his narrow red tie and sent a slight whiff of some sort of lemony aftershave her way. It smelled traditional, discrete, as balanced and steady as he himself seemed. "Right now, I'm looking for a direction." Again, there was that hesitation. "I'm sorry about your family. I know this must look like one more cop digging around in a very raw wound."

He held out a hand and she took it, surprised at its warmth. Standing this close, she could see tiny laugh lines around his eyes. He looked like a man who didn't let the nature of his job stop him from enjoying life.

He lifted his coat from the hook, slipped his arms into the sleeves, and stepped out on the landing. He turned, the faint light from the kitchen casting his face in shadows. Miller reached out to stop him. "May I ask a favor? If you find out anything else, will you let me know?"

His eyes narrowed and he studied her, as if weighing his options. "I'll do what I can, although I can't promise anything."

"Please. I need some answers." She cringed at the pleading tone of her own voice.

"I'll be in touch." Again he paused, and she caught a softening in his face that turned his cop face human. The connection felt almost physical, a sudden unexpected attraction that felt inexplicable with this stranger in a suit.

She watched him make his way down her stairs and disappear into the murky night.

Chapter Two

Every case is the same, except when it's not

Late Friday night, July 8th

Matisse fumbled in his glove compartment and retrieved a crumpled pack of Camels. He lit one, drew deeply, and stared up at the narrow beacon of light coming from Miller Abel's kitchen. He'd parked his car at an angle, a hundred feet down from her gate. The moon slid out from behind a cloud and turned her dirt road into a backdrop for a gothic romance.

What the hell just happened? He'd bounded up the steps, confident he could turn Miller Abel into his inside source. Then the 'guy' turned out to be a woman, and Matisse found himself feeling as awkward as an adolescent on a first date, struck dumb by her. He could hardly call her good-looking, although she'd clearly been worth a second glance once upon a time. Now she was too thin and too pale, with faint purple circles under her eyes and her disheveled dark hair twisted carelessly about her small head. What was it that stirred him up? She stared at him with the saddest eyes he'd ever seen, pale gray, like the lake during a storm. And there was something else hidden behind those eyes. If he'd been called on to name it, he would say rage, tightly leashed, yet ready to erupt, a feeling he himself struggled with for a year when his mother died unnecessarily.

He grimaced. Instead of feeling pity, he'd gotten a hard on, for a woman whose entire world had tilted on its axis six weeks ago. Matisse didn't even know what he'd said to her, how much he'd told her. He'd been so sure he could use Miller Abel as an inside source. Instead, he's escaped at the first opportunity, feeling like a fool. He couldn't see himself dropping her into a cesspool of danger after what she'd gone through. And he sure as hell didn't want to hang around here late at night with thoughts of nailing her.

He swore silently at the Hammond PD, who hadn't bothered to fax over more than a one-pager to him with only a brief description of their case and where it connected to his own. He should have double-checked before jumping on the name 'Miller.' He'd run at it like a dumb agent, fresh out of Quantico. He'd shown up at her door tonight hoping to get a jump on the case and make up some time since he'd wasted the afternoon tying up the loose ends of his last investigation.

He stared at the glowing end of his cigarette. He'd never developed the taste for tobacco until his infatuation with alcohol skidded to an abrupt halt five years ago after a drunken off-duty cop slammed into his mother's car, killing her instantly. So tobacco became his addiction of choice. Now, after three years of weaning himself down off his pack a day habit, he felt satisfied with his single smoke a day. At least nicotine wouldn't wipe anyone else out around him.

He took another drag. *Back up, Matisse. Get a grip on yourself and get all the facts first.* To start, he'd rolled into Whiting late in the day, too late to meet with Chief Santos, still determined to get ahead of the game and check into the Hammond Police in the morning with an ace-in-the-hole. It seemed like a natural fit since Miller Abel worked in the mill. With an accusation of conspiracy in dumping wastewater directed at both the steel mill and the water department, Abel would have a major stake assisting in the investigation. Factor in the murders of the family and his point man job in the mill, and

Matisse knew he could run this guy. He hadn't even bother to back-check the obvious, depending instead on the limited info in the fax: The director of the Hammond Water Department and his family murdered six weeks ago, one lone survivor. They'd given him a name, occupation, and contact information. Nothing more. No one bothered to add the sex of the survivor, and Matisse had been too eager to get a jump on the case to wait until the meeting with Santos.

The last of the storm rumbled over the rooftop, leaving the moon free to shine. Then the fog rolled in fast off the lake right behind the rain, creeping silently towards his car. He twisted on the ignition and let the engine idle, listening to the low purr of his Lexus. A fancy car for a mid level FBI agent, only because he'd managed to do some big time investing before he'd quit environmental law.

He checked his watch. Ten-thirty. He needed some sleep and dreaded the lonely motel room waiting for him.

So what about Miller Abel? He silently cursed fate, searching his mind for some way to use her. The ethical problem belonged to him alone, not the FBI. They didn't give a damn whom he called in for his investigation as long as the job got done.

What a surprise to find her living in a dingy building next door to a mud flat, an unlikely address for a successful engineer. At least she'd managed to keep her job after the murders, so she must be functioning on some level.

Matisse stabbed his cigarette out in the ashtray. Tonight the token cigarette tasted like shit. He forced his mind back to the question at hand. Could she be up to doing some snooping for him? He tipped back his head, relieving the tension in his shoulders. *Damn!* He didn't want to use her. His instincts said she had to be too wounded to make a good inside source.

What were his options here? The weeks had come and gone since the murders and the police murder case was growing cold, shriveling up any link to his own investigation. Maybe, just maybe, she could keep an ear open and listen for gossip pertaining to water irregularities at the steel mill, then pass along to him whatever came her way.

The fog closed in, settling about his car. Matisse pushed the window power button and the window rose. He left it cracked an inch, pushed the gear stick into first and eased away down the alley, running parking lights. Time to get back to Motel 6 and do some Googling on Miller Abel.

****

The Hammond Police Department made no pretense of decorating, just your basic low budget squad room, until you hit the office of the chief of police. Stepping into the room felt like stepping back in time. The walls were covered with pictures and awards from the past forty years, neat bookcases were stacked with manila files, and wooden furniture that looked reassuringly worn filled the space. The whole room cried 1940s movie set, when the police department ran on sweat and shoe leather, not procedural manuals and computers.

Lou Santos looked to be on the far side of sixty, short, stocky and probably fighting a losing battle with weight. Dressed in a neat blue suit, dark handkerchief peeping out of his lapel pocket, he looked like a man with a wife who loved him. In fact, he looked like a man sure of his place in his community, capable of whatever the job required.

"Chief Santos, I'm Special Agent Matisse with the FBI. Can you give me a few minutes to go over some background information?"

"Glad to meet you, Agent Matisse." The man motioned to a low-slung armchair. "Have a seat."

Matisse eased himself down. He stretched his legs out in front of him, a small relief for his aching back from one more night on a foreign mattress. His late night with his laptop left him feeling as hung over as if he were back on the booze. *Christ.* He wondered if he was already getting too old for the world of crime investigation.

"So what can I do for you?" Santos said.

"I need a little more information on Miller Abel. Some background info on her."

"What kind and for what reason?" Santos' voice rose a notch.

"I stopped by her place last night, hoping to fill in some blanks about her father. Turned out 'he' is a 'she.'"

"You thought Miller was a guy?"

"Yeah, the fax I got was brief. No one mentioned the engineer working at the steel mill was female."

"Humph." Santos gave him an eagle's stare, honing in on Matisse's face. "And what's the fact that she's a woman got to do with your case?"

"Both our cases are growing very cold, very fast. Everything depends on getting something going here. My only hope is to connect the dots in the two cases right away." He weighed his next words. "My nose tells me they are related, and Miller Abel is sitting in the middle of that connection."

Santos rubbed the back of his neck. "What have you got in mind?"

When Matisse didn't answer right away, Santos leaned forward. "I was close to her family, ya know. She's got no one left now except me to protect her."

"I understand. I promise you I did some thinking on this before coming to you. My argument is she's our best link to both cases." Matisse studied the man closer. A cop with a father figure fixation was one more problem to deal with in his investigation.

"Working on the assumption I can establish Miller as my inside source, I want her to keep her eyes and ears open and see what she finds that intersects with my investigation. She's got all the right moves for this. An inside track at work. She knows everyone in town. She's trusted, and most important, she wants to see justice done."

Matisse waited for the man to start squawking like an over-protective father. The guy surprised him by asking a more direct question. "What's your case exactly?"

"The Bureau's been tracking a lot of chatter the past six months about a threat to the Chicago water supply. When I got your request to come take a look-see at what you'd found, my ears perked up. This could be way bigger than a local murder case." Matisse kept his voice light and stuck to the basics of his case. No need to give the guy specifics. "The lead you sent us is our first good one with a water connection."

"You're not seriously thinking Charlie Abel is a suspect, are you?"

"If I thought that, I sure as hell wouldn't be courting Miller Abel for my inside source."

"So you've got a serious terror threat going, and you want me to let you bring Miller into your investigation?"

Matisse straightened up. This man made him feel as awkward as a kid in the principal's office. "I didn't say that, Chief Santos. I don't like the idea of using her, or any woman, that's for damned sure. Last night I was there to get some questions answered and see if she could come up with anything her father might have said. She mentioned some trouble with a local environmental group."

"Yeah. They're always stirring things up with the mill. Nothing new there. I don't see what she can give you that's not public knowledge." The guy wasn't giving an inch.

"Like I said, she's known, has friends, won't stick out like a sore thumb if she gets herself into one of that group's meetings. Nothing dangerous. I just want her to do a little snooping. Is that going to be a problem for you?"

"Damn. She's a nice girl from a nice family, and she's been through hell."

Matisse paused, wanting a couple more inches from the man. "I'll just get her doing a little listening and reporting. It might not be a bad thing for her, give her a focus, a purpose right now."

"Hell, Matisse, I don't know. You seem like a sincere guy, for FBI. Just go easy on her. And for God's sake, don't send her into anything dangerous."

"I don't intend to." He forged ahead, despite the scowl on the man's face. "What can you tell me about her background? Work, friends, interests?"

"She was born in Hammond, grew up here, got a lot of friends. Or used to. She's turned into a loner since the murders." Santos' face twisted up like a bulldog's. "Her career choice has always been a puzzle to most of us. A good looking girl, she had options, so why the heck would she want to spend her days in that grimy mill?" He shrugged. "I'm old fashioned, Matisse. I know I'm out of my depth with the way women are these days. And Charlie always said she loved her work." He shook his head. "He sure loved his girl."

"You and Charlie Abel go way back?"

"'Nam. We flew together–in a Huey. I was part of Charlie's crew."

"Good guy, huh?"

"Yeah, the best. We didn't see each other often the last couple of years. You know how it is. You get busy. Life gets in the way. We usually met up every month or so over poker. He was always bragging on those kids, both of them, especially Miller."

Matisse tossed his Starbuck cup in the trashcan and leaned back, resisting the urge to relax. "She seems to be holding up all right. Except the place where she lives is damned desolate. I saw it's a new address for her. She make the move after the murders?"

"Yeah. She'd moved into a condo not far from her parents' house a couple of months ago. She had her life going good. And then she walked in on that goddamned massacre." He spat out the words with the sort of general rage against life of someone who'd seen it all.

Matisse considered Santos' words. "I'd like to get a look-see at the original of the file you sent me. That possible?"

Santos reached across his desk and picked out three pink butter mints. He popped them into his mouth, leaned down, and yanked open his right bottom drawer. The manila folder he pulled out looked dog-eared. He held it out to Matisse. "If you need to keep it for a while, you'll have to sign a release."

Matisse fanned through the slim file; only two pages, a copy of an email, and a page of hand-written notes. "The notes were verified to be in Charlie Abel's hand-writing?"

Santos shuffled through papers on his desk and Matisse caught a mumbled 'yes,' or something that sounded as close to a 'yes' as he was likely to get.

"What about other leads? The kid? Her brother?" Matisse persisted. He couldn't help feeling sympathy for this guy, his own investigation floundering, forced to call in the Feds.

"Jake? We've done a check of everyone remotely linked to him. Zip." Santos rubbed the back of his neck again. "The kid ran a little wild sometimes, maybe, but basically a good boy. Into motorcycles, you know."

Matisse lifted an eyebrow. "Nothing there?"

"Nope. A lot of people are into motorcycles. A helluva lot of the doctors and professional people hereabouts. No leads."

"You got anything new going right now?"

Santos shook his head slowly. "We've still got a couple of people we're following up on. You'll keep me updated on whatever's happening with Miller?"

"Will do. I'll do my best to make it easy on her."

The man visibly relaxed, his face twisting into the closest thing to a smile Matisse had seen. "Sorry. Don't mean to make your life harder. We're a small town and we stick together." He nabbed a few more butter mints and reached down for something more. He pulled out a small paper-wrapped package, bound with a rubber band. With a quick check out his window at the squad room, he handed it off to Matisse. "This is something else we're working on. Besides the files I gave you, and the list of people who knew the Abels. I don't want this to go anywhere yet. Just check it out and see what you think. If it's what it looks like, it would blow a dark hole in the trust we have around here for our friends."

Matisse reached for the packet and pulled off the rubber band. Inside was a small roll of deposit slips for a bank account. And a picture of a small child, a girl, semi-nude, staring provocatively, almost defiantly at the camera. He looked up at Santos, questioningly.

"Yeah, I know. Shit. I don't know. We got into the account attached to the deposit slips. About 5K had been deposited, then withdrawn a week before Charlie died. That's weird. I suppose I can come up with an explanation, probably purely innocent. But the picture is something else."

"Who is it?" Matisse asked, knowing the answer already.

"It's Miller."

The silence in the room felt like a giant sinkhole had opened up. "What do you make of it?"

This time Santos didn't meet his eyes. "I don't know what the hell to make of it. It looks like pornography to me. There's no way in hell Charlie was molesting his kid. No way. Hell, where the fuck did he get the picture? And why did he have it stuck away in a safety deposit box he'd only had for a few months?"

Santos leaned forward. "Check it out, will you Matisse? And keep it quiet. No word of this to any of my men."

Matisse nodded, rewrapping the small package and shoving it into his jacket. "You have my word." He stood up. "Any problem with my talking to some of your staff now, then heading over and having a chat with the water department people?"

Santos leaned back in his desk chair. "Naw, no problem. And if you've got the time, stop by Milski's next Saturday night and have a beer with me and some of my detectives."

Matisse tried to hide his surprise at the guy suddenly inviting him to play on their team. "Be glad to. I'll be staying here for the next week or so. Where's this pub?"

"On the corner of Michigan and First in Whiting. You can't miss it. Been there for seventy years. Not much else around here managed to stick it out that long."

Matisse reached out and shook the guy's hand. He couldn't help liking this man with the dogface hiding a soft heart. Miller Abel was another story. Once a good-looking, successful woman, she was as prickly and distrustful as anyone with her circumstances. Worse still, beneath that cool reserve, he felt her anger bordering on rage. For some reason that seemed to fuel the unpredictable attraction he felt towards her, setting him up for a combustible situation. How the hell was he going to get her to work with him without the whole thing blowing up in his face?

Chapter Three

The beginning of going nowhere always feels like somewhere

Saturday, July 9th

Heat waves shimmied off the black asphalt, turning the parking lot into an open-air sauna. With the temperature already ninety degrees in downtown Hammond, the inside of Matisse's car felt hot enough to melt his badge. Last night's storm had done nothing except pump humidity into the air. It felt worse here than in Chicago, the lake breezes having little impact on the miles of factories and deserted warehouses with barely a tree in sight.

Hell! Matisse slid gingerly onto the leather seat and thought about his cool apartment in Chicago overlooking the lake. He slipped his ignition card into the slot and pushed the AC up to high. As the engine idled, he dreamed about his red Corvette eating up his savings in a Gold Coast rental garage. He thought about the safety deposit box with the cash and the picture. Then he thought about Miller Abel. What the hell had he gotten himself into?

It took ten minutes to cool the interior enough to touch the steering wheel. He slammed the door, did a quick one-eighty around the parking lot and out into Saturday morning traffic. Santos words dug into him and he weighed them carefully. The man might frown on using Miller Abel, but he hadn't tossed any direct threats Matisse's way. Yet.

Matisse reviewed the woman's history and thought some more about how she'd looked last night, a determined pale face beneath that mess of hair. Her kitchen could only be described as a wasteland, as sterile and white as a morgue, except for the pile of books and newspapers leaning against the far wall. Like that stack, how close to the edge she teetered might be anyone's guess. On the other hand, with her history and credentials, she'd be the perfect inside source. People wouldn't question her right to ask questions about her family's deaths, and more important, a shortage of time to get his investigation going forced his hand.

Matisse glanced over at the folder on the seat, containing a piss-poor email and some scribbled notes from Charlie Abel. And then there were those vague web threats his office had dug up. Ricin poison was something a lot of people remembered from that Japanese subway incident ten years ago. With the possibility of hundreds, even thousands of Chicago residents dying from drinking water laced with ricin, what the hell right did he have to be waffling over how to deal with his own libido rather than jumping on the rare opportunity to use Miller as an inside source.

Matisse cut a left at Main and sped towards the Hammond Water Department. If he got nothing there, he'd make another call on Miller Abel.

The water department occupied two stories in the seediest part of Hammond, next door to an abandoned building that was the former city hall, now moved to a better neighborhood.

Matisse waited for an opening in the unrelenting traffic even on a Saturday. He turned into the angled parking slot facing the front door. On the sidewalk, a man in a plaid beanie who had to be well into his eighties flipped up the kickstand of his motorbike. He balanced a Dunkin Donuts coffee cup in one hand, poetry in slow motion. Matisse smiled to himself. The old guy had more guts than he did, especially in this heat.

Plaid beanie maneuvered his bike into the street, still clutching his coffee, and sped off. Matisse shook his head and watched senior after senior parade down the pavement, no one under fifty. Hammond, Indiana, Miami of the north. What the hell kept a well-educated woman like Miller Abel living here where the average age had to be sixty-five or seventy? If family had kept her around before, what kept her now?

Matisse climbed out of his car into a blast furnace. He loosened his tie to keep from suffocating and made a dash for the entrance. A limp black wreath hung on the thick-paned front door, an announcement of the recent loss of their boss. The standards were different in the North Chicago neighborhood where Matisse grew up. His mother's death had been a private affair, with no announcement of her passing to the world.

He shoved open the heavy glass door. Inside, the air felt cold enough to give him freezer burn. He shifted his shoulders about uncomfortably, worried his damp shirt would turn to ice on his back. A mocha-skinned woman held court at the front desk, barely visible behind a gigantic cloisonné vase sporting purple irises. As stern as a judge holding court, the woman leaned around the flowers. "May I help you?"

"I'd like to speak to the director."

"I'm sorry. He's recently passed." Her face gave nothing away.

"FBI." He flipped out his badge. "I need to see whoever's in charge."

"I'll see if Mr. Winston is busy."

"Fine." Interesting. She obviously still considered Charlie Abel her boss, the other man fighting a battle to get a foothold, even after six weeks.

A man who looked to be mid-forties strode towards Matisse. With his receding hairline and expanding girth, he was heading for middle age fast. He held out a hand to Matisse. "Henry Winston, How can I help you?" His navy sweater looked expensive as did his shoes, not top of the line yet beyond middle management's reach. Matisse knew, having been part of the corporate world of money not that long ago.

Matisse showed his badge. "Robert Matisse, FBI. Sorry to bother you, Mr. Winston. I'd like to ask you a few questions."

The man blinked once. "Follow me."

He led Matisse to an office overflowing with papers covering every free space, including a small walnut desk wedged between back-to-back filing cabinets. "Sorry about the mess. With our recent loss, we've had trouble sorting things out." Winston indicated a chair across from him. "Please. Have a seat."

"This won't take long, Mr. Winston. Just a couple of things I need to clear up."

The man pushed aside loose papers and perched on the edge of the window radiator. "What's this about?" Despite his casual stance, his face looked as tight as an over-wound clock. Henry Winston was expecting Matisse. Someone, maybe Santos, had given the man a heads up.

"I know you've already given a statement to the Hammond Police. The FBI is doing a separate investigation and I need a few more answers."

Winston shrugged. "I'm glad to help in any way I can."

Matisse pulled out his Blackberry, taking his time to survey the office. The disarray looked total and sudden, as though someone had torn apart the place in a desperate search for something. Had Charlie Abel kept his office like this? He texted in a brief note to himself to ask the daughter.

"Can you tell me a little more about the mess you're in here? Anything specific or a sudden change of leadership issue?"

"I don't get the drift of the question. If you told me what you're looking for..."

"Mr. Winston," Matisse tried to keep the impatience out of his voice, "I'm running a separate and perhaps related investigation into the death of Mr. Abel. I'm with the Special Anti-Terrorist Unit of the FBI and I need some answers fast. The water department is my main focus right now. Since Mr. Abel was the director and he's no longer available, I'm relying on you to give me some answers." Matisse kept his gaze fixed on Henry Winston.

"Well, I'll do my best. Charlie, he left this place in a mess. I can't find anything. Some of the water quality testing spreadsheets are out of order, some are even missing, and the last six month EPA inspection data has disappeared. I don't mind telling you I'm having a hell of a time keeping things going right now. That's why I'm in here on a Saturday."

"So this disarray isn't unusual for your former director?"

"Oh, you know," Winston replied slowly, "it's a matter of different styles. I'm more of a 'by the book' person, while Charlie's been around so long, he ran a lot of things from memory. Pre-computer, you might say."

"He didn't use a computer at work?"

"Oh no, he used one. And even before Charlie's death, I'd say we'd been having a lot more problems, what with shifting all our accounts on-line and the usual delays caused by moving into the digital world."

"Any other problems besides the lost files?"

"Like what?"

"I'll be honest with you, Mr. Winston. I'm tracking a threat that came into the water department earlier this year. I need anything you can give me that's come up recently relating to water management that strikes you as unusual. In particular, I need to know about your relationship with North American Steel. In particular, the run-off and waste management data."

"I see." The guy's eyes slid sideways, looking as jumpy as a mountain lion stranded in downtown Chicago. Either the normal fear of a minimally effective man faced with a job no one had trained him to do or something more. Whatever the cause, this man refused to share specifics. "Is this anything to do with that email the police found in Charlie's files?"

"Yes. That's one of the things I'm following up on."

"Well, I can tell you he never mentioned it to me. Like I told the police, I'm as clueless as the next guy. As far as wastewater, all the factories around the lake adhere to strict EPA standards that include monthly testing. I'd have to say you're barking up the wrong tree if you think something illegal is going on with North American."

"So your testing records are lost? As well as the EPA's results for the past six months?"

Winston leaned forward and straightened a folder sitting on his desk. "Yes."

"That seems remarkably coincidental. Do you have a suggestion for why the files disappeared around the same time as the email warning?"

He shook his head. "Sorry. I don't really know how to explain the lost files. As for the email, Charlie followed current trends, you know, environmental things. I'd say his curiosity made him keep that email. I doubt if he thought much more about it. No," he said, "I can't see how anything about that email would be relevant. There are too many checks and balances to have something illegal slip through. As for Charlie's murder, I don't see any connection there either. Charlie's been doing this job for thirty years and nothing much has changed, except better assaying techniques and computerized tracking and reporting methods. And our new software."

"What about Homeland Security regulations? All water departments were required to upgrade and revise back-up security after 9/11. Any problems with that?"

"Nope. Like most cities, we haven't got the bucks to do a really great job with security, so we're doing the best we can. Put in new fences around the water treatment plants, alarms, added an extra guard, stuff like that. Charlie constantly worked on ways to get more funding for improved security," he said. "Is there something else here I should know that you're not telling me? There's been nothing in the news about the murders. How about a hint of what's going on?"

Time to take a left turn and set up a roadblock for the man's curiosity. "It's classified right now, Mr. Winston. As far as the Hammond Water Department goes, we've found nothing implicating anyone to any crime. I'm working on a separate case and simply following up on all leads. Answer a few questions, show me some files, let me talk with your people, and we're done."

"All right. Sorry I'm a bit strung out right now. Murder isn't something you expect to happen to friends. And then with my new responsibilities..." His voice trailed off.

"Did the police take Charlie Abel's computer?"

"Yes. They brought it back last week." He pointed to a bulky outdated looking PC sitting on a table against the wall. "I can tell you, five weeks without it left things in a bigger mess."

"And as far as Homeland Security regulations?"

"You mean problems? As far as I know, we haven't had any difficulties meeting the regulations, other than Charlie complaining about lack of funding."

"So, as far as you know, aside from the one email, the water department, and Charlie Abel in particular, never received any threats or warnings, either directly or indirectly, related to this office?"

Henry Winston shook his head. "You'd do better to look at their son, Jacob. He ran around with a nasty crowd. These days, every other crime in the news relates to some nice family getting itself murdered because of their kid. Usually it's drugs."

"I'll keep that in mind. I would appreciate it if you'd let me have a few minutes with the rest of your staff."

Winston's face twitched. "Glenda is the only one here on weekends. You can talk to her if you don't interrupt her work for too long. The rest of them won't be in until Monday morning."

"How many people work for you?"

"Four in this office and eight more over at the water treatment plant including two part-time guards."

Matisse stood up. "Thank you for your time, Mr. Winston. If you don't mind, I'll question Glenda. Mrs.— ?"

"Bridgewater. Mrs. Bridgewater. Fine. Will you keep me in the loop on this, Agent Matisse?"

"Be glad to, if anything significant turns up. I wouldn't lay awake nights worrying about my questions. They're just standard procedure."

Glenda Bridgewater turned out to be one more dead end. She'd received no suspicious calls and spotted nothing strange in Charlie Abel's manner in the weeks before his murder.

****

Matisse pulled into a drive-thru a little past noon and scanned his phone messages as he waited for his cheeseburger. Five years on the job and he still couldn't get used to fast food. Maybe he should pack a lunch or stop at a deli once in a while.

Four messages: one from his office, one from Lou Santos, one from his father. He'd only turned his phone off for an hour and a half and every goddamned important person in his life had called. He looked at the last number. The caller ID read Anonymous.

A greasy-haired kid appeared at the window, and Matisse yanked off singles and offered them up. "Keep the change." The kid could probably use some kindness. His face was a walking billboard for unhappy teen.

"Here's your order." He tossed the bag at Matisse who snagged it mid air. So much for kindness.

Matisse parked under an overgrown maple. The leaves cast shade the color of a shallow pond in late summer. He left the engine running, fighting a losing battle with temperatures reaching one hundred. He unwrapped his burger and took slow bites, his thoughts moving in tandem with his jaws.

What about those missing records, the lost files? Since the focus of Matisse's investigation dealt with threats to the water system of the entire Chicago area, anyone connected with water had to be a central focus of investigation. Matisse pulled out his notebook and scribbled down a note to do a background check on Winston.

Finishing his burger, he tucked his trash into the sack, slurped up the last of the Coke, and punched the cell phone autodial. "Dad. What's up?"

"Robert. Thanks for calling back so fast. Your sister's coming out, and I was wondering if you have time to go out to dinner with us?"

"Sure, just let me know what night and I'll arrange it. How's she doing?" With a great job, a good marriage, and nice kids, his sister always did fine. Envy seemed futile. He loved her and he'd blown his chances for the full life. So instead, he'd gotten good at ignoring the twinges of loneliness that shot through him from time to time.

"She's staying with me for a couple of nights. Says she needs a change of pace." His dad lived in Evanston, not exactly down on the farm. Something in his dad's voice rang warning bells in Matisse's head. Kim wasn't a woman who needed time off from her life.

"When's she expected?"

"She's got business in the City Monday, then she'll be free Tuesday and Wednesday. How about meeting us Tuesday night? We could go see a show and you can stay over at my place, then head back to your job Wednesday."

"I'll put it in my schedule, Dad. I'm not sure about staying over. Let me see how things develop here."

"Where are you? Not at home, I take it?" His father knew better than to ask too many questions. This time apparently curiosity got the better of him.

"I'm not far, in northwest Indiana. I'll be there Tuesday night for sure. If I can stay over, I will."

"Swell. It'll be like the old days." No such luck. There was no more traveling back to the old days with Matisse's mother dead for five years.

"Okay, Dad. See you Tuesday."

Matisse called back Anonymous.

"Hello?"

"This is Robert Matisse. You were trying to reach me?" Matisse waited.

"Mr. Matisse, this is Miller Abel. I'm sorry to bother you on a Saturday. I have a few questions I'd like to ask you."

"No bother. I'm working. What can I do for you?" Another pause, her hesitation palpable in the silence. "You all right, Ms. Abel?"

"I'm okay. Sorry. I'm trying to frame my question, so I don't sound like I'm losing my mind."

"Take your time."

He heard her exhale.

"I'd like you to give me a straight answer to something."

"If I can.

"You came to see me for more than a few answers, didn't you?"

He sighed and shifted around, pushing aside the sack of trash. "What makes you think that?"

"You had some sort of agenda last night, and I had the feeling you veered away when you discovered Miller Abel was a woman. It had to be more than surprise at my name."

"Yeah. You're right. I wanted something else. I'm still mulling it over."

"What is it?"

He squinted into the sun reflecting off the shiny top of a black sedan moving down the street. It slowed momentarily, then sped up. Matisse tracked it around the next corner and out of sight.

"Agent Matisse?"

He sure as hell didn't know where he wanted to go with his plans just yet and didn't need her pushing him. He preferred women who were polite and subtle. "Listen, Ms. Abel, I'd rather not talk about this on the phone. Is there some place we can meet?"

"There's a bar ten minutes from me. It should be empty this time of day. Will that do?"

"That should work. Give me the name."

"Milski's Pub. It's in downtown Whiting."

"Okay. I have a couple of things to do first. Can you meet me there in an hour?"

"Yes. I'll meet you there at three." She hung up without a goodbye.

He leaned back, aimed the cold air vent at his face and closed his eyes. She'd sounded confident, professional, with no hint of the fragile woman he'd met the night before. Maybe they could work together after all.

Chapter Four

A barroom is as good a place as any to bind us in partnership in the serious work of the world

Saturday afternoon, July 9th

Milski's felt as cold as a tomb with the bodies inside still alive. Miller, her back to the wall, studied the room from the darkest corner. A dead jukebox stood beside her, its red and yellow face hogtied with its own cord, as if someone had hated the last song and resorted to murder.

At the bar, a man in work overalls crouched over his beer. A wizened man in a Cubs cap camped out at a nearby table playing Solitaire. The only other patron, a leather-clad biker, lay draped over the pool table. The stooped, silent bartender ignored them all, busy building a miniature Louvre pyramid from shot glasses at the far end of the counter.

A flash of daylight followed Robert Matisse in the back door. He did a quick one-eighty of the room, and honed in on Miller. He stopped at the bar and exchanged words with the bartender. She watched him hand over some bills in exchange for his drink and stroll towards her.

FBI dress code must not apply on weekends, since today Matisse had shed his suit and tie for khakis and a T-shirt. His clipped dark hair caught the glow of white from the Czech flag flashing in neon behind the bar. Backlit around his head, the light cast him in the role of angel. The rest of the bar crowd fared less well, blue hue turning them all into ghouls.

Miller pulled back the hood of her sweatshirt and watched him walk across the room. At first glance he presented the predictable FBI anonymity. On second glance, maybe not since something in the easy way he wove between tables drew most of the eyes in the room. In her former life, she might even have found him attractive.

"Ms. Abel." Faint light struck the high planes on his cheeks and turned his face hard. Clothes or not, still Mr. FBI.

"Special Agent Matisse."

He pulled out a chair opposite. "Call me Robert. Or Matisse."

"Matisse, as in painter."

Her comment drew a brief smile from him, a sense of humor probably the last thing he'd expected from a woman in her situation.

"Club soda," he said, raising his glass.

"Because you're on duty? Or don't you drink?"

"Gave it up a few years back." He took a small sip and leaned back, looking like any normal bar patron. He suddenly leaned forward. "Tell me something about yourself. What made you decide to become an engineer?" The casual question came out of left field, while his face still said this is business.

She took a drink of her soda. "This is pertinent to your investigation? Or are we doing social chit-chat?"

"Chalk it up to a little curiosity."

He probably was curious, far from blue collar with his uptown subtle looks. He'd probably be a wonder at spouting feminist theory. Yet she couldn't see him dating a woman doing a grimy job in a dead-end industry dominated by men. If answering his curiosity got her inside of his investigation, she'd give it a shot, irrelevant as it seemed to her life today. Or maybe when they gave him her name, they'd given him her condo address by mistake, the one she'd given up for her ghetto by the lake. She studied the huarache dangling from her foot, a Salvation Army special. Six weeks ago she'd have dismissed them as something worn by North Shore Chicago nannies. He must be damned confused.

"You haven't answered my question," he said. "What made you choose engineering as a career?"

"The answer is 'I don't know.' I liked all sorts of girly things growing up, playing with dolls and all that. I could make up some psychobabble about pleasing my dad," she shrugged. "Frankly, it's not worth discussing. I wanted to be an engineer, and I am one."

The air conditioning groaned on overhead and arctic air tossed her napkin to the floor. She shivered and tugged at the zipper of her hoodie. In the past she'd have been happy to show off her body, especially her best feature, great boobs. Although the fifteen pounds she'd lost in the past six weeks shone a spotlight on her ribs.

Someone like her with all that trauma in her recent past, he must distrust her mental state. It was easy to see the evidence of her pathetic life these days. If she had any hope of getting information from him, she needed to convince him she was stable.

He waited, apparently serious about the question of job choice.

"It's a little sexist, you know," she countered, "asking that."

"Sorry, must be showing my age."

"You'd have to be past sixty to have escaped the women's movement," she snorted. "Either that or you grew up in the South."

"I grew up in Elgin, Illinois."

"How old are you, Matisse? Late thirties?"

"You're being polite. I'm forty-five, look my age, and feel it today."

"Why's that?"

His grinned. "Cheap motel, lumpy bed. A few years ago you could have put me down in a swamp or the desert, and I'd be fine. Now I'm bitching about a mattress." He leaned forward. "I sound like a senior citizen."

"Who are you trying to convince?"

"You've got a sharp tongue, Miller Abel. Somehow it's not what I expected, especially after last night."

"I have bad nights sometimes. Don't you?"

"Sure. And no one's going to argue you don't have a right to them." He shifted back, balancing on two chair legs. "Off night? You seemed to me like a nice person drowning in a nightmare, struggling to resurface."

"You missed that nice person by two months. I've lost the being-nice bug, or even civil most days. Does that bother you?"

"No. It helps. I'm starting to get a sense you can take care of yourself."

Miller leaned forward and placed both hands on the table, tired of small talk. "Good, then we're on the same page. Because I'm here to discuss your case and how I can help you."

"All right. Let's get down to business."

"So we are going to do business?"

"Maybe."

Her eyes strayed to the leather-clad biker with the pool stick strutting towards the bar. He leaned over to speak to the bartender and Matisse followed her gaze. "Know that guy?"

"Nope. Why?"

"Just wondering. He's been watching you. Or me. He's got his ear cocked our way."

She glanced over at the pool table. "I never saw him before. Maybe he's bored. "

"Maybe. I'm a cop, remember, and distrust is my primary operating mode." He stood up. "Want something from the bar?"

"No, I'm good."

Matisse crossed the red and white twilight zone into the blue neon of the bar. He stopped short of leather guy, who shot Matisse a nervous glance and headed back to his game. The kid couldn't be more than twenty-five, small, with the hungry look of a young wolf. Canis lupus in biker gear, his restless movements stirring up danger as he went.

Matisse ordered another club soda and came back. He shoved his chair closer to hers. "Okay, let's have it. What do you want to know?"

"Did you give me the real reason for stopping by my place last night?"

"What do you mean?"

"The few questions you asked me seemed a little simple, stopping by so late at night. I had a sense you would have said something else, if I'd turned out to be a man."

"Got me," he said. "You're right. I did have something more in mind. I'm working on a case that involves a threat to the Chicago water supply. And since your father was the director of the Hammond water department that connects directly to the Chicago system—and since someone murdered him, it's possible there's a connection. When you consider the email to your father warning about a water issue, I can't ignore the possibility, however small, the cases are connected. That's basically what brought me to Hammond."

"You really believe there's a link?"

"Maybe. Chief Santos made the decision to call us in. Responding more or less routine."

"I don't think he's got any leads to my family's murderer." Miller leaned forward, watching Matisse's face with the shadows dancing off it.

"I'm here to make sure there IS no link. It's a long shot. I get paid to ignore the odds and follow up on every lead. When I saw you worked at North American Steel, it seemed like a natural fit to ask you a few questions."

"And?"

"And see if you could do a little inside work for me. Keep your ears open at your job, maybe even go to a couple of the environmental group's meetings." He drank his soda, taking his time. "Since you turned out to be a woman, I nixed the idea."

"I don't see why that matters."

He frowned, suddenly looking closer to her father's age than hers. "I'm about ninety-nine point five percent sure it won't be dangerous. It's the last point five percent that worries me since nothing's guaranteed in life. Asking a man to be an inside source for me is one thing. Asking a woman, especially one who's been through what you've been through, is too much. So I decided not to make an offer."

"So you're reconsidering?"

"Yeah." He drew the word out. "I'm reconsidering. Chief Santos is against your working with me, by the way."

"Of course he is. He's known me all my life and he's protective, more so now."

"If he gets a whiff of any threat, he'll come after me, you know?"

"How will you know?"

"What?"

The question burned in her belly, a low simmer ready to erupt into flames. "How will you know if it's dangerous?"

"If something happens to you. Let's just say I'm not going to let you get anywhere close to danger. If I use you, you follow my rules and you're only going to be eyes and ears; no action."

"So you will let me work for you?" The snap of breaking billiard balls punctuated her words, turning her stomach to a knot. Her brain screamed '*Say yes!*' She suppressed it. There was no way she'd plead.

"Last night I would have said absolutely no way. Today you're different." He tipped back the last of his club soda and slid the glass across the table. "Which one are you, Miller? The pale shadow I met last night? Or the strong woman opposite me today? Tell me it's the latter and we've got a deal. I don't want to be responsible for you falling apart."

A man with a conscience behind today's cop face. She felt a moment of interest, almost an attraction for him. It made her take a second glance across at him. He hadn't shaved today, probably not style as much as convenience on a Saturday. Still, it suited him.

"If I haven't gone crazy sitting in my empty apartment doing nothing, it's not going to happen now. At least I'll have something to focus on to keep busy." She fiddled with the empty coke can, then pushed it way. She felt way too eager for this job. "So, what will it be? Will you let me do this?"

"Hell, I don't know." He fixed her with an eagle's stare. "You're not going to take no for an answer, are you?"

"No." She waited.

"Okay. Let's give it a go for a few days and see how it plays. Like I said, all I need is for you to be my eyes and ears in places where I can't go. Just look, listen, ask some simple questions and report back."

She leaned closer and almost touched his arm before drawing back. He was still a stranger, an empathetic one maybe, certainly not her friend. "Thanks, Matisse. I appreciate the chance to do this."

He didn't respond, probably wishing himself back in Chicago, or anywhere other than sitting in a chintzy bar in the Region discussing his case with an unstable female.

"Let me make this clear, Miller. I'm not looking for a partner here, just someone who's already inside to keep watch for a week or two and update me."

"I understand."

He pulled out his Blackberry, discussion over. "First, I need everything you can get on North American Steel's runoff system. And maybe do some talking with your father's people at the water department, set up some kind of meeting under a pretense of some sort?"

"I haven't bothered to get over and pick up the contents of my father's desk. I could probably arrange something about that."

"And the Lake Coalition group? Can you get yourself into one of their meetings? Get friendly with a couple of their members?"

"You want me to join the group?"

"You don't have to join. Just go to a few meetings. If you already know someone who's a member, that would make it easier. I did some checking of membership and found quite a few employees of North American Steel listed."

"So I've heard. Odd bedfellows, you're thinking? The steel business is looking to go green, like most corporations are right now, and American has been doing a lot of hiring of middle management with environmental degrees. People in business can care about the earth too."

"So do you have any friends already belonging to the Lake Coalition?"

"I'll check around." She didn't mention she'd dropped all her friends six weeks ago, and they'd think something bizarre if she suddenly checked back in on them. "What else, Matisse?"

"That's enough for the next couple of days. Do some fact finding and get me access to the water data. And more general information about the Lake Group. There'll be no heroics involved," he warned, "and everything stops at the first sign of danger."

"All right. How do I get hold of you?"

"My cell phone. We can set up a regular meeting every few nights. Some place private. No need to make it public after this."

"My place?"

"That will work. I'll stash my car someplace and hoof it to your apartment."

"There's an alley behind Lake Street, two blocks over. You can park there."

"I'll find it. Let's make that eleven. Will your neighbors get suspicious with a man showing up that late?"

"I don't know my neighbors. And a strange man showing up at my door might be mildly interesting to them. In fact, it'd probably seem more normal than my life looks these days, if they bothered to consider it. Actually, I doubt whether they give a damn what I do."

"All right. Give me a day to get a plan and a checklist for you." He stood up. "I'm going to hit the john. Be right back. Don't leave yet. I want your schedule, and we can work out the days we'll be in contact."

Matisse had barely slammed the men's room door when the pool hall cowboy sauntered over to her table. He wore the kind of steel rimmed shades favored by cops. "You're Jacob Abel's sister, aren't you? Miller? I'm Joe Sedlack. People call me Sed." He placed a surprisingly well-kept hand on the table. "I knew Jacob. Met him at the Lake Coalition meetings."

"Jacob was part of the Lake Coalition?"

"Probably like me, not exactly a member although I remember seeing him at a couple of meetings." He stopped. "I was really sorry to hear about Jacob. He was a good kid." He slipped off his shades. Up close, his features were finely chiseled with a high brow and unexpectedly piercing eyes, his face revealing more uncertainty than he'd want anyone to see.

"Yes." What else was there to say? She didn't know this guy, didn't want to share intimacies with him. She especially didn't want to talk about her brother with a stranger.

"What's up, buddy?" Matisse grunted from behind Sedlack.

The kid took a step back and Miller almost felt sorry for him. Six inches taller, forty pounds heavier, and twenty years older, Matisse had the advantage.

She fingered the empty pop can. "Matisse, this is Joe Sedlack. He knew my brother. Joe, this is Robert Matisse."

Matisse gave him no more than a brief nod and slid into his chair. "Sorry to interrupt. We're in the middle of something here."

"Catch you later, Miller." Sedlack gave Matisse another quick glance, replaced his shades and left.

"You know that guy well?"

"Never met him before."

"It's unfortunate he saw us together."

"Why? Every regular guy in Whiting can see us sitting here."

"They don't know me from Adam. I'm just some guy hitting on a much younger woman." He gave her an ironic looking grin. "But the fewer people who catch on to why I'm here in town or that you have any connection to the FBI, the better."

"Even without your badge flashing, Matisse, you sort of broadcast law enforcement. If you'd been less cool, he'd probably have assumed you were a friend of my dad's."

This time he did grin. *Hell.* She'd clearly insulted him by putting him in the same age group with her dad's friends. "You may have it all wrong about him, Matisse. Did you consider *he* could have been hitting on me?"

He didn't answer, then gave her a brief nod and reached for his Blackberry. "What did he say his relationship was to your brother?"

She repeated what Sedlack had said, her stomach twisting. Any mention of Jacob always felt too raw.

Matisse stopped texting and glanced up. "Your brother belonged to that group, too?"

"According to Joe Sedlack, they met there. Jacob never mentioned him it to me."

Matisse went back to texting, glancing up as he did so. "You have any idea what he does for a living?"

"No. He didn't say."

"Let me know if he turns up again in your circle. How does Monday night sound for our first meeting? Too soon?"

"No, that's fine. I'll be working Monday, so that'll give me a starting point.

"If you get nothing, don't worry. I'm not expecting much. Just whatever you hear or see, anything you can think of. Names, strange coincidences, anything at all that seems related to water use. I'll come up with more specifics by Monday night. If something urgent turns up, email me right away." Matisse stood up. "Anything else you need from me?"

She fought back an irrational urge to grab hold of his shirtsleeve and beg him to stay. Despite all the bravado she put out to the world, she felt afraid. Irrationally, with him she felt safe.

He, on the other hand, clearly had nothing else to give her.

"No." She stood up. "I'm good."

"I'll give you a couple of minutes lead time out. Monday night. Eleven o'clock."

Miller tossed her can in the recycling bin at the door and stepped outside, blinking in the midday sun. She resisted an urge to take a quick check over her shoulder at Matisse. Instead, she hurried to her car.

Heat rose off the black asphalt pavement around her car, suffocating her. She cautiously slid across the seat, the plastic hot enough to sear a steak. She left the door ajar and eased her hoodie over her head, flinging it down on the passenger seat.

Matisse. She felt a flash of something too much like yearning. Not the sharp zing of sexual desire one would have felt around an attractive male. This was a more basic need to be comforted and protected. She made a face. Too much like paternal love, it felt humiliating. She didn't want to make Matisse into her substitute father, and he sure as hell didn't want to be one. For the first time in weeks the hollow place in her chest softened and shrank a bit.

She slammed the door of her Honda, shutting out the image of Matisse along with that feeling, ignoring the sense of it crouching there, a lion of need ready to pounce at the next urge she felt.

Going slow, she paused at the exit to let a red-haired kid on a bike whiz pass on the sidewalk. He reminded her of Jacob. She stomped on the accelerator and turned east towards home. She caught sight of a gray pick-up in back of her, similar to one she'd spotted twice before that day. She shrugged and drove on.

Chapter Five

Good friends and nuns are sometimes useful

Saturday evening late, July 9th

Miller bounced along the alley. The tires of her Honda seemed to hit every rut in the road. After leaving Matisse, she'd killed the rest of the afternoon trying to ignore replays of their conversation in her head. She'd cruised the grocery store first, picking up useless items, and onto the library as she nursed a good case of despair. At the Oriental Star things began to look up. She captured a corner table and entertained herself spying on families eating from a Chinese 'lazy Susan.' She killed another hour over cold tea until the owner's son flipped the Open sign and gave her a polite nod towards the door.

A second night of fog made her feel as jumpy as heat lightning. The dense fog had already subdued the day's heat and pulled night in fast behind it. She snatched her grocery bag, the white cartons of leftovers, and pushed open the car door.

The dew, stinking of fish and mud, soaked through her huaraches before she reached the landing. She fumbled for the door key dangling from the Carabineer clip. This one reminder of Jacob was all she could allow herself. She'd stashed the rest of him—his clothes, his IPod with its hip-hop music, his worn running shoes retaining the shape of his feet—in brown Goodwill bags and dropped them in a donation kiosk.

Where the hell was her apartment key? She blindly worked her way through each key. Not there. She methodically made another try. No door key. *How the hell could that happen?* She kept it separate from her car key, tucked away in her outer purse pocket for easy reach at night. She went over her movements at the bar. Had she dropped the key there? She thought about Sedlack and shivered. She'd stashed her purse under the table on the floor. Had he somehow managed to find it and get the key out?

Footsteps echoed from below and Miller shoved aside the dark thought.

"Hello! Need some help up there?" The volume of the woman's voice could compete with a bleacher full of fans at the Indy 500.

"I'm locked out."

"Can I help? I'm your downstairs neighbor just moving in. I'm an expert at breaking into places, since I have a habit of locking myself out. Come on down, while I search boxes for my flashlight."

Miller shifted food cartons about, squeezing the Dim Sum against her chest. The voice sounded a hundred miles below her at the bottom of the steps. She lurched her way down, taking the last step off into an abyss suddenly lit up by a stream of light from an open doorway under the stairs.

"I'm Mary Catherine Doherty. Come inside while I look."

Miller followed her into a room painted fuchsia and daffodil, a kaleidoscope as surreal as the bleachers at Wrigley Field in mid August. The walls were still bare and everywhere pictures leaned against crates and furniture. Much of the artwork was movie posters.

In sharp contrast to this fun house, a four-legged mahogany table dominated the middle of the room. Atop it was a radio with black knobs and a gold dial, looking straight out of a 1930s B movie. The similarity of this place to Miller's began and ended with the floor plan.

"Here, hand me those things and take a load off."

Miller stared up into a face as clear and unlined as a baby's. Black brows crawled across her broad forehead like a parade of caterpillars. Her raven hair hung straight, the bangs fastened back with a glittery red barrette. If the coiffure belonged to an early Bette Davis, the rest of her, down to the red shoes, cried out Judy Garland. She extended a hand. "Call me Sparky."

Miller felt a grin forming at the woman, quicksilver fast, and ready to leave everyone else in the dust. "I'm Miller Abel." She reached out and shook thin fingers that sent an electric charge up her arm.

Sparky, crouching in front of a box, glanced up. "Miller Abel? That's your name? I'd have thought you were a man with that name."

"That's the second time in two days my name's been mistaken."

"Sorry," Sparky said. She dug into the box, flashing Miller with the velvet soles of the red slippers. "Now where did I put that flashlight?" Miller glanced around the room. Anything could get lost in this Technicolor world. "Here it is," Sparky said and pulled out a work-man-sized flashlight, a two-handed job. "Like I said, we'll have to break in."

"Break in?"

"Yeah, don't worry. It's a snap. I leave the keys in-side lots. Let's get to it."

Miller gathered up her groceries and trailed out the door behind the woman, feeling like a lost child. Five steps in the fog and darkness swallowed her up, leaving only the squeak-squeak of shoes on wet wood.

Juggling the packages, Miller clutched at the drip-ping railing and climbed. She stopped, her heart accelerating at the unfamiliar sight of two faint yellow lights in the fog accompanied by the low purr of a motor. A repeat of last night. The car moved slowly, as menacing as a jaguar waiting to pounce.

Sparky stood on the landing above. "Expecting someone?"

"No."

"Hmm. Maybe they're lost. Got an entry light up here?"

"No outside light." What good were lights when broad daylight hadn't saved her family? "You still have a plan for getting in?"

"Through the window. Want to join me? Downstairs it's simple. Eighteen feet up it will be a little more challenging."

Miller joined Sparky on the landing, glancing down. It must be well over twenty feet to the ground from here. Thank God she'd left the window open, since the woman seemed determined to make a circus entry.

"It looks about two feet from the landing to the window ledge. Here. Grab hold of the flashlight and point it out that way so I can see." Sparky handed her the light.

"You sure you want to do this? There's gotta be another way. Call the super, maybe?"

"I'll be fine. You hold onto my feet. Can you do that? I'll lean out and grab the ledge." Sparky pulled herself up onto the 2x4 railing and grabbed the roof easement. Miller caught hold of the woman's thin ankles, the narrow slippers curling around the railing. "Okay. I've got you."

Without hesitating, Sparky leaned out and seized the window frame with both hands. She swung a spidery leg across the gap, planted the other foot firmly on the wood ledge and hung there. Then suddenly she folded herself up, shoved the window up and disappeared inside. The entire scene played out without a word.

Seconds later, the kitchen flooded with light and she flung open the back door. "Come on in!" Sparky motioned.

"That was some performance," Miller said. "Are you circus trained or self-taught?"

"Just showing off. Almost everything I've done for twenty years has been on my knees. You know, as in praying. So I'm ready for some excitement these days."

Miller closed the door behind her. "Have a sit, Sparky, and I'll make us some coffee."

"I'd love some tea, if you have it."

"Only regular tea. Nothing fancy."

"That's fine. I'm used to nothing fancy." Sparky dropped down on a chair.

"You've spent twenty years kneeling?" Miller asked, pulling out her plain white mugs.

"Yeah. Not what you think," she said.

Miller wondered vaguely what one might think.

"I was a nun, retired now. The Sisters of St. Elizabeth."

Miller studied the woman. She looked less like a nun than anyone Miller had ever met. "I didn't know nuns were allowed to retire."

"Well, sort of retired. I started out in an order with a vow of silence, my first mistake. I should have known I could never be quiet for long." She grinned.

"You were silent?"

"Heck no!" She snorted. "I lasted about six months there. Then they moved me from Indianapolis up to Chicago, and I spent a lot of time working at their resale shop," she said. "Handy for me although not a good fit for someone who's taken a vow of poverty. Then I went from one job to another, including teaching, which I happened to be pretty darned good at. Five months ago the convent and I mutually parted ways." She cradled her mug. "Hey, your apartment is an exact duplicate of mine. It looks like you've just moved in, too. If you need an interior designer, I'm your gal."

The muscles of Miller's face twitched. Sparky had a way about her that brought on the urge to share, even secrets. "I moved in five weeks ago. I'm not much for decorating these days."

"Well, when you're ready, let me know. I'll be happy to go shopping with you. I've got a friend who's up on all the resale shops in the Region. Jessica Bean. Know her?"

"Sorry, no."

"I just met her. She lives in the next building, up-stairs. I'll have you both over one day." Sparky stood up and made a quick tour of the room, glanced out the window, and returned to her seat. "So, you have any family in the area?"

The left turn cut a gash across Miller's mind, leaving the last happy thought dangling. "No. I lost my family. Six weeks ago."

Sparky merely nodded at the explanation.

"What are you doing now, since leaving the Order?" Miller asked.

"Moving on to what's next. Nothing. Everything." Sparky raised her mug and took a taste. "I'm taking some time to see where life's pointing me, enjoying having no bells chiming and not a lot of rules dogging my heels. Just being."

"Well, thank you for helping me get inside."

"My pleasure. I enjoy a good challenge. And a new friend. Interrupts my struggling with unpacking." The woman's clear blue eyes never left Miller's face. "Any idea where your key galloped off to? You don't want it floating around the neighborhood. You could come home late one night to a robber."

"I don't know. Didn't notice it missing until I pulled out my keys tonight." Miller paused. "Where are you from?"

"The North Shore." Sparky peered at her over the mug rim. "Where'd you go today? Any possibility you dropped the key somewhere?"

"Ran errands. The library. Things like that." Three hours doing Internet searches on Robert Matisse, the Lake Coalition, and environmental terrorism in general. "Milski's." she added.

"I've been there, One of my favorite bars. Better start there. That's the easiest. Anywhere else?"

"No." Where else would someone with no life go?

Sparky went over to the sink and washed out her mug. "I've gotta get going. I'll give you my cell number. Don't hesitate to call me, if you need something."

Miller crushed the paper in her hand and watched Sparky disappear down the steps into the mist. What could she possibly need from this woman?

She checked the time. Just after nine.

Miller pulled out her phone. One message. She checked it. Nothing, a dead line. She didn't get many messages these days, except work calls, and those were usually emergencies when a piece of machinery broke down. The people who used to be her friends eventually gave up calling when she never called them back. Except Lexie, who unrelentingly left a message once a week, inviting her over for dinner or out to a bar.

Where was that damned apartment key? Panic hovered just below the surface as she reached for the yellow pages. She found Milski's number and punched it in.

"Milski's."

"I was in earlier. I've lost a key and was hoping someone found it."

"Hold on. I'll check." Bar music blared in the background accompanied by the clanging of billiard balls. She heard an indistinguishable shout at someone, then "No keys today. Got a set from yesterday though."

"Thanks." She hung up and considered her next move, drumming nervous fingers on the table. What was Robert Matisse doing right now? Did he have plans or was he busy with FBI business? He could only be the kind of man who belonged to someone. Probably out this evening with a wife or girlfriend. He'd choose a nice place to take a woman. The woman herself would be nice. He must be cursing the fact that he was stuck in Hammond for two weeks with his investigation.

Restless energy surged through her and she checked her watch. Was it too late to call Lexie? Six weeks of ignoring her didn't make it easy to ring her up for a quick chat. Would she hang up? What the hell. It was worth a try. Miller punched in Lexie's number.

"Hello?"

"Lexie, it's Miller."

"Miller." The pause was too long, well beyond socially acceptable. Miller found no energy to fill it in. "It's so good to hear your voice."

"I'm sorry I've been avoiding your calls, Lexie." She searched for small talk to explain pushing away everyone in her life. "It wasn't you."

"I know. You need to do what you need to do." Another pause, more awkward. "I wish there was something I could offer you."

"There is, actually. I've been thinking about going to one of those Lake Coalition meetings." Her voice trailed off, the words sounded so fake. "I need something to keep my mind busy." Hell, how pathetic did that sound? "You happen to know when they meet and where?"

"Sure. I'm seeing a guy who goes regularly. Blackie's Tavern in Hammond. Not sure if it's every Friday. Want me to find out and call you back?"

"No, thanks, Lexie." Miller tightened her hold on the phone. "I'll call Blackie's." She swallowed down another thanks. Tossing casual lies at Lexie hurt. "It's good to hear your voice."

"Miller." Questions hung between them, unspoken. "My invitation's still open to get together sometime for dinner."

"I know. Look, Lexie. You've been great. I need a little more time. I promise you I'm not gone forever." Miller stared out her window. A distant buoy clanged, guiding some sailor home.

"I know, kiddo. Call me when you need me. I'll be here. Hell, I'm not going anywhere for the next ten years or so with two kids under six."

Miller knew every aspect of Lexie's tough circumstances. Most people who stayed in the Region were trapped by similar economics, similar responsibilities, or just a general sense of failure. They all had one thing in common including herself—the lake, always there, a reminder of freedom, a mental, if not a physical escape from desperate lives. Despite the complaints, Miller knew Lexie loved her kids and even her waitress job at a local bar. She probably even loved the grit and guts it took to survive in their dying community.

"I promise we'll get together again, once I get some things straightened out." Miller cleared her throat, her voice rusty. Her chest seized with the overwhelming desire to turn back the clock, back to those days when the only problems she and Lexie shared were worries about the guys who might ask them out. Her previous life was just a dream world, before the nightmare began.

"I won't go away, Miller. I'll be right here, waiting. Just know there are people out here who love you."

"Thanks, Lexie," she whispered, the fist in her chest tightening.

"Stay in touch, okay? Just stay in touch from time to time. Promise?"

"I promise. Thanks." She stared out in the direction of the lake and watched a faint light wobble and disappear.

Chapter Six

Real danger comes from no action

Sunday afternoon, July 10th

Miller glanced up at the sky as she crossed her yard. The dull steel sky hung low, stubborn rain threatening to let go. Why was it that the clouds over the lake always felt closer than other clouds, just out of reach? Two seagulls cried overhead, tugging and scuffling like schoolboys over food.

Miller opened the passenger side of her car and reached across the seat for the stack of library books forgotten in the car last night. Her apartment key continued to be missing. Harassing the super this morning had produced a duplicate from the back of his desk drawer.

Fingering the key, she glanced at Sparky's apartment. Some sort of shiny fabric now hung in her windows, in sharp contrast to the weed-infested front yard.

Miller ran up her steps and inserted the key into the lock. It worked fine. Miller pushed opened the door. She crinkled her nose. As usual the place stank like somebody's unwashed socks. Despite whatever scrubbing she did, the smell lingered, as if a reminder of other tired lives preceding her own in this place.

Shoving the door with a foot, she deposited her books on the table.

Something felt wrong. She moved about the kitchen, her heart speeding up.

Nothing. The skin on the back of her neck prickled.

She moved to the table cautiously looking about for some evidence that someone had been in her apartment.

She reached out to flip the light switch. Nothing. She took two steps to the backpack she kept on the hook by the door and pulled out her .38, Lou Santos idea. He'd bought the gun for her after the murders and made sure she learned how to fire it.

She paused to let her eyes get accustomed to the gloom. She fumbled in the kitchen drawer for a flashlight. The hand holding the light shook as she took the four steps down the narrow hall, pistol in the other hand. The bathroom door stood shut and she pushed it open with a shoulder and stepped back, her stomach clenching.

Drip. Drip. Drip.

The memories flooded in on her, the stench of blood, followed by the vision of bodies sprawled about. Death.

Sweat broke out on her forehead and she felt lightheaded. Sucking in air, she stepped into the bathroom. Faint light filtered down from the small, skylight above. She nudged the shower curtain back and spotted the source of the dripping. The bathtub.

Leading with the S&W, she crept cautiously down the hallway to her bedroom. Again, she nudged open the door with a shoulder and made a slow circuit of the room with the flashlight. No one.

She turned the light on the faded white chenille bedspread, lifted its worn edge, and took a quick peek beneath the bed. Nothing.

No street noises penetrated this room.

Methodically, she shone the light into each corner, then moved to the closet. She set the flashlight on the floor with the light pointing towards the door and silently grasped the doorknob. With a flick of her wrist, she wrenched the door open. The space held only a few clothes, too narrow and shallow for much more. No feet appeared beneath her clothes.

That was it. There weren't any other rooms in the apartment. If someone had been inside, he was gone now. She sagged against the door frame in relief.

A faint sound came from the front of the apartment. She slammed the closet door and headed that way, the revolver level.

Sparky stood on the landing, dressed in black, peering in through the screen. "Miller!"

"Come on in. It's open."

Sparky wore black tights covered by some sort of black pinafore, over a short-sleeved T-shirt. She looked like a member of some senior special ops team. "I saw you drive up and thought you might like to come down for coffee." She squinted at the revolver hanging from Miller's hand. "Is that real?"

Miller slid the gun out of sight into the open kitchen drawer, ignoring Sparky's question. "I found my door unlocked. I think someone's been inside."

"Did you ever find your key?"

"No. I'll admit it seems a stretch to think someone found it and knew where I lived; unless he followed me." Miller shrugged her shoulders, barricading off her fears. "Your offer still hold? I could use that coffee."

"Sure, come on down. You going to call the cops?"

"No. I've seen too much of them in the past six weeks. Nothing looks disturbed. It was probably some kid who didn't find anything to steal. I'll have my lock changed tomorrow. The fuse boxes for the apartments are out back. I'll be right back."

"I'll go do it for you." The woman didn't wait for a reply but turned and left. Miller pulled her door shut, checked to make sure it was locked and followed in Sparky's wake, swept up as easily as a swimmer in an undertow. Sparky found the box and flipped the switch.

Downstairs, Sparky's apartment lights glowed. In less than twenty-four hours, the woman had her entire place looking like she'd lived there for years. "Come on in." Sparky motioned her inside. "Have a seat." Miller watched her dig around in a cupboard and pull out two swan-shaped mugs.

"How do you take your poison?"

"Black, thanks," Miller replied.

Sparky put her mug down, dug out a pack of Camels, and pulled an ashtray towards her. "You mind?"

"It's fine."

She lit up and took a puff, grinning. "Can't seem to give up the habit. Just took it up a while back."

Miller drank her coffee, searching for words that might be considered light hearted banter. "Good coffee."

Sparky waved vaguely with one hand, smoke circling her body. "Thanks. As for smoking, the convent didn't allow it. They didn't allow a lot of things bad for me. I'm doing an experiment in trying them all out. So far smoking and coffee are my favorites. Alcohol and drugs numb me out. Not my thing. If I'd been born thirty years later, I'd probably look into meth." She paused on a puff. "Hell, I'm not that desperate for fun." She grinned. "Do I shock you?"

"No. I'm hard to shock these days."

"I suppose so." She leaned forward to peer into Miller's face, black hair swinging forward. "That's both a good and a bad thing. Good if you're open minded. Bad if you're immune to life. Which are you these days?"

Miller considered. Disabled by life lay on the tip of her tongue. Disabled did not necessarily imply incapacitated. Getting in action looked easy. Finding an action that produced a worthwhile outcome seemed harder. "I don't know. Maybe a little of both right now."

Their differences in philosophies might only be a matter of degree separating them. Attacking life as a connoisseur versus attacking it as a nihilist, blindly seeking vengeance. The void between thinking and doing seemed as wide as Lake Michigan these days.

"Well, it's always good to consider things like that. As for my experiment, I still have quite a few forbidden fruits to try. Men, or maybe more specifically sex. I'm leaving that for later, starting with something easier. Violin lessons." She blew a smoke ring over her head. "What I really would like to do this year is have an adventure, something dangerous and exciting. I think perhaps you might be the one who's going to bring me that." She narrowed her eyes at Miller. "There are no accidents, you know. The Buddhists believe every person you meet has a lesson to teach." She reached over and patted Miller's hand. "Don't be frightened. I won't impose myself on you. I'm here if you need me, that's all. And eager to be part of what you're up to, if you care to invite me along."

Miller looked around the vivid room, fighting the urge to bolt. "Thank you. I appreciate the offer. I've got only vague plans right now, looking for an opportunity to take some action."

"That's good. Very good."

"You know anything about that environmental action group that meets in Hammond?"

"Nope, not a thing."

"I thought I'd attend a meeting this week. Want to join me?"

"Sure, I'll be glad to tag along. What are you after?"

"Information right now." She stopped wondering if she'd already said too much.

"Care to tell me what you're looking for, specifically?"

"Sorry." She shook her head.

"Well, like I said, I'm happy to go along. Just give me a buzz." She stubbed out her cigarette in her mug and stood up. "Want more coffee?"

"No, thanks. I need to get going."

"Sure you don't want to call the police about the apartment?"

"No. I'll pass." She stood up. "They'd think I'm flipping out or something since nothing seems to be missing." She turned back. "Thanks for the coffee. And the company. If you really want to go along to the meeting, be ready Friday night by six-thirty."

Sparky grinned. "Okay. See you then. And if you need me sooner, just give a yell."

A feather light rain began to fall as Miller climbed the steps to her apartment. She paused at the landing and turned, leaning over the railing to inhale the damp night. The whole place seemed to vibrate with the familiar rumble of the eleven o'clock train.

Miller shut her eyes, searching for the name of this unfamiliar feeling. Gratitude.

Maybe there was hope for a future.

Chapter Seven

Secrets belong to the night

Monday, July 11th

Miller took her place at the window. She raised the cup of black coffee to her lips. Sleepless nights were bad and mornings could be worse when consciousness brought the return of memory, like a slap to her face. Sometimes her mind refused to grasp reality. This Monday morning was different. There was some possibility of action, something she could do that might lead her to a killer. Tonight she would meet with Matisse.

She studied the seamless lake and listened to a lonely cry of a gull soaring low. Even she could still appreciate the memories of childish expectations the sound awoke.

There was no time for reveries now. She needed to get Matisse a lead for his investigation, something important enough to turn his opinion of her from unpredictable to invaluable. She took another swallow and mentally cataloged options for information gathering, most of them too risky. She checked the stove clock. Seven-fifteen. In thirty minutes she needed to be pushing open the heavy gray fire door to her office.

The obvious place to start had to be the steel mill's water quality data, and Greg Zelenin was the man for that. As environmental specialist, his job at North American Steel included tracking air and water quality. Specifically, he made sure the amounts of airborne and water waste was at, or below, the minimum allowed by the EPA. Air quality measures were taken daily, and water quality measurements were done on a weekly basis.

She'd gone on two dates with him what seemed like a lifetime ago before the murders. He was tedious, yet she could tolerate his boring civilities long enough to get a look at those records.

What about legal data? The complaint files? That data would be in the assistant director's office. Getting access to that office could be trouble. The easiest way would be to copy the key card and go in at night when she'd been called in for some machine emergency. Wandering on over to the office area then wouldn't present a problem.

Tonight she needed easier access to data, not confidential, but still useful.

She headed to her bedroom, threw aside her standard work gear of jeans and tank top and pulled on a pale green T-shirt and floral skirt she'd forgotten to get rid of from her former life. Thank God she still had it in her to dress up and do the girly, flirty thing, if only for old time's sake. She scowled at her duplicity, even in the midst of life falling apart.

Trembling, she hurriedly touched her lips with her tongue, ran to the bathroom, and yanked open the vanity drawer. No fancy makeup these days, just lipstick, something pale followed by a few licks with the hair brush. The girl-next-door look hid the haggard desperate real woman beneath. Grabbing up her office gear, she raced out the door.

Only a few minutes late, she charged into the small office she shared with another mechanical engineer, Hank Satorius. The room was crammed with back-to-back desks, computers, and file cabinets. There were old fashioned paned windows, dirty from years of neglect, clean enough to catch a faint glimpse of lake. The office smelled of burnt metal and stale tobacco. The administrative offices began four doors down and a world apart.

Miller tossed her work clothes on Hank's chair and picked up the telephone.

"Greg. Hi. Miller Abel."

"Hey, Miller. How are you?"

"Fine. And you?"

"Well, thanks."

Enough small talk. "I'm working on a problem we've been having with our run-off at oven five. Would you be willing to sit down with me over lunch and discuss possible causes?" It sounded plausible and happened to be a helluva lie. She held her breath until he bit.

"Sure. When?"

"Today, if possible. Would you mind going out for something? I'm sick of cafeteria food."

"No, that's fine. What time?"

"Noon? Let's make it somewhere fast. McDonald's or Rose's?"

"Rose's, it is. I haven't eaten there since high school."

"I have errands to do first," she said. "I'll meet you there at noon." Not that there was anything irregular about this situation. Engineers and EPA specialists meeting for lunch to exchange data happened all the time. Still, there was no need to be seen driving off with the water quality engineer, especially since she planned on breaking into the backup files if need be one of these nights.

Rose's used to be the place to be seen. These days the shabby tables and chipping paint made it too seedy for someone like Zelenin and a little too reminiscent of adolescence. Two car customers ate from metal trays affixed to windows. Inside, two men occupied counter stools at Rose's, both white haired and on the down side of seventy. Miller picked a table near the door, black topped, chrome-sided, with the standard mustard and ketchup jars. It looked the same fifteen years ago, except now there were more chips and dings in the chrome and enamel.

Zelenin sat opposite her, his gray eyes so light they seemed myopic. He had a good looking face, one that rated a second glance from most women although she'd never found him attractive enough to let him anywhere close to her bedroom.

He rambled on talking shop, taking the coward's way, with no mention of the recent tragic events in her life. Who could blame him? Most of her old friends avoided mentioning her family, avoided her eyes, probably hoping the whole thing would gradually fade away. No one wanted to come close to the road she'd been forced to travel.

The waitress took their orders, scooped up her menus and cruised off, heading for the kitchen. Miller watched her fiddle with something on the wall, producing a low hum, followed by the slow movement of automatic blinds sliding down over large plate glass, casting a faint green glow over the table.

Miller turned her attention back to Zelenin. "I'm sorry to interrupt your day with this problem, Greg," she said. "I've got a problem with oven number five. It's showing discrepancies in product. Your data is the first stop. I'll need to look at the water disposal records to see if I can detect irregularities. My first check is always settings, and I've done that. Nothing turned up, so I need to go over water temperature and output files next."

Zelenin's stiff smile barely reached his lips, and she wondered if he was relieved or sorry this lunch had nothing to do with their past. "Sure. I'd be happy to gather the data and send it to you. Or if you want, I can give you access to the database You'll need to do it on my computer though. I can't give you access otherwise."

She studied his pale blue shirt, his sports jacket in dark gray, as stiff as his smile and flashed on Robert Matisse's perfectly pressed white shirt. Matisse, with his FBI frown seemed way more interesting than the handsome face opposite her. "I'd really prefer to search your database myself, if that's okay. I won't know what I'm looking for until I see it. You know how that is." She flashed him a quick smile. "I thought maybe I'd stay late tonight. I'd like to get this situation handled as soon as possible, since the quarterly report is due this week." She leaned forward.

"Sure." He shifted about and she saw something un-readable cross his face. "Tonight will work. I leave at five. If you stop by around four-thirty, I'll go over my database with you and show you where the hard copies of the water quality data are found."

She exhaled and leaned back. She had no explana-tion for why the hell she felt so nervous. There was nothing irregular about her request, just her paranoia about doing anything she didn't normally do. Or maybe it came from her fear of being caught out lying about her real agenda—to snoop around, get damning evidence anywhere she could, and catch a killer.

With the small talk exhausted after the first five minutes, the forty-five minute lunch dragged on like five hours. Miller heaved a small sigh of relief when Zelenin crumbled up his wrappers on his lunch tray and got to his feet.

He'd parked his new Toyota hybrid beside her run-down car. Of course his vehicle would be environmen-tally safe and predictable. He unlocked his door and turned back, squinting into the midday sun. She gave him a quick involuntary smile, not for his good looks or even his file sharing. Most likely it was a combination of guilt for blowing him off years ago and feeding him bullshit now.

He took a step back and cleared his throat. "I was wondering if you'd like go out sometime? Maybe for a drink after work one night? Nothing fancy."

She blinked. Did he actually want to spend more time being awkward together? The back of her neck prickled. Was there something more to Zelenin? Something he knew? Or something in her questions about the water testing that put him on alert? She shook off the thoughts. Paranoia was a dangerous disease. "I'd like that, Greg. What night?"

"Friday? Have some dinner and shoot some pool? Milski's."

She fumbled for her keys. Why not? One more action to keep Matisse happy that she was out doing his investigating. "All right. Friday, at seven. I'll meet you there."

She glanced back over her shoulder as she exited Rose's parking lot. Zelenin hadn't moved and she could see him inside his car talking on his cell phone.

****

Miller listened carefully as Zelenin gave her a thorough rundown of what he kept in the EPA database and the hard files. Nothing special about that. He'd do the same for any authorized co-worker. At last he stood up, gave her a quick grin, and warned her to lock up when she left.

Data in traditional paper files were the most difficult to corrupt. She started there, pulling out everything relating to water waste management. She reached for her phone and started clicking pictures of page after page. It took her an hour and a half to get the hard copies. Before moving on to the computer files, she got up, went to the door and peeked out. Zelenin's office was at the far end, her own office at the other end of the windowless hallway where all adjunct salaried staff resided. She looked both ways, saw no one and heard nothing.

She spent an hour searching the online EPA database, stopping to print relevant water file data. In the end she found a few leads, where numbers didn't quite match up or she noted a couple of missing days. All in all, she didn't find much in the way of pertinent information.

As she reached over to switch off the computer, she spotted his email app. She took a quick automatic glance over her shoulder and double clicked on the mail icon. It took her twenty minutes to scan his files, not opening anything unread.

Then she scrolled through the last of his saved emails and poised over the 'quit' button when she saw the file marked 'personal.' She held her breath and opened Zelenin's personal email folder.

Knock-knock! She jumped at the sound, the door inches behind her chair.

"Yes?"

"Cleaning service. Will you be long?"

She paused before answering, waiting for the adrenaline rush to let up. "No, I'm just finishing up now. Give me a few more minutes."

Taking a deep breath, she scanned down the personal file and stopped at an email from a Jasper Clawson. The subject was 'Missing files.' She opened the file, scanned the text, and emailed the file to herself. She carefully deleted the 'sent' copy from his file cache.

She shut down the computer, stood up, dredging up a polite smile before she opened the door. The cleaning person turned out to be young, late teens or maybe early twenties, her hair spiked, two nose rings in her small nose, reminding Miller of a baby calf. "Sorry, I hope I didn't inconvenience you. I'm working late tonight."

Stupid, why apologize to this girl? The kid probably could care less who got what from where. Miller moved around the sudsy bucket. Shades of Cinderella. Only in the Region did the cleaning staff work with such antiquated tools.

****

Heading towards midnight and the heat felt unbearable in her small kitchen. Miller turned her back on Matisse and opened the door an inch, hoping for even a thin bit of relief. Nothing, not even a hint of breeze found its way inside. She paused and listened, hearing only the occasional rasp of a bullfrog.

She reached for the straight back chair and resigned herself to the inquisition. He'd brought out his professional face tonight, leaving the kind one hidden far behind his eyes. She focused on his questions, feeling too hot to resist them.

He shifted through the printouts spread out over her table. "How normal is it for you to be studying this kind of data?" He'd been sorting through the files for thirty minutes, his eyes pinned to them. He surprised her by being able to read them. "If you check chronology, there are some missing days. And I've noted some missing references to the poor quality readings. Any idea where those might be? Some sort of problem file they keep separate? Maybe administrative staff pulls them out?"

"You're pretty good if you can get that much from those files. I didn't realize the FBI trained their officers in waste water data."

"I did environmental work with a private corporation before I came to the FBI."

"Oh." There wasn't anything else to say. She leaned back and considered her options. Since the details were clear to him, she'd have to make sure she made a thorough study of what she passed over to him—or hid what she wanted to investigate herself before passing on the information. She resisted glancing towards her backpack dangling from the hook by the door. Inside lay a crumpled single copy of one of Zelenin's emails with the name of a warehouse where North American stored its outdated paper records. Tomorrow night she'd check it out herself. She'd leave him out of that drama for now. Once she determined if there was anything useful at the warehouse, she'd pass it on to him in bits and dribbles, making sure she was necessary to his investigation.

He slid a file over in front of her. "What do you see in these items you've highlighted for me?"

"Nothing that would be considered an environmental emergency. It's more of an area to watch, a red flag around the water treatment and probably not urgent. Quite a bit of unidentified minerals turned up in the assay on release. It could happen one month. To have it happen three months in a row is a bit odd."

"Would your water quality friend have anything to say about this?"

"I can call him. He asked me out for Friday but I'm not going."

Matisse looked doubtful. "Is that normal? Socializing with this guy?"

"We've been out a few times before. Not recently. He didn't find anything odd about my agreeing to go out with him. He's not that suspicious, Matisse. I asked him out for lunch and he returned the invitation. We're not a hot item, if that's what you mean. Just casual acquaintances. Anyway, I declined."

"And he wouldn't think it strange if you talk shop on a date?

"No, not at all," she snorted. "In fact, that's about all we did have to talk about. He's not exactly a mental giant when it comes to charming small talk. Aside from his good looks, which he relies heavily on, Greg's not got much going for him. I'll call him."

Matisse grunted back at her. Miller bit her lip to keep from grinning. Here they sat, a couple of Neanderthals, hunkered down around a kitchen table on a hot night in the twenty-first century. His concern did seem genuine despite the cop façade. He was just the sort of man you'd take a ride from, if you were stranded or someone you wouldn't hesitate to give money to, if he came to your house asking for donations.

"Anything else?"

She stirred her iced tea, listening to the tinkling of the ice cubes. And another thing, he caught on fast, more astute than one would assume. How much information did she dare offer? "I found an e-mail to Zelenin that sounded a little strange." Tell as much truth as possible and you won't get caught in a lie.

"You got into his email?" Matisse's voice rose a notch. "This is just a 'listen and report' assignment, not Deep Throat."

"The email stood open," she fabricated, "so I took a quick peek." Reaching across the table, she pulled out a manila folder from under the spreadsheets and sifted through pages before flipping a page over to him. He'd get a look at the email, just not the last page. In a day or so, after she checked out the warehouse, the last part of the email, mysteriously lost, would turn up.

His eyes moved quickly down the page, then back to the top, making a slower trip. "The message is dated two months ago," he said. "The email address is the same as the one on the warning sent to your father. In fact, almost the identical email. Does this EPA guy usually get this sort of correspondence shuffled to him?"

"No, not at all. Any sort of complaint letter would go to administration, probably to the assistant director."

"May I keep this?"

"Be my guest." She stood up and reached for the ice tea pitcher on the counter. "More iced tea?"

He nodded and pushed the glass towards her. "I need you to think hard. Do you remember anything your father might have said about his work and money. Or a safety deposit box."

A wave of fear swept over her, draining the room of its warmth. She kept her back to him while she poured his tea and composed her face, then turned and set his glass in front of him. His own impassive face showed nothing except an expression she'd already begun to expect when he talked business. While he might feel kindness towards her, he kept his own concerns and feelings close, showing nothing in his body language. At least not with her.

"What's this about, Matisse?"

He reached into his shirt pocket. "Mind if I smoke?"

"No. My dad smoked. Mostly outside though, since my mother hated it." Miller reached for the small jar she used as an ashtray and handed it to him. He paused to light his cigarette and take a drag. He exhaled a thin stream of smoke that drifted lazily towards the open crack of window. "So what's this about? You mentioned that safety deposit box on your first visit."

"Santos didn't mention your father's safety deposit box?"

She shrugged her shoulders. "No. Lou Santos is a family friend. He and my dad went to high school together. I'm not in his confidence when it comes to his investigations."

Her kitchen felt too small for this man, his hawk-like eyes too direct. Miller tugged at her sweatshirt, drawing it closer, wishing now that he'd leave.

"Along with that email I mentioned, we found some deposit slips in a safety deposit box at Lake County

Federal. Looks like about five thousand dollars had been direct-deposited into a private account," he said quietly.

"You're not going to convince me my dad had anything illegal going on, you know."

"Calm down, Miller. No one's accusing anyone of anything. I'm just asking. That's all. Do you remember any references to a separate bank account? Maybe a personal account for something?"

"No. Wouldn't it be easier to ask the bank, find out who opened the account?"

He took another sip of tea and set the glass on the table top. Condensation from the glass formed a ring on the table and he wiped at the puddle with his fingers. "We've talked with them. The account was opened about eight months ago. "

"Isn't there usual information you provide when you open an account?"

"Dead end. The social security number is bogus. The address is a post office box. The deposits were cash." He rubbed his hand across his forehead."

Miller studied the table, avoiding his eyes, feeling like a teenager with this man. Was he going to go on? Give her more leads? She needed something more she could check on. "Is there something else about this whole situation you're not telling me?"

He took one last drag and stubbed out his cigarette. "There was nothing else in the deposit box—except a picture," he replied.

"A picture? Of who?"

"Of a little girl."

"What's the secret, Matisse? You're acting like it's some big deal. It's probably a picture of me Dad was saving."

Matisse's eyes didn't meet hers. He didn't smile.

"Well?" She asked, knowing he'd just shut the door on any more information.

"Look, I'm sorry to bother you with this. I know the questions are painful. It's important that I cover my bases."

Miller sighed, ready to end this late night discussion. She watched his long fingers loosening his tie, his shirt looking as pristine at eleven at night as it must have been when he put it on this morning. "All right. Do I have the right to ask what you're thinking? Can't you tell me that, at least?"

"I don't know what I'm thinking. The deposits aren't in your father's name, although he kept the slips. I can't tell you what that means. I promise I'll keep you updated on what we find."

He sounded like the nice guy again, sympathetic, slipping off the cop façade. A sudden need rose up inside her, the hunger for something from him almost physical. It only made her desire for him to leave all the stronger. She felt pathetic, a lonely woman, with no friends or family around, the man who cared most about her in life, her father, gone. And this older man, a good looking one, a man who clearly would be nice to small children and lonely, lost women. She pulled her eyes away, afraid he'd spot her hunger for some small sign of warmth. "Thank you. I'd appreciate that," she said.

Matisse shrugged. He looked eager to leave himself. "Anything else? Anything at all that might be important you can think of?" he asked.

"Nothing." She glanced away, not about to mention her lost key or that someone broke into her apartment. He was nervous enough about using her, so why add fuel to his fire? "Anything new on your end?"

"No. A lot of FBI work is routine, backtracking, checking, rechecking. Most of my time is spent doing mindless work, asking questions that get me no place."

"Have you been with the FBI long?" The words popped out automatically, useless small talk couldn't stop, losing the battle between need and common sense.

"Four years. I worked for the private sector before that, a lawyer. Environmental law."

"Sounds like a big change."

"I liked environmental law. As it turned out, my job was working with big business to twist the EPA rules to suit themselves. So I decided I could make more of an impact from the law enforcement end of things," he said.

"Do you have family?" The words came out before she could stop them. "Sorry. None of my business."

"No, that's fine. I have a sister. She practices law, environmental as well. And my dad, he's retired. Another lawyer."

"Wow, a family of lawyers. What about your mother? A lawyer too?"

"No, a realtor. She died four years ago. A drunk driver."

Miller tried to think of something to say other than 'I'm sorry.' No words came to her.

"It gets easier. Although sometimes I wish it wouldn't." His rough voice held regret.

The small knot in her throat moved down into her chest. "What do you mean you wish it wouldn't?"

"At first I wanted the pain to stay, so I wouldn't forget her. I couldn't stand the thought of time passing and the pain easing with the memories, making her death seem insignificant," he said. "I don't suppose that makes any sense."

She exhaled slowly and the knot in her chest loosened. "I know exactly what you mean. I keep holding onto the pain. It's the only thing I have left of my family." A light breeze slid in and she felt it brush her face like fingers. He leaned over and touched her cheek.

"It will get better, I promise," he said. "One good thing came out of my mother's death. I gave up drinking. Oh, I'd have argued from here to hell and back that I wasn't an alcoholic. My friends weren't fooled. I drank. Now I don't."

She studied his face. Those drawn lines around his mouth were probably a product of the remnants of alcoholism as well as exhaustion. "Thanks, Matisse."

"For what?"

"Sharing something human about yourself. You're not just a suit."

"Human enough to call me Robert instead of Matisse?"

She grinned at him. "Maybe. I like Matisse. It suits you."

"Okay. I'll be waiting for Robert though."

"And if I start calling you Robert, what will you make that mean?"

"We'll see. It'll depend on the context." He stood up and dragged his jacket off the chair. She thought she saw a flicker of desire mixed in with confusion on his face. "Listen, I have an appointment tomorrow night, so I won't be around. Starting Wednesday, I'd like to set up daily meetings or at least a call. That work for you?"

"All right. I don't have much of a life anyway these days."

"I don't know about that. That guy at Milski's was all over you. And there's the EPA specialist who invited you out. Sounds like you've got some action going."

"Sure, Matisse. A kid who thinks he's the Marlon Brando of the new millennium and a guy who thinks discussing air quality ratios is scintillating." She didn't bother to mention Brando called her earlier tonight and set up a date with her for Wednesday. She'd acquiesced only because he was one more lead and one more information carrot to dangle before Matisse, if the kid knew anything.

Matisse looked relaxed now, his hands shoved into his pockets, even with the cop stance in safe mode. She thought she saw another flash of desire on his face, or perhaps it was just her own hope she saw written there. His smile did move from his mouth to his eyes and transformed his face.

She inhaled sharply as desire surged through her own body, a physical longing that made her feel weak. If he knew her real agenda, it would turn that smile of his to anger immediately. Hunting for a killer might be way too dangerous, but the surge of adrenaline it brought put her unexpected desire for him to bed.

Chapter Eight

No crime is as great as doing nothing

Tuesday night, July 11

Bam! Miller jumped at the slam of the heavy metal door behind her, echoing into the darkness of the interior of the building in front of her. She waited, not moving, for some sign to show her she was alone. It was a risk coming over tonight, hoping for a way inside the warehouse. Matisse would drop her from his investigation like a hot potato if he knew she planned on breaking into the warehouse, if necessary, to get more evidence. That the door was unlocked seemed prophetic. However dangerous, she could not turn back now.

Built in the early 1920s, the warehouse belonged to the heyday of bootlegging. This had been the world of Al Capone and the Purple gang. Someone had managed to keep the wood and shingle firetrap from burning down by misdeed or pulled down by some enterprising manufacturer for the past seventy years. So here it remained, like a lost ship on a weed infested field, three blocks from the lake and a hundred thousand miles from modern civilization.

Miller tracked the cement floor ahead of her for twenty feet until the floor dissolved into the darkness. From outside, the building looked about the size of a football field. Inside it loomed endless and silent, as foreboding as a mausoleum. A single light bulb, encircled with a misty aura, hung from the ceiling on a thin cord that reminded her of a hangman's noose. She followed the dim light upward until it disappeared into the wooden ceiling beams above her head. The place smelled of wood mold and spiders, not inviting to a woman alone.

Miller patted her pocket and found her pistol. Five lessons at a shooting range in Gary left her feeling more like a kid holding a cap pistol than someone who knew what she was doing with a gun. The S&W .38 felt cool and solid in her hand. She fumbled with the safety and flipped it off with a click that bounced off the walls like a Ping-Pong ball. In the other hand, she clutched Sparky's heavy-duty flashlight.

Zelenin's information in her pocket gave no hint of where to start her search. She snapped on her flashlight, did a quick walking tour about the immediate space. Shining the blue LED light in front of her she took a tentative step. The sound of her own breathing grew louder as she walked, competing with the pounding of her heart beating in her ears. She paused to listen, took another step, and paused again.

She heard nothing. She felt disoriented, as if she'd been dropped in the middle of a dark highway with no idea where she was.

Her breathing grew louder to her ears with each step she took across the floor. She could feel the coldness of the cement through the soles of her sneakers, shuddering when her foot came in contact with something squishy. She was afraid to shine the light down on whatever this might be, probably nothing more than mouse or rat droppings, or maybe the remains of an animal who'd sought shelter from the winter.

She turned and shone the beam on the imprints of her shoes in the dirt behind her. She'd left a trail as clear as if she'd written "Here I am!" for all to find.

Ahead of her were boxes stacked to the ceiling, row after row of gray, dust-covered cartons. Moving faster, she strode down the aisle, the boxes marked with various logos and captions: Hammond Sewage and Disposal; Calumet Electric and Light, Second Bank of Hammond, and on and on. Every business in Hammond must use this warehouse for record storage.

She began counting her steps as she hurried along, keeping her light fixed on the rows—five steps, ten, twenty, fifty. She tried to make some order out of the storage system, some sense of it. As she moved towards the back of the building, she noticed the boxes got grayer, less sturdy, more decrepit. Here spider webs and dust clung to them, the boxes looking too tired to fall over with no one to bury them.

Keeping the rows as her guide, she moved more slowly here, surveying the hundreds or even thousands of boxes.

She made it to the far wall, turned, traversed the back wall, and started a long hike back towards the front of the building following the far wall. She'd reached halfway when she spotted the name *Calumet and Northern Steel* on the boxes to her left, shoved all the way against the wooden slats holding up the wall. She kept her light focused on these boxes, stack after stack. Her own footsteps seemed to grow louder, echoing upward into the mist.

Two more rows and the labels changed to *North American Steel*. When had Calumet gone through a name change? Ten years ago? Eight? She studied the dusty boxes, more solid looking, newer than the Calumet ones. She stopped in front of that row, running the light over each box, searching for signs of recent visitors.

Crash!

The sound echoed off the walls, impossible to detect where it came from.

Her hand jerked up and the automatic flew out of her fingers, skidding off into the center of the room, with a sliding sort of sound. Adrenaline flooded her body, making her feel so weak she almost dropped to her knees. She pursed her lips to keep a scream from escaping. Her head swirled with terror, the thoughts random and jagged. She stood stuck in place listening, hearing nothing–no footsteps, no sense of another human being nearby.

She took a deep breath and cautiously made a circle in the dark around her. On the second sweep, she spotted her pistol lying in the center of a side aisle, fifty feet away. She darted over to the Smith & Wesson, reached down, and snatched it up. It felt cold, as though the deadness of the place infused itself into her gun. Once again she swung her flashlight upward into the rafters. The mist hung in the air above her, obscuring the wood beams a hundred feet overhead.

Again, nothing moved. The silence felt like a giant vacuum, as if waiting for something to fill it.

It was time to get some evidence and get the hell out of this nasty place. Ignoring her pounding heart, she retraced her steps back to the newest boxes, searching for signs of disturbance. Nothing, nothing, nothing. Six rows later, she found a stack of boxes without a sign of dust.

Shoving the pistol into her jacket, she caught hold of the nearest carton, tugged it out, and slid the lid off the box, revealing rows of manila folders. She pulled a folder out and peered inside. Here were last year's water quality testing results for North American Steel. It took a few minutes that seemed like forever to search each folder, checking for dates.

With the next boxes she found what she wanted. Records from two years ago, last year and at the bottom of the stack were four folders from this year. Someone had stuffed the top file with sheets of blank white paper. Why? There was no time to consider explanations.

Beneath the blank file, three more folders were stashed, each one containing water quality records from this year. In the manila folder on the bottom of the testing records lay a single yellow sheet lined with her father's handwriting. She'd know his scribbles anywhere. They looked like some sort of notes he'd made.

She stuffed the last folder into her jacket and zipped it up to her neck. She plopped the lid back on the box and shoved it to the back, above and behind two other older boxes.

Bang!

What the hell was that? An animal trapped in the building running into something? Had she left the door open, letting in a gust of wind?

Suddenly the flashlight went off, leaving her in the dark.

She stuffed the flashlight into her pocket and clutched her pistol tighter. Her legs trembling, she retraced her steps, stumbling into what seemed to be the center aisle. She stopped and searched for any signs of light coming towards her. There it was, the exit. In a slow, loping sprint she ran down the aisle towards the door.

She almost made it. Something hit her mid knee and her arms flailed about in a slow motion dance. She stumbled and fell to her knees, her breath catching. She bit her lip or maybe her tongue and the bitter, warm taste of blood filled her mouth. Disoriented, she heard the echo of feet in the dark somewhere, running hard, fading away.

She shoved her legs out in front of her, first one, then the other. The right knee stung, but the pain wasn't disabling, thank God, so no broken bones. She rolled over and pulled herself up in the dark. What happened to her pistol? Vomit rose into her mouth and she swallowed twice, fighting the nausea. With trembling fingers, she felt about her on the dirty floor. She swung her free hand about in a wild circle until she encountered the gun, knocked it away again, and heard it slither to a stop somewhere to her left.

Her senses told her she was alone now. She gave a short laugh and stifled it, tottering on the edge of losing control. She wiped the blood from her mouth and leaned forward circling the cold cement with trembling fingers.

At last her little finger made contact with cold metal. Her S&W.

Clutching at it, she pushed herself to her feet.

Operating on instinct now, she hobbled to the exit. The door stood open, letting in faint light from the building across the highway.

Limping, she made her way to her car. *Christ!* At least she'd parked close to the building, out of sight of the street. Her heart hammered with each faltering step. She expected a hand to reach out of the dark and grab her or the sharp, quick pain of a knife in her back.

Panting hard now, she reached her vehicle and grappled with the car keys stashed in her back pocket. At last, she slipped into the safety of the familiar, reached for the lock and pressed it down. It took three tries to get the key into the ignition and turn it on.

With the headlights off, the Honda crept forward. She held her breath until she'd exited the parking lot and left the warehouse three blocks behind.

Pulling to the side of the highway, she let the engine idle until her breathing calmed down. She'd stopped making the inadvertent little moaning sounds ten minutes ago. This scene played out like a stupid comedy, definitely more Stephanie Plum than Lara Croft.

She flipped on the interior light, took a quick look at the cut on her lip in the rear view mirror, and unzipped her jacket. Then she pulled out the stolen manila folder and flipped it open.

She flipped through the loose pages and noted again all the dates were this year. They were in sequence right up to May tenth, four days before her dad's murder. The single yellow sheet looked as fresh as if he'd written on it yesterday, his words dancing across the page, as if he'd left her a note before stepping out for a few minutes.

The notes were from the water department, not North American Steel and they were notes her father made to himself, or rather questions with his characteristic bullet points beside each thought:

who changed the figures on the bottom line of pages 1-10?

who signed off on these sheets?

why would anyone want to change the water quality figures for only the days North American Steel did water testing?

someone at the water department?

someone from North American Steel?

someone else?

Her dad, as usual, kept meticulous reminders, and left nothing to his head. She began to cry softly. She allowed herself a few minutes of grief, then swallowed hard, pressing down the pain that felt like a fist around her heart. The thing to do now was to focus on what needed to happen.

Miller shoved the pistol into the glove compartment, pushed open the squeaky door, and stepped out into the humid night.

It was close to one in the morning. All the drive-through places were shut down for the night, except Rose's, who kept a vigil for another hour to cover bar stragglers needing a cup of coffee to push them home.

"What'll you have?" The kid at the window called out, boredom dragging the last word out so long she almost lost the meaning.

"Coffee. Black." Why the hell else did they stay open for? Did normal people actually stop by here in the middle of the night for a burger and fries? Miller leaned towards the window and fished out her wallet. The kid exchanged the Styrofoam cup for the single bill she offered, and slid the window shut, without offering change.

"Keep the change," she called out to the shut window, as she juggled the covered coffee. At least he'd put a lid on the cup. She maneuvered the gear stick into first and swerved out of the drive-through, towards a spot in the dark along the empty street.

Taking very slow sips, she gave herself fifteen minutes for the remnants of her jangled nerves to compose themselves. She speculated about possible invaders of the warehouse besides herself. No security people would investigate a noise and then take off like a cat with its tail on fire. Her knee throbbed and her body trembled as if she'd received a head-on tackle. She squeezed her eyes shut, trying to focus on what happened. Had someone followed her to the warehouse? Had he seen her digging into those boxes? Was this a real threat to her? Or was it a random attack from someone breaking into the warehouse? She stared at the folder sitting on the passenger seat. What did she have? What had she stumbled upon? Was it the same thing that brought a killer to her parent's house?

Downing the last of her coffee, she flipped on her lights and headed for home, her hands still shaking almost too much to steer. Then she remembered she'd left the flashlight behind.

Chapter Nine

Infinite highways can seem ordinary

Tuesday Night late, July 12th

The lonely highway stretched ahead of Miller as she drove. She rolled her window down and sucked in peaty air. The dim glow from the dashboard lit up the interior making it feel as friendly as sitting beside a campfire, the low hum of the car lulling her towards a sense of safety.

With marshland to the right and crumbling, abandoned factories across the highway, this deserted stretch of land looked like a dreamscape—or a nightmare, with a dark, deserted factory looming between her and the lake.

She jerked the wheel and stomped on the brake pedal just as a railroad crossing bar dropped down with a thud fifteen feet in front of her car. Even in the middle of the night, it didn't pay to be distracted. The red blinking light from a sluggish freight train lumbered towards the crossing.

In neutral, her car burped out a staccato idle. Miller shifted about the muscles in her cramped thighs. She leaned back and eased her fingers under the rubber band she'd wound carelessly around her hair earlier that evening and slipped it off, running nervous fingers through her loose hair.

If only removing a rubber band could solve the root source of her headache; that sense of standing on the edge of a void with no place to go. In the six weeks since the murders, she'd even managed to get used to standing too close to an abyss.

Miller squinted into the dark, following the long line of piggybacked container cars. No end in sight. Hell. She slouched down and pictured Matisse listening to her review of tonight's adventure with displeasure in his eyes. He'd lecture her, looking disappointed at her lack of good sense. No, first he was the law. If he heard the true story of tonight's escapade, he'd shift his face in annoyance and split so fast, he'd leave her spinning in her tracks.

Matisse was probably one of the last civil men in America under fifty. Any behavior like hers tonight, bordering on anarchy, would be taboo to him. She almost smiled as she pictured him in his khakis the other day at Milski's, the way his thighs stretched and filled them, with the slight bulge over his zipper, the too tight material wearing down the fabric. Matisse, a man closer to her father's age than her own, ran the gamut from father figure to sexual fantasy for her. He was sexy as hell. And too Freudian by far.

Why did sex always have to be such a problem for most women? Something to be considered and weighed out? She doubted if Matisse suffered over stupid doubts? If he wanted a woman, he'd do what other men did—let the body rule, the consequences taking care of themselves.

She rolled the window all the way down and leaned her head out, letting the velvet night air cool her. Car after car of the slow moving freight train rumbled past and she followed them with her eyes, the motion soothing. What was it about a long line of dark, deserted train cars that felt so peaceful?

She shut her eyes and listened to the rumbling of the wheels over worn, uneven tracks and drifted off, dreaming of a sunlit beach.

The water shimmered. She squinted at romping kids and mothers holding the hands of their toddlers. Joy bubbled up in her throat.

Boom! She turned reflectively to the east. It sounded like an explosion somewhere beyond her view. She scanned the point where the water merged with sky. A thin billow of dark smoke rose up at the horizon, followed immediately by a wall of water, the color of blood, rising up and speeding like an express train towards land and the boisterous families playing in the water, oblivious to the threat.

Another loud boom echoed in her head, scattering the nightmare.

She started up and craned her neck, struggling to figure out where she was. Her car had died at the train crossing as she slept, with the headlights on, illuminating the upright crossing gate. In the distance a train whistled.

Her lights blinked once, twice, dimmed and then flickered out, leaving her staring into the blackness.

Heart hammering, she turned the ignition switch. A brief grrr and then nothing.

She tried again. Not even a whimper.

A shiver of fear shot through her and replaced the warmth of the night. She checked the rear view mirror automatically and saw no lights, only empty miles between herself and help. Her heart fluttered in her chest, and she wiped her sweaty fingers on the legs of her jeans. She forced herself to stay calm.

In the distance the lights of Whiting and home twinkled, three miles off, too far and too dangerous to trek home from here. She felt transfixed, gripped by inertia, the scratching of the crickets, mocking her fears.

Just call someone!

Blindly she reached for her purse, fumbling for her phone. She fingered the keypad in the dark, hesitating only a second before pressing the autodial for Matisse. Who else could she call at two in the morning?

It rang once, twice, and a third time before he picked up.

"Matisse," his voice hoarse, muffled by sleep.

"Matisse, it's Miller. Look, I'm sorry to bother you. I'm stranded in my car out on the Industrial Highway across from the old Headlands Plant. I'd call for a tow, except nothing's open this late."

"What the hell are you doing out there at this time of night?"

She hesitated searching for a response. *Just a little B&E, Matisse.* Where else could she say she'd been? At work? He could check that out too easily. A good rule about lying—keep it as close to the truth as possible. "I couldn't sleep and decided to take a drive. I ended up not far from the Beacon Warehouse, so I stopped to take a look."

His displeasure almost crackled at her through the phone. "What's so interesting about the Beacon Warehouse?"

"The water department stores its files there." Enough. He didn't need to know every other business in town used it as well, including North American Steel. He'd find out soon enough, once he got around to asking where the company stored its EPA files.

He paused again, then grunted, "Lock your doors and stay in your car. I'll be there in fifteen." He paused. "You all right?" This was clearly an afterthought.

"I'm okay. It's just a dead battery. I stopped for a train and fell asleep with the lights on." She craned her neck, loosening the tension. "I owe you, Matisse." The words echoed into dead air. He'd hung up.

Her phone said two-fifteen. She reached up and touched the cut on her lip, it throbbed slightly now and was crusted with blood. She could see no open wound.

She glanced up as something caught her eye, a flash of light reflected off her windshield. She checked the rear mirror. A large car—or maybe a truck—crawled slowly towards her, headlights gleaming like the eyes of a giant cat on the prowl.

If she was lucky, it would be a patrol car doing nightly rounds or maybe a delinquent truck doing a late pick-up. Who else would be on this road at this time of night?

She reached across and flipped open the glove compartment. She fumbled inside for her gun. The cool metal felt like a friendly hand in the dark. She flipped off the safety and lay the Smith & Wesson on the seat, ready.

The lights grew close, slowed to a near stop a hundred yards behind her, flashed her with its brights and revved up. When the eighteen-wheeler accelerated around her and its red taillights disappeared with a roar, she nestled the automatic in her lap and leaned back to wait.

Twenty minutes and two more vehicles slid by her dark car before she made out a faint light reflecting off Matisse's Lexus.

He pulled to a stop with his headlights facing hers, popped his hood and leapt out, leaving the door ajar.

He wore a lightweight jacket that flapped open as he jogged over to her window. In his hand, he held a man-sized flashlight. As usual, another competent male.

"You okay?"

"Yes." Her voice sounded tremulous and too weak.

"Pop the hood."

She reached down for the release button and the hood snapped free.

Matisse anchored it open, leaving the flashlight on the fender. He fiddled for a few minutes, strode over to his trunk, and returned with cables.

"Put the car in neutral and switch it on."

"Grrr-rrrr."

She paused, then tried again. "Grrr-urr."

With a roar the engine turned over, ran ragged for a few seconds before taking hold. She pumped the gas pedal until the engine idled evenly.

"Let's get out of here. Follow me." His index finger punctuated the words, a man pissed and short on small talk.

Matisse performed a three-point turn and waited as Miller struggled to get her stubborn Honda into first gear. At last, she edged her car up behind his Lexus. His car leapt ahead and she jammed down the gas pedal to follow.

In the last fifteen minutes the moon had risen above the lake and was reflecting off his car. She followed him easily, keeping his red taillights in view when he got too far ahead.

He slowed when they got to the intersection of Front Road and turned down her dirt lane. He pulled to a stop and she braked hard behind him. Before she could shut off her lights he leapt out of his Lexus and motioned to her.

She hesitated long enough to slide her automatic under the driver's seat before stepping out of her vehicle. His silent anger scorched her.

He caught hold of one arm above the elbow. "What in the hell were you trying to do tonight, Miller?" His frustration bit into her.

"I was lying in bed thinking about the missing documents, and then I remembered the warehouse. Since I couldn't sleep, I made a quick trip there." He'd taken another step towards her, too close, his heat white-hot.

She pressed a palm to a chest as hard as a brick. "Back, Matisse. I know. I'm not actually part of your investigation and not authorized to do my own thing. You made that clear enough. Well, I get your point except since when does a U.S. citizen need authorization to do some investigating of one's own?"

"Since you took it upon yourself to search for information the Federal government is after. It's my investigation, my files you're searching for. I can't believe you were stupid enough to go to that damned warehouse alone. It makes me wonder if you buried your sanity two months ago with your family."

She shoved harder, feeling the physical assault of his words. "Low blow, Matisse."

He dropped her arms and took a step back. "Sorry." He rubbed his eyes, looking more tired now than angry. "You are the most fucking annoying female. If I find out you've been withholding information from me, you're going to be removed from this investigation. No more inside source work, nothing. If you go off half cocked again, that's it." He stopped suddenly and motioned at her. "Get in my car."

"Why? It's almost three in the morning."

"We can't stand out here debating this. Someone's likely to call the cops. Thirty minutes of your time is all I'm asking."

She climbed in his car, barely getting her door shut before he did a quick turn, and headed down her alley, spitting dirt and dust.

His car smelled of warm leather and tobacco. The dashboard panel in the dimly lit interior looked as complicated as a small plane. Miller leaned back and shut her eyes, the car's gentle rocking motion putting her on autopilot.

Ignoring her, Matisse turned onto Morton, heading away from Whiting.

"Where are we going?"

"For coffee. There's an all-night diner down the street."

"For God's sake, Matisse, I don't want coffee. I had some an hour ago. At this rate, I won't be able to sleep until next week."

"Thirty minutes to debrief, and I'll get you back home to your bed."

She sank back again, resigned. "All right."

Ten minutes later he pulled up to the curb outside a place right out of Edward Hopper's world. A lone counterman was leaning on his elbow leafing through a magazine.

The night air hung heavy with humidity, the deserted fluorescent-lit street as bright as daylight.

He took hold of her elbow and steered her toward an empty booth clinging to a back wall.

"Sit."

Miller dropped down heavily on the vivid pink vinyl seat. Etta James wailed 'At Last' from the small jukebox on the chrome table.

One other customer, a kid, hung draped like a lover over an ancient pinball machine in the other corner.

The counter guy, somewhere between forty and a hundred, wore his oily dark hair in a stringy ponytail revealing grey roots. He wiped at the long counter with small circles, looking up as Matisse approached.

Miller studied him as he leaned down to give his order. In wrinkled khaki pants and a T-shirt, the cotton clung to him in the heat like skin. For his forty plus years, his body looked ten years younger and solid; no creeping middle-aged rolls of fat, no slouching pecs or biceps.

As though reading her thoughts, he turned and gave her his piercing cop look. She tried hard to not read anything into it, despite the crackle of disapproval in the air.

The man exchanged mugs for cash and Matisse strode back to her booth. Miller cautiously tried her coffee and waited for Matisse to browbeat her, too tired to resist.

Instead Matisse picked up his cup and took a gulp of coffee, looking more exhausted now than angry "What did you really have in mind, Miller, with the warehouse visit? What were you going to do if you found something?"

She shrugged, astounded he assumed she found nothing. "I don't know. Probably read it then pass it on to you, if it seemed like something that mattered."

He straightened his legs, stretching them out under the table within inches of hers. It was a casual move that belied the lines gouged around his mouth. "I'm assuming you didn't find anything, since I don't see anything being handed over to me." He took another swallow of coffee. "What were you really doing in the warehouse?"

She drank her own coffee, ignoring his question.

"And what the hell happened to your face?"

She flicked her tongue to the corner of her mouth, feeling for the cut. "I fell and bit my lip."

"What were you doing when you fell?"

"Running out of the warehouse." That was true. "You know how women are, scared of the dark, freaking out?"

He pulled a napkin from the metal container, reached across and dabbed at her lip. "So how did you find a way to get inside? And for God's sake, don't tell me you broke in."

"Someone left the place unlocked and a light was on inside, so I went in."

"Shit."

It was the second expletive she'd heard from him tonight and loud enough to make the kid at the pinball machine look up and smile.

"Let's have it, Miller. What'd you find?"

"Rows and rows of storage boxes, some municipal. A lot of businesses store their stuff there."

"Anything from North American Steel?"

"I saw some of those."

He pulled out his phone and stopped. "I'll get a warrant in the morning to search the place. What's the name of the place again?"

"Beacon Warehouse"

He pulled out his Blackberry and took notes.

Matisse looked up. "You never did tell me where you got that name. And why you decided it was a good idea to search it."

Hell

"And why you ran."

"Greg Zelenin said something that reminded me the old records for North American Steel were kept at Beacon. So like I told you, I couldn't sleep and decided to go over there and see if I could find anything. I got lucky with the door unlocked and was doing some serious searching when I heard a loud noise, sort of a crash, and I ran." She took another drink of coffee. "I fell as I ran out."

He rubbed the back of his neck. "Well, you're alive at least. That's about the politest thing I can say right now." He drank his coffee and tapped into his Blackberry. Miller waited in silence, afraid she'd doze off.

At last he put away his Blackberry. "How the hell are we going to manage this, if you pull this kind of stunt the second day of working together?"

Miller kept her gaze on the mug in her hands, avoiding his eyes. "I know, Matisse. I'm a real pain these days. My friends will attest to that. If you can find any." She chanced a look. His mouth was drawn up in a straight line, more frustrated than angry. She sighed, needing a little kindness right now.

"Drink your coffee and let's get you home." He shoved his phone in his pocket. "Are you sure you're not hurt?"

She shook her head, not trusting her voice.

Fifteen minutes later, the car purred and floated along her rutted road like an ocean cruiser.

He pulled to a stop and turned.

"Thanks, Matisse. Sorry to be so difficult."

"You're that all right. But we can still salvage a working agreement if you're promise to play by my rules." The words were terse, the tone gentle. "I'll wait for you to make it inside."

Feeling like a truant child, she fought a sudden urge to confess every sin and bad deed she'd ever done. Instead, she ran for her stairs and escaped him for now.

Chapter Ten

Desire has no understanding

Wednesday, July 13

Matisse awoke sprawled out on his back, full sunlight streaming through the window. He threw his right forearm across his eyes. The sun was bright enough to blind a man. He glanced at his watch. Eight o'clock and only four hours of sleep. Not nearly enough. He stared down at the tent in his top sheet. The sight of his rock hard erection brought a quick follow-up image of Miller Abel from last night. What right did she have to call him out at two in the morning? And what the hell right did she have, with her too pale face and fragile body, to make him think of sex?

He grunted, disgusted with her, his libido, and the morning.

He hauled himself up, reached for his phone and punched in Santos' office number. Santos promised he'd do his best to get the warrant within the next couple of hours.

Matisse got to the squad room of the Hammond Municipal Building at 10:15. Santos was waiting for him. "I've found a vacant office for you to use while you're here." He held out a small key and motioned for Matisse to follow him. He unlocked the office door and flicked on the lights. The search warrant lay in the center of the desk, along with a phone number of a J.R. Cantner, who owned the warehouse and lived in Chicago.

By eleven, Matisse stood at the front door of the warehouse behind the manager, an A.P. Guzman, according to the name on his worn shirt. It took an hour to do a thorough walk-through of the building. Signs of Abel's presence were evident everywhere—footprints in the dust, interspersed with recent-looking scuff and skid marks, and a couple of toppled boxes not far from the door.

"Who the hell did this?" The manager sounded more nervous than angry. Matisse caught on immediately. The guy had gone off and left the warehouse door unlocked. Now he could barely summon up curiosity over a possible break-in, probably sure the owner would find out he was to blame and fire him instantly.

Matisse reassured the man he wasn't there to inves tigate a B&E. The man stepped aside and Matisse pulled on rubber gloves and led the way, making a circuit of the warehouse. He almost missed them, the boxes marked Hammond Water Department. They were shoved back out of the way, sitting sideways, leaving clear slide marks in the dirt. Three boxes, all disturbed. He pulled them out, removed each lid and meticulously searched through the contents.

Inside, he shifted through page after page of reports tucked into manila folders. Not until the third box did his heart speed up. The heading on these files all said North American Steel. Could these be the missing data files Miller dug up in her search of Zelenin's records? If so, what the hell were they doing in the water department's boxes?

The manager stood by silently watching, clearly nervous, even with Matisse's reassurances there would be no questions about a break-in.

Matisse glanced up at the man and went back to the boxes. He stacked the reports from North American Steel to one side, thought briefly about sending them to

CSI for fingerprints and passed on the deal. Probably the most prominent would be his and Miller Abel's.

"I'll need to take these with me. I'll write you a receipt for the things I take. You can give the Hammond police a call in a week or so, and they'll let you know about releasing them back to the warehouse."

"Okay, not my problem, as long as you promise this isn't going to lead to any questions about how someone got inside. I've been manager here for ten years, and I can't afford to lose this job."

"Like I said, I'm not interested in how anyone got in, just what's turned up here," Matisse said.

"Well, you're not the first one interested in these things. I had a request from some guy at North American Steel to go through boxes a month or so ago. Before that, I had a water department employee request access to their shit. Then a cop or someone who said he was a cop, wanted to look around a few weeks back."

Matisse cleared his throat. "Hammond police?"

"Don't know. Can't remember. Think it might have been Chicago. Or maybe the sheriff's office."

"You keep a signed release when you let people come in here?"

"With businesses, we do. Not the cops. Not you."

It was a waste of time to pursue much more with this man. He was clearly more interested in covering his back than providing information. "I'll take a look at those entry records anyway. Give me few more minutes to finish up here, and I'll meet you at your office. Is it up front?"

"Yeah. Sure. Your call." The man gave him one last nervous look and left.

Matisse finished searching the rest of the boxes, made another circuit of the place, wrote himself a note to follow-up on the files, and headed for the office and A.P. Guzman. He almost missed the large flashlight lying beside a box. 'Abel' was written on it with what looked like nail polish. *Shit.*

To the right of the metal entrance, a sign on an unpainted wood door read 'private.' With less than six feet of clearance, the door looked so insignificant Matisse had missed it.

The 10x10 office contained a small table with an ancient computer, a dangling overhead light matching the one in the entrance and a straight backed, battered chair. Assorted stacks of boxes and papers covered the floor. Guzman pulled out a clipboard, flipped over several pages of a yellow pad and handed it over to Matisse, pointing with a cracked fingernail. "There."

Matisse studied the signatures. The last one looked like 'Zclcnin,' the friend of Miller's from North American Steel. Guzman took back the clipboard and flipped some more pages. He pointed to another name, Henry Winston, Hammond Water Department. Matisse noted both names. He wrote a receipt for the files he'd taken and held it out. "Did the police who showed up here a few weeks ago ask for anything specific?"

"Nope, just wanted to search around. I let 'um."

"They took nothing?"

"Not that I saw."

"So you have no records of that visit at all? No receipts?"

"Nope."

Matisse made a U-turn in the vacant lot and headed towards downtown Hammond. His stomach complained about the lack of food, and he a made quick stop at a fast food place.

He drove as he ate, pulling in front of the station as he stuffed the last bite of burger into his mouth. It definitely would be a good time to make more of an effort to manage his food intake.

Matisse dropped his laptop and holster at his new desk, and headed for Santos' office. He knocked on the door.

Santos opened it. "What'd you get? Anything useful?"

"Some files from North American Steel misfiled in a water department box. And a lot of questions."

"Let's have 'em. I can see by your face you've got something for me."

"The manager at the warehouse said they'd had a lot of visitors in the past two months. Including the police."

"Police? Did he give you a name?"

"Nope. In fact he wasn't sure what police. At first he said Chicago, then he switched to sheriff's department. He had no records of a visit and no memory of what they'd done in the warehouse. It could be it's got nothing to do with what I'm after. Or your case. There were some other visitors as well. The water quality guy from North American Steel who I assume is Zelenin, and Henry Winston from the city water department. The warehouse manager said it's rare for him to get visitors. Just file drop-offs at the door."

Santos made a quick turn around his desk and pulled up his chair. "Hell. Well, take a seat and give me your thoughts."

"First, let's eliminate the Hammond police."

"Easy enough. I'll check the duty roster and then put in a call to the sheriff's office and the Whiting PD.

"Good. It's not likely the law enforcement person was out of area but it won't hurt for me to put out some feelers to Chicago, as well."

"So where are you going with this, Matisse?"

"I'm not sure. It's possible this is connected to my case. Whether it's got anything to do with yours is your call."

"What put you onto the warehouse in the first place?"

"Miller. I had her doing some checking at her work. She was going through EPA records and spotted some missing months. She found the warehouse reference." He didn't look at Santos, instead pulled out his phone to study his messages. The man didn't need to know Miller had made a midnight trip there last night.

The expression on Santos face would have curdled milk. "Just make sure she doesn't get caught up in something here."

Matisse headed out before any more assertions—or questions—came his way.

A call to Edward Zabrowski, one of the guards at the treatment plant, came next. Matisse got his voice mail at the Water Department and left a genial, innocuous request for a call back.

Now Zelenin. Matisse got another voice mail. This time Matisse swore and called back, asking for the director of the company. The switchboard put him through to a vice president.

"Jeffrey Owens' office."

"This is Special Agent Robert Matisse with the FBI antiterrorism task force. May I speak with Mr. Owens?"

"Just a moment, sir." It was more like three minutes before a low, resonant voice came on.

"Jeffrey Owens. May I help you?"

"Mr. Owens. I wonder if you might have a few minutes of your time today. I'd like to ask you some questions."

Matisse caught Owens' hesitation, brief as it was. "My girl said you're with the FBI. Can you tell me what this is about?"

Matisse rolled his eyes. His girl? What era did this man live in? "I'm investigating a water issue having to do with the Chicago water supply. I've been called down to

Hammond to check up on some local concerns that have turned up. Mostly routine. It should only take a few minutes of your time. Would now work?"

"Well, let me have my girl check my schedule." Silence followed, interspersed with the sounds of paper shifting about and drawers banging. "I can see you at three, Agent Matisse."

"I'll be there."

Matisse killed the next hour copying and logging in the EPA records he'd found. Boring as hell although a great way to bring clarity and focus to his case. It also kept his mind from wandering back to speculations about Miller's agenda.

Three o'clock turned out to be shift change at North American Steel and the parking lot ran thick with SUVs and trucks.

He snagged a spot in visitor parking and hoofed it to the entrance.

In the twenty-five feet between his car and the door of North American Steel Headquarters, perspiration already ran down his underarms.

Inside the front entrance, Matisse made his way to a young woman at the reception desk dressed in some sort of gold camisole, better suited to the bedroom than the male world of steel, especially with the temperature in here on the wrong side of sixty degrees.

He told her who he was and took a seat to wait for Owens. By the time the man turned up, the goddamned cold had already turned his sweaty shirt and pants into an icy wet suit.

"Agent Matisse? I'm Jeffrey Owens."

Matisse rose and turned. A man younger than expected held out a hand and shook Matisse's with a firm grip. Probably closer to forty then fifty. Most women would call him handsome, his face the kind to light up the cover of People magazine. Matisse knew the type, had met him often in his law job. This was a man who covered all his bases, including an attractive wife, two charming kids, a house on the right block, and no debt.

"If you'll follow me." Matisse felt like he just got an invitation to join a church.

Owens led the way down a carpeted hall that smelled of new furniture and no dirty jobs. It made Matisse wonder if any of the steel workers ever saw the inside of this area.

The office faced Lake Michigan, with wide windows letting in late afternoon sun streaming across an oak desk. "Can I get you something? Coffee or something cold?"

"Sure, I could take a Coke, thanks."

He pushed a small button and spoke into a small box in his desk. "Carrie, can you bring me two Cokes, please?" He pointed to a plush seat opposite. "Have a seat, Detective Matisse."

"Special Agent."

"Of course."

A knock sounded twice and the door opened. The blond receptionist came in carrying a tray and placed it on the side table near Matisse's chair. "Is that all, Jeffrey?"

"That's it. Thanks, Carrie."

Jeffrey's eyes followed the girl a second too long before refocusing on Matisse. "What can I do for you?"

"I'm with the FBI anti-terrorist unit out of Chicago. I was called in by the Hammond police regarding a potential threat to the water system here." He paused, waiting for a sign of something, anything. The man popped his Coke tab, took a drink and leaned back against his desk, as if an anti-terrorist agent showed up every day. "Can you tell me if you've had any correspondence in the past six months from environmental groups? Specifically, any threats?"

"Regarding?"

"Your waste water procedures, or anything relating to a connection with the Hammond Water Department?"

The man's face shifted slightly from mild interest to something like displeasure, two straight lines barely visible between his brows. "The EPA tracks all that for us, as it does all the industries around the Lake. We have those records, if you'd like to see them."

"I would. I've left a message for Mr. Zelenin."

"I'll make sure he gets hold of you." He did a flick of his wrist and checked the time. "I'm sorry I can't continue this. I have an appointment in five minutes. As for threats, I don't recall any, recent or not, from the local environmental group. There have been newspaper reports, of course, voicing concern over industries impact on the lake."

"So you've had no threats to your company in the past six months to a year? Not even a warning?"

"We receive prank calls from crazies from time to time who want us to stop making steel. And some emails along those lines these days. Some claim they're worried about the environment, others complain about the outsourcing of our steel products manufacturing to foreign shores."

"Do you keep a record of those?"

The man rubbed his aquiline nose with one finger, staring off to the left of Matisse. "I'd have to check with my assistant. Greg Zelenin tracks those things related to the EPA. The outsourcing concerns come to me. We run a very tight ship these days, with fewer than two hundred employees. We're run for the most part by robotics."

"I'd appreciate copies of anything you've received in the past year." Matisse stood up and handed the man his card. "Anything within a mile of a threat; a warning, a fear, however you want to call it." Matisse watched the man place the card carefully down on his desk. There were no signs of business or anything close to clutter in the room. "How quickly can you get back to me? Email will work. I need it by the end of this week. Can you get me something by then?"

"Of course, Agent Matisse. I'll have my assistant get right on it." He stretched out a hand and Matisse shook it, feeling a distaste for this man. Too fastidious, too good-looking, and too successful for his liking. He'd seen too many men preened on success and the entrapments when he'd been a lawyer.

The sun shimmered over the lake, turning it from blue to white gold. No clouds today, and even with the lake breezes, the heat weighed down on Matisse, his body feeling as if it added forty more years to its age. He wondered if Jeffrey Owens felt his energy dissipate when he stepped out of his cold storage of an office. Probably not. The man looked like he never wilted, as perfect as a Ken doll.

Matisse ran the A/C in his car while he put in a call to the Chicago office for updates. He got back a lot of confusion over the owner of the bank box and nothing on any of the traces he'd run on those people scurrying around the edges of this case: Joe Sedlack, Henry Winston, Greg Zelenin, even Jacob Abel. He added Jeffrey Owens to his background check list. Matisse signed off, defeated for the day.

He ran through his voice mails. His sister. Just a quick hello and sorry she hadn't been able to make the dinner last night, asking about a reschedule next week.

And Andrea Hutton. He pressed autodial.

"Robert. I got you."

"Hi Andy. How are things?"

"Good. Actually, not so good. I'm up against a wall over here, running on empty. Want to meet tonight for a drink? I need a new bar—and a fresh ear."

"The booze joints in Gary not meeting your expectations?"

"Oh, I've found some great clubs. I thought a change of venue might work. The cover of foreign soil and all. Got some free time tonight and an acceptable watering hole?"

"Yeah, I can manage it. Meet me at Milski's Pub."

"Milski's. You've got to be kidding. Sounds like something made up for a two bit screenwriter who heard the Region is full of Eastern Europeans."

"That's it. Milski's is a Whiting landmark. Track it down with your GPS and we'll meet, say around seven tonight?"

"Can do. I'm looking forward to it, Robert." She paused and he held his breath, knowing the offer coming.

"Depending on how tired we are, I'd love to extend it beyond just a drink."

"I'll take a rain check on that, Andy. I'm in a hole here, in fact a six foot deep shit hole with my investigation. The overlap of murder and my case is eating me alive. Having some downtime sounds like another life."

"Okay. The offer still stands, if you change your mind."

He dropped his phone on the passenger seat. Stretching the truth with Andrea left him feeling like he'd eaten a mouthful of stale cookies. His sudden distaste for recreational sex took him by surprise, and he wondered if it had more to do with an attraction to Miller Abel and less with the murder of her family.

Chapter Eleven

Betrayal shows no logic

Wednesday evening, July 13th

Joe Sedlack arrived twenty minutes late for their date. Not that Miller was surprised. If asked, she'd have said he'd be someone she'd expect late to every appointment. The set of his shoulders, the clothes he wore on Saturday, all argued against someone who followed the rules.

She stared at her face in the mirror, wishing she had other plans tonight or no plans. After last night's fiasco with Matisse, she needed to prove herself to him. So tonight she perfunctorily dialed his cell phone, relieved when she got his voicemail. She left a simple message only. She'd set up a date with Sedlack for this evening and expected to have some new information for Matisse the next time they spoke.

She dressed carefully, a little sexy maybe, yet nothing too blatant. Just a halter shirt with crossing back straps and a skirt, one of two she now owned. She'd even bothered to pull her hair up in a topknot and put on some lipstick.

Miller suspected Sedlack might not show. She glanced out the window. There he was, propping his Harley behind her car. A man and his motorcycle. She smiled, thinking how humans think themselves unique and not part of the common likes and dislikes of everyone else. Men.

His boots hit her steps with heavy thuds. She picked up her bag when she heard his quick rap on her door. Her mind still skittered around for an excuse to avoid going out with him tonight.

What in the hell was she doing going with this guy? In less than a minute the former Miller Abel would have shifted his attention to her friend, Valerie, whose ideal of manhood always included black leather on a cycle. The notion of spending an evening with this character sounded way depressing and was most likely a dead end. She couldn't picture Sedlack involved in anything that didn't include a mirror, a camera, or an opportunity to make an impression.

She stepped back and let him in. He smelled faintly of fuel and leather, a sharp contrast to Matisse. "Hi, Joe."

"Hi, yourself. Sorry I'm late. Had to run an errand for a friend."

She clicked on the light above her sink, did a check of the room, and led him out onto the landing. In the last five minutes, the sun had dropped below the horizon and a slight breeze stirred off the lake. The sky shone pale orange, heading for mauve and eventually deep blue.

A tiny burst of pleasure, so small it almost eluded her, shot through her like that first infusion of good coffee in the morning. Following immediately came a feeling of guilt, even at the tiniest moment of joy.

She followed him down her steps and out her gate. He'd parked the bike behind her Honda. "Milski's okay?"

She took a helmet from him and tucked in stray strands of hair. "That'll do."

Joe jumped on the starter and the roar of 400 rpms flooded the silence. The noise reminded her of Jacob, when he'd drop by to bring her something from her mother or play his latest mix of music or share a joke. The night suddenly grew smaller around her and less friendly, the memories a small fist squeezing her heart. At least the old familiar ache kept her company, like a good friend.

The crowd at Milski's overflowed onto the sidewalk tonight. The early shift crowded around the bar, lingering over a last beer. Both pool tables clanged and popped.

Joe swaggered to a small table along the wall, and she averted her eyes as he called out to friends. Hell, she knew half the people in the place.

Sedlack pulled out her chair and she took it, grateful he'd picked a table in the semi-dark. No one she knew would expect her to be out at a bar six weeks after the murders, especially not with someone like Sedlack.

"What'll you have?" he asked.

The choices were minimal, and she ordered without caring what she ate. "A Heineken on tap and a hamburger.'

"With all the extras?"

"No thanks. Just the burger."

"Be right back."

He brought the beers and pulled his chair adjacent to hers rather than across, partially blocking the aisle to the dance floor.

"You don't come here much, do you? I think last Saturday's the first time I've seen you in this joint."

"No, not much. I've spent a lot of time in the past few years working on my career. It's a little more important as a woman to put time in." She shrugged, aware of how ridiculous that must sound to him.

"So why bother? Fitting into the world of money and all that, I mean?"

She almost smiled, his response predictable, and his face so earnest in his belief in his own unique worldview.

The food arrived and saved her from replying. She bit in, chewing slowly, following the action around the room to avoid Sedlack's eager face.

Mid bite, she spotted Matisse sitting against the wall opposite. A chill shot up from the nape of her neck to her scalp. She glanced away quickly, grateful for being unnoticed. She waited a beat and took another quick look. This time he sensed her eyes on him and turned to look. He'd seen her.

There he sat, along the far wall at a small table, looking relaxed and happy. He looked engrossed in conversation with the woman opposite him. In her mid thirties, she was professional looking with light brown, almost blond hair brushing her shoulders. By the cut alone—smooth, sleek, classic and demanding a trim every four weeks—Miller recognized a woman with cash to spare. She wore a simple dark shirt and slacks, understated. In most females, an outfit like that would imply on the job—or an abundance of confidence. Miller squinted across at the woman's left hand. His partner or a girlfriend?

She yanked down on the frivolous halter top and mentally shrank. The woman with Matisse looked like an adult with an important job to do. She fit well into his world. Miller fiddled with her burger, feeling stupid sitting across from a kid like Sedlack. What made her think Matisse might be attracted to her? A lonely woman, living in a rundown apartment, in a town clinging with white knuckles to the edges of prosperity. Especially when this lonely woman lived on the fringes of sanity, flirting with destruction.

They were discussing her, she could tell from the quick glances her way. The conversation seemed intense and serious, Matisse doing most of the talking, the women's face a question mark.

The woman shot another quick look across at Miller. This time Miller caught a straight-on glimpse of her features, pretty, not loud. Probably closer to Matisse's age than she'd first surmised, the woman looked around forty and a throwback to the '50s, one of those women who wore pearls and required a napkin in her lap when dining.

"Something got your interest?" Sedlack asked.

"Someone I know."

Joe followed the direction of her attention. "Isn't that the guy you were in here with last Saturday?"

She hesitated. "Yeah. He's with the FBI. He wanted to ask me some questions."

"About what?"

Joe Sedlack, unabashed and arrogant as he was, had no fear of prying.

"The murders." She spoke the words quietly, waiting to see if he'd back off.

Instead, he leaned forward, his beer mid way to his mouth. "The FBI is interested in your family's murder?"

The words hit her like a hand shoved hard into her chest. How long would it take before she got used to the word 'murder' in the same sentence with 'family' without falling apart? She struggled to pull a blank cover over her face.

"He said it was routine." She shrugged, debating how much to reveal here. "My dad worked for the water department in Hammond and the Hammond police called the FBI in over something they thought might interest them."

Honesty. What the hell? Why prevaricate over this. It would be easy enough these days to check up on Matisse. And just maybe, telling the truth would pull some secrets out of the secrecy surrounding her family's deaths.

"Yeah? Doesn't sound routine to me. What's an FBI investigation got to do with the water department?"

"He's with the anti-terrorist unit, something about possible eco-terrorism. He's investigating a threat to the Chicago water supply."

"I suppose it's the usual Homeland Security crap. What the hell do they think they're up to all of a sudden worrying about the environment?"

Miller shivered and looked around the room. How much was too much time to spend safely with this badass from the dark side? He might be nice looking, but he sent out enough strange energy to be a character in a Stephen King novel. "So you don't like them investigating environmental cases? Or are you just generally against government investigations?"

"I don't like any government investigation. And I don't trust guys who hang out in bars wearing suits."

"He's not important."

"You got that right." Joe sucked on his bottle, his eyes fixed on hers. "Sorry, I didn't mean to go off on you like that." He didn't look sorry and didn't look like being angry gave him a problem. Looking like a meth addict, his eyes glistened with a rush of adrenaline. "I go to the Lake meetings sometimes."

Where the hell did that come from? "Oh really? You're into the environment?" If he belonged to the green movement, she was a closet member of the Hell's Angels.

"I took in a couple of meetings. Like I said, I met Jacob at one of those meetings." He signaled the waitress to bring him another beer. "Want to go along with me to the meeting this week? I have some unfinished business there."

She ignored his invitation, took another bite of burger, and resisted the urge to take another look at

Matisse and his girlfriend. "What's your interest in the Lake Group?"

"I like shaking things up this town."

"You like anarchy?"

He shrugged and she knew he hadn't caught her meaning. He poured down the last of his beer and plunked the can down. "I don't suppose you belong to the group, especially with that job of yours?"

"No, I'm not a member."

"Looks to me like the Coalition is having some fun with the big boys who own North American Steel. Probably out to cause havoc."

"Since a former EPA specialist started the group and a lot of the members still work for North American Steel, I doubt they're out to trash the company and risk their jobs. I'd say it's more likely the members are conscientious and care about protecting the lake." Suddenly she was tired of nodding as he ran his diatribe against the world. Who cared about his happiness? "I'm a little tired, Joe. Let's call it a night."

"This early? It's barely nine o'clock."

She tossed down the remains of her beer and reached for her bag. "Six weeks ago I lost my family. It's going to take some time to work my way up to an evening of fun." Let him figure out she was beyond boredom.

He flashed a shark's smile and she weighed the possibility of calling a cab. Miller wove between the tables and made for the back door, feeling the eyes of Matisse and his girlfriend on her back.

Joe Sedlack drove faster on the return trip, carelessly sneaking through yellow lights and sometimes red. The earlier light breeze revved up into a strong off shore wind smelling of the lake that pushed aside the odor of burning iron ore, a constant reminder that this was a steel town.

Her anger evaporated by the time they reached her alley. Being angry at this kid seemed irrelevant. He pulled up to her gate and she climbed off. "Thanks for the evening, Joe. Sorry I'm not more sociable."

He parked his bike and reached for her.

She ducked easily. "Let's not wrestle, Joe. It's not going to go anywhere."

"Sure about that? It might be just the thing to make you feel better. I could come up for a while and we could work our way into it, easy like. I'm in no hurry."

He reached for her arm and she scuffled with him, feeling like a five year old fighting over a toy. "No, thanks."

"I'll call you in a day or two. We can try it again."

She clearly didn't need to worry about putting a dent in his ego. "We'll see." The idea that Sedlack could have something useful for her persisted. Whether he was some way involved in murder seemed ludicrous, although Miller couldn't imagine anyone actually committing murder.

A door banged under the stairs.

"Miller. That you?" Mary Catherine Doherty to the rescue.

"Hi, Sparky."

She ran down her dirt path and out the gate to Miller. "What's up? You going for a ride? Beautiful night for it."

"Just back. Sparky," Miller said. "This is Joe Sedlack and his Harley. Joe, this is my neighbor, Sparky."

"Hey, cool bike." She wore something that shone in the dark, almost lighting up her face. "Where'd you go? Just cruising around?"

"Yeah. Over to Milski's for a beer." She glanced at Joe who stood silent, as if unsure whether to be a polite child or a sullen teenager. "Thanks again, Joe."

She turned to Sparky "Where you off to?"

"Coming home."

"Want to come up for a while?" Miller asked, feeling an unexpected yearning for Sparky's direct personality.

"Sure. I'll follow you. Lead the way."

Miller hurried up her steps with Sparky at her heels. She shivered as she fumbled for her key, the roar of the Harley in the distance unexpectedly menacing.

****

"Known that guy long?" Sparky asked.

"No. I just met him a few days ago."

"He related to your investigation?"

"I never told you I was investigating anything."

"That's what you're doing, isn't it?"

Miller forced a smile, but Sparky was too quirky to get angry at. "Maybe."

Sparky did a quick scan of the room. "You know your problem? You're bored. No TV, no music. You need something to do besides sitting at your window staring out into the night, even if it's only writing sad poems. "

"Music might be nice. I could see myself getting a CD player or something."

"An IPod. You need an IPod."

"Sparky, you amaze me. For someone who's spent years in a convent, you're way ahead of me." She smiled up into the lean face, as guileless as a baby's. "Poems and music. Humpf. Maybe I'll go out tomorrow after work and get myself a couple of blues CDs."

Sparky gave her a pat on the arm. "Good. Let me know what you like, and I'll give you a couple of mine. I have at least five hundred CDs stashed away in boxes in my bedroom." She pulled a chair away from the table and plopped down, as much as a woman with shanks as lean as a race horse could plop herself anywhere. "So back to the investigation. Don't try and fob me off with the mention of music and poetry. I want to hear what you're up to. This Joe character is part of it, right? And the suit I saw leaving late last night?"

"You accuse me of standing around at my window. Sounds like you're spending your time watching my comings and goings."

"So what about the man in the suit? Very cute. Nice. A bit old for you. Still, I approve. He has good energy. He a boyfriend?"

"Sorry. No."

"Then he's something to do with the law, right?"

"He's FBI, with the anti-terrorist group out of Chicago."

"Wow. I knew adventure was in the works when I met you." Sparky grinned at her. "You're going to have to keep me in the loop, right?"

What could she say to that? No, I don't want anyone? "All right." Sparky could have her uses. Her B&E skills were impressive.

Sparky met her eyes. "So, nothing's going on between you and the biker boy? Or you and FBI-man?"

"Sorry. Nothing going on." Except an insane fantasy to seize hold of Matisse and beg him to stay the night.

"I know I get way too personal, but who can help it? I'm a former nun, for God's sake. I've had so little experience with sex, I've got to start some place. If voyeurism is the best I can do to start with, it will have to do. I'm working up to finding some action myself."

Miller laughed out loud, the rumble in her chest as unfamiliar if she'd sung a snippet of an aria. "You're something else, you know?"

"I am, aren't I? You've got to let me in on your game plan, you know."

"Game plan?"

"Your investigation. With Matisse, right?"

"Not exactly. He's working on a possible connection between my father and an FBI case."

"Oh, well, that sounds promising. Can you give me a hint of what you're doing?"

Miller did a mental grimace. Sparky would keep pursuing this until she got something to gnaw on. "I'm Matisse's inside source at the steel mill. And anywhere else he needs eyes and ears."

"You've got to take me along when you're out on duty."

"Well I'm not exactly 'on duty.' I go about my daily life, dig around when I can, and report back to Matisse."

"Like tonight?"

"Yeah. Joe said he knew my brother. And he goes to the Lake Coalition meetings, so with both those things, I thought he might have some information. I came home early because he's too weird and I couldn't hack it."

"And last night? Something happened? You and Matisse got in around three in the morning."

"I did some digging around in a warehouse across town and got into a bit of trouble. I banged up my knees and my lip. And almost got caught. I did find a small lead or two. One of them I passed on to Matisse. Not the other."

"So you're playing your own game along with the FBI's. Good idea. Don't tell me what the lead is. I don't want to know. Just promise me you'll give me a shout out when you're ready to set off on another search."

Talking with Sparky about all this made it sound like an episode of I Love Lucy. And here stood her Ethel, begging to tag along.

"All right. You're still coming to the Coalition meeting with me, right?"

"Sure thing." Sparky stood. "Buzz me when you're ready to leave Friday, and I'll be waiting at the bottom of the steps." She reached for the door knob and turned back. "Should I get a gun?"

"Gun?" Not I Love Lucy, more like Cagney and Lacey. "Uh. Do you own one?"

"No. I'd like to try one out, though. In fact, I think I'll hit up a friend for a few lessons at a shooting range. And maybe buy myself a small firearm. One of those ladies' Saturday night specials." She twisted her blunt features up like a Pekinese. "Yours is a .38, as I recall."

"Not a lady's gun exactly. It's small yet not too small." Miller followed her out onto the landing "I don't think you need to get a gun, Sparky."

"Friday night is probably too quick to get one anyway." She paused. "They're pacifists, right? What can happen at an environmental meeting?"

Chapter Twelve

Suspects are never guilty, until they get caught

Thursday, July 14th

Matisse picked up a double espresso at Starbuck's and dragged his tired bones down Main Street. Thank God for the advent of good coffee in America. Ten years ago if he'd ordered any kind of coffee that didn't sound American in a Midwest city, he'd have been tossed out on his ass, and proclaimed a yuppie.

He sat his paper-sleeved Doppio on the warped wooden desk and shoved his holstered gun into an empty drawer. The Hammond squad room looked overdue for a facelift. No cubicles in sight, the last redecoration had to be pre-1960. Paired desks, parked front to front, occupied the hundred square foot room as haphazardly as Dodgem Cars suddenly out of power.

Matisse's office was basic, just a desk facing an un-occupied one, allowing for a clear view through the window to the highway beyond. He could make out a strip of pale blue in the distance that could only be the lake. The cooler weather must have brought out the bad guys last night, since the place sounded like a kindergarten on the first day of school.

He pulled out his Blackberry and deposited it carefully to one side on the empty desk. What the hell was he going to do about Miller Abel? His groin tightened at a sudden fantasy of her, damp with exertion, tousled hair spread out on the pillow. In his dream world, he'd replaced the look of despair with one of pleasure.

Sucking in stale squad room air, he reminded himself of the stubborn look she gave him during one of his lectures, like a terrier with a bone annoyed at its owner yanking it away. He cursed himself silently for being caught in this situation for all the wrong reasons, when every aspect of her life was at cross-purposes with his own.

And what the hell was he doing, letting his thoughts keep wandering back to sex? A 45-year old man should be well past adolescent drooling over a woman, especially this woman. She was from a small town and raised in a blue collar world. Aside from holding a professional job, their lives met at no point. And she was too young for him. Or rather, he was too old for her. She didn't need his North Shore life and for sure didn't want anything from him. His instincts whispered something different. She wanted what he wanted—blazing, mind numbing sex. For him, he craved a brief, hot fling to dispel the loneliness of two weeks in a strange city. For her, it probably had more to do with hoping to blast away the shell shock of grief that he knew well. It would make itself at home in her body, dulling her life down and threatening never to leave. She happened to be a nice girl suffering from a trauma that forced their paths together for a few weeks. That was all.

He sighed and reached for his cell phone. Three messages. A quick return call to his home office he handled easily. He left a reassuring message for his dad to the second message. The third, a call-back to Andy, he skipped.

He liked Andrea. She'd come to the Chicago office two years ago, a good agent with a caring ear, something not available from most. Recreational sex was a common phenomenon in the Bureau between agents, and he and Andy indulged without regret. Since he'd arrived in Hammond, he felt only distaste for the activity.

He shoved aside the Starbuck's cup and pulled out a yellow pad. Greg Zelenin, Henry Winston, Joe Sedlack, Jeffrey Owens. Anyone else? He retrieved the list the Hammond Police compiled. Wayne Cornell, a chemical expert with North American Steel and the man who'd organized the Lake Coalition Group; someone who knew a lot about the environment, water, and the steel industry.

Matisse stared at the names, searching for some connection to money, some connection to the water threat. Who needed money and how did it tie in with the threats the Bureau was tracking? It was more than six weeks since the Abel murders. Too damned much time. Alibis sprang up abundant after that long, and memories clouded or faded completely.

Matisse rubbed at his forehead, a dull headache threatening. He reached for his phone and dialed Cornell. It rang five times before his voicemail picked up. The computer generated response requested callers leave a message. Matisse said to call him, nothing more.

He turned back to his list from Santos and studied it. Someone already crossed off several of the names. One stood out. *Dmitri Versakos.* Written in sloppily, probably by some cop in a hurry to finish evidence cataloguing. Next to the name a scribble read *"From Charlie Abel's address book."* The investigating cop crammed in more information below the name: *"Left Hammond in 1988 for Florida. Returned 2009. Check him out."*

Matisse glanced at two cops dragging themselves into the squad room, coming off duty. He dialed Zelenin. The voice on the other end sounded young and professional. He offered no resistance to Matisse's request for a meeting. Not even a question about what an FBI agent might want.

Henry Winston could wait. He'd thrown a quick question or two at him last Saturday. There's been no connection in his background check to environmental groups, no sudden cash in his bank account, and no recent spending sprees. He might dislike the Eddie Haskell of the water department, but the man came in low on his list of suspects. Probably his worst crime was ineptitude at his new job and he knew it.

Matisse stood up, shifted back his shoulders, and headed for Santos' office. The door stood open and the man himself stared out the window, his back to his door. "Lou, got a minute?"

Santos swung around, looking more tired than Matisse felt. "Sure. What can I do for you?"

"You got any background info on a man named Dmitri Versakos? He's on the initial list of Abel acquaintances to follow up, yet I don't see where anyone has done that."

Santos reached across his desk and selected a yellow butter mint. "Shit. Well, his being on that list is probably nothing significant. More than likely just some diligent cop cataloging every name he found. The guy hasn't lived around here for twenty years. We took all those names out of Charlie's address book. We included him mainly because he moved back to the area a couple years ago. He was Charlie Abel's boss at the water department in the old days."

"Anything I should know about him?"

"Not much. He went through a nasty divorce, something to do with cheating or sex or something. What else is new?"

"You know the guy?"

Santos shifted back in his chair, sucking on his mint. "This is a small town. I know almost everyone. I met him a few times. Nice enough, I guess. Greek. Came from a big family in Chicago. Anyway, he picked up and left for Florida more than 20 years ago. Charlie Abel inherited his job as manager at the age of thirty-three. As

I recall, someone we tracked him down in Florida and got word he'd moved back to the Chicago area a year ago. That's why we left him on the list."

"Do you know what he did in Florida? Who he worked for?"

"Nope. Can't recall if my detective passed that on to me. I don't think it was a utility job." Santos scratched his chin and studied his mint plate. "Seems to me it was some sort of computer business."

"I'm spending the day following up on your list, so I'll track him down, Lou."

"Thanks, Matisse. Send me a copy of your report, if you don't mind. For the record."

"No problem. I've got a couple more calls, and I'll be out the rest of the day. You can reach me by cell, if you think of anything else."

****

Matisse pulled into Visitor Parking next to the ornate steel entrance of North American Steel. He strode through the fancy doors and into a dim hallway of gray walls with thin yellow trim, probably someone's idea of steel industry chic. A deep red carpet pointed the way to administration, the minimalist interior probably in the best of taste in the 1990s.

The EPA office began four doors past the offices of the director and CEO but at least 100 K down the income ladder. Matisse paused and listened at the door. No sounds came through. He knocked twice and pushed it open.

A man looked up, surprise on his even featured face. Matisse offered his hand, "Mr. Zelenin. I'm Special Agent Robert Matisse of the FBI." He assessed the man quickly, weighing his approach.

"Have a seat, Agent Matisse."

The small room contained a desk overwhelming the five by five foot square space filled up with too many bookcases and file cabinets surrounding the desk like armor.

Matisse waited, letting the man begin the dance.

"How can I help you?"

"I'm with the Chicago Antiterrorist Division of the FBI. I'd like to ask you a few questions about your water control records."

The man gave him a forced smile. He was a nice looking guy, in his early thirties. Given the make-up of people in the Region, he was probably of Ukraine descent with those even, sharp features of every Olympic gold medal skater from Russia.

Matisse felt illogical annoyance tighten his stomach. Zelenin probably grew up in the Region, a good fit for Miller's world. She said she dated him a bit. He looked like a shoe-in for a boyfriend. Suddenly Matisse felt fifteen years too old and miles out of place in this world.

"Is there some problem, Agent Matisse?"

"Not so far. Just following a couple of leads on a possible connection with a case I'm investigating. The Hammond police called me and asked me to follow up on some possible problem involving the Hammond Water Department."

He let the information out slowly, waiting to see if this man would jump in to justify the loss of EPA records. Instead, Zelenin stared at him silently, his face blank. "I'm trying to track down some water data that we haven't been able to get our hands on. Some of the EPA records on waste runoff from North American Steel. I was told you're the man to talk to."

"If it has to do with anything EPA, I'm your man."

"Can you tell me if all your waste byproducts go through the Hammond sewage processing? Or do you dispose of any of it yourself?"

"We use a standard filtering process, as required by the EPA. Our system is a series of tanks, with the treated water eventually exiting into the city system."

"Have you noticed any discrepancies in the measurements, say, in the past six months?"

"With our runoff?"

"Yes, or anything out of the norm?"

"No. Nothing I can think of. We did have a problem with some data files coming up missing earlier this year."

That he bothered to mention the lost files pushed him down Matisse's list. Why bother to tell the FBI something that might never even come up missing? Unless he knew it would be obvious to the EPA and come to the attention of the FBI. "Did you ever resolve it?"

"We have back-up files on everything. We filled in the missing data with the duplicates."

"The originals never turned up?"

The man shook his head, the mild expression on his face sticking.

Matisse saw his type often on the North Shore. The kind of man one would run into at the park, pushing a stroller, holding a toddler's hand; responsible, prosperous, conventional, and predictable. The kind of man Matisse might admire intellectually, but he'd never choose a friend who tried so hard to be a good guy that he couldn't be authentic.

He reached in his pocket for his Blackberry. "I'll need to see a copy of all those missing records," he said.

Zelenin's mouth twitched, the first sign of disturbance in his even features. "It will take me a few days. Will Monday work?"

"That's fine."

Zelenin shifted about restlessly in his chair. Time to go.

"Just one or two more questions. Do you know anything about the Lake Coalition Group?"

"I know about them, of course. Wayne Cornell had this job before me. He started the group a few years ago. I'm not a member."

"You disapprove?"

"Not really. I just think it's a waste of time. I've been hired to manage North American Steel's environmental responsibility. An integrity watchdog, you might say. I do a damned good job, as does the EPA. Wayne Cornell is an arrogant Greenie. One of those guys who thinks the system's flawed, no matter how hard we try to make things work. He wouldn't be happy if the water tested as pure as a mountain stream."

Matisse kept his face impassive as he tapped notes into his Blackberry. "So has Wayne Cornell accused North American Steel of environmental violations?"

"Although I don't follow Wayne's every move, I'd say he's too afraid of losing his nice house and good standing in the community to accuse North American Steel of anything outright. He likes the spotlight put on him, of being a pure environmentalist, a do-gooder. I doubt if he'd ever do anything really, if he found real issues with the water."

Zelenin's words surprised Matisse, the first indication of his having some thoughts on the subject and sharing them. Matisse would have bet his Lexus the man never took a position on much of anything that might stir up controversy. Yet he'd turned the tables and accused Cornell of exactly that; playing life safe.

Matisse stood up and extended his right hand across the desk to Zelenin. "Appreciate your candor, Mr. Zelenin. I think that's it for now." Matisse headed out the door, turning back to throw out one last question. "Did you know the Abel family well?" The question was an afterthought to fulfill his agreement with Santos to keep both cases in the forefront of his investigation. He had serious doubts Zelenin could be a murderer, especially one so heinous. The man was too much of a 'nice guy' in his own mind to commit sudden or premeditated acts of such violence.

"Miller Abel's family? I know of them. I didn't know them personally. This is a small town. Most people's names are known, but I didn't run in their circle. They were older than me."

"Did you know Jacob Abel?"

"Nope. You'd do better to ask Wayne Cornell that question, since with all the social activism going on with kids these days, Cornell would be more likely to have run into Jacob somewhere."

"Jacob was part of the Coalition Group?"

"I have no idea. I'm just saying he looked like a kid who'd be into fighting the system, what with the motorcycle and his friends."

"What friends are those?"

"I couldn't give you names. I'm going by appearances. I've run into Jacob around town a few times. In clubs mostly. The kid was underage, of course. He seemed like a pretty good guy, a little wild maybe, but not a bad kid."

For not running in their circles, the man had a lot of opinions about people he claimed to not know.

"Thanks for your help. Here's my card. Can you send those files to me as an email attachment?"

"I'll have to convert them to PDF."

"Fine. I'll expect them by Monday. And if you think of something else that seems out of place, anything at all, even the smallest thing, either with North American Steel or your records, ring me up."

"I thought you were investigating some sort of terrorist threat. Is there a connection with the Abel's murders in all this?"

"Probably not, other than the Hammond police turning up a few things in my jurisdiction during their investigation of the Abel case. Since Charlie Abel worked for the water department, there's a natural link there. I'm ruling out anything other than coincidence."

Matisse let himself out into the cool gray hall, cursing silently. All in all, the interview had been a waste of time. The only fucking information of use was supposition on this guy's part.

****

Dmitri Versakos picked up on the third ring. "Hullo." His two-pack a day voice made him sound ninety, although, according to his background info, he was only five years older than Charlie Abel, which would make him fifty-eight.

"Mr. Versakos. This is Special Agent Matisse. I'm with the FBI, the Chicago Anti-Terrorist Division. I'm doing some work on a case in connection with the Hammond PD. I'd appreciate it if you'd give me a few minutes of your time today for a couple of questions?"

"What about?"

"The Hammond Water Department. I can't be more specific over the phone."

"You know I've been gone from that job for over twenty years? I don't know what I can tell you."

"That's fine. I'm tying up some loose ends. Just need to ask you some questions. You're on my list. It'll only take a few minutes of your time." Matisse's headache pushed its way from a small cave in the back of his head to just behind his eyes.

"If you come by my office, I can probably see you now. You know where I work?"

Matisse got the address and punched it into his Blackberry. "I'll be there in thirty. Thanks, Mr. Versakos."

Matisse took the Gary exit off the toll road. He hadn't had occasion to drive through Gary in years. It looked like the city was still vying for the armpit of America award, especially since Pittsburgh cleaned itself up a few years back. He drove past empty lots buildings used to occupy. Five minutes later he pulled up to one of the municipal buildings that still huddled in the downtown, as if fearing the future.

Versakos' small Internet company occupied the third floor of a building that looked stuck in the early part of the last century. Especially the upper floors that could have been used to film The Maltese Falcon.

He could make out "Abner Grable, D.D.S." stenciled on the milk white glass beneath a printed sign pasted over it announcing "Patriot Internet Company" in red, white and blue.

The connection to patriotism escaped Matisse when he stepped inside. The A/C ran loud enough to drown out the door opening and closing behind him and the dark-haired woman pushing forty behind the desk in the outer office didn't look up. She'd dressed for a faulty cooling system in a skimpy yellow striped sundress. One strap fell off a plump shoulder, and she shoved at it as she glanced up with a thin smile. Probably attractive ten years ago, her hair looked worn out, her make-up only serving to etch in the wrinkles she meant to cover. She continued to fight, but age looked like it was wining this battle.

"May I help you?"

"I have an appointment with Mr. Versakos at noon."

"He's stepped out for a minute. Take a seat." She motioned to three straight back chairs pushed up against wainscoting that looked like real oak. A sign of wealth a hundred years ago, now only a sad memory of the Region's former prosperity.

Ten minutes after Matisse arrival, Dmitri Versakos opened the door and stepped inside. He was dressed in bright colors, a red plaid shirt and white cargo pants, probably very hip with the retiree crowd in Florida. He came forward with a smile and a hand out.

"Agent Matisse?" He wore his suspiciously dark hair pulled back in a ponytail affected by hair stylists, furniture designers, and rap stars.

"Mr. Versakos. I appreciate your time."

Versakos opened the door to his inner office. "Come on in. It's a little cooler in here. The air conditioner is at the end of its days, I'm afraid." He pulled a face. "Although these historic buildings look good, they're not big on infrastructure."

The AC in the inner office looked too tiny for the three, eight-foot windows, and the motor raged so loud Matisse decided it probably compensated for size with volume. Matisse was forced to yell just to hear his own voice.

Two bulky computers piggybacked a metal desk someone must have salvaged from some public school closing in Gary. Matisse got the message like a red flag flying in his face. Whether it was playing the horses, an addiction to on-line poker, or just bad business sense, this guy was short on cash.

"Had lunch?" Versakos motioned to a plate of something that looked like canapés, another holdover from cocktail parties of the last century. "Raw octopus." The man's smile was a little apologetic. "I'm Greek."

"No, thanks. I've eaten." Which was true. Matisse had managed to finish off a forgettable burger as he maneuvered his car into an angled spot in front of the pawn shop across the street.

"So what have you got?" The words were those of a gambler, a man used to the language of the bluff.

"Pardon?"

"What's this about?"

"I'm working on an investigation possibly connected to a Hammond PD case, the Abel murders." Matisse watched Versakos closely to see how the body responded. Nothing. Not even a quiver of recognition that the name Abel meant anything. "You know about the murders? Six weeks ago, three people?"

"I read about it in the papers. Horrible thing." He squinted and the wrinkles around the man's eyes deepened, his mouth drawing downward simultaneously.

"According to my information, Charlie Abel worked for you some years ago."

The man looked confused this time, and it looked real. "Don't recall the name."

"He worked for you at the Hammond Water Department."

Versakos pushed his food aside. "Charlie? Oh yeah, I remember him. He got himself murdered?"

It was a callous statement, yet he seemed genuinely surprised. Either this man was very good or he knew nothing about the murder. "I know you've been gone for quite a few years, Mr. Versakos. We contacted you because the police found your name and number in Mr. Abel's address book. Have you had any recent contact with Charlie Abel, since you've been back? Either in person or by phone? Or email?"

"I don't think so." He shrugged. "Wait a minute. I think I did heard from him last year through one of those social networking sites. Linked-In or Facebook, maybe. You know how it is? You get those emails requesting a connection and delete them without a second thought. I don't participate in that crap, except running ads through some of the bigger social network sites."

Matisse made a mental note to check Linked-In and Facebook to see if Charlie Abel belonged to either. And why did this man say he didn't remember Charlie Abel, then change his mind and reveal Charlie sent him an email? Versakos had to have read recent newspaper coverage of the murders, so why bother denying he knew Abel? *Hell, one more thing to add confusion to this crazy investigation.*

"I left the world of Hammond behind when I moved south twenty years ago. I didn't stay in touch with anybody from my old life up here. Too many sad memories." He reached for a cracker. "Bad divorce. Lost my kid and everything else I owned."

Matisse made second mental note to track down the divorce records. "So you had no contact over the years with anyone from the Hammond water department?"

"Nope. I cut my ties to the Region a long time gone."

Matisse signed and switched tactics. Clearly this man would give him nothing more on his connections up here and Matisse would need to dig into it himself. "You know anything about the Lake Coalition Group?"

He shook his head, too quickly to Matisse's mind. "What's that?"

"A local environmental group that started two years or so ago. You ever heard of Wayne Cornell?"

"No. Don't know the name."

"What about Joe Sedlack or Greg Zelenin?"

Versakos shook his head and glanced down at his watch, losing interest in Matisse's questions. "Names aren't familiar, I'm afraid." He shot another pointed glance down at the watch. "I have an appointment in a few minutes that I need to get ready for." The grin that followed looked abashed, a stupid expression on a man in a ponytail with his shirt revealing a tanned hairy chest. "I've started a sort of Internet dating company for the average guy. A blue collar E-Harmony thing. Its working out pretty good. I'm sorry I can't give you any more time. Like you said, I've been gone a while. My ties to this place are all in Gary these days." He stood up, signaling the interview was over.

"Thanks for your time, Mr. Versakos." Matisse stood up and followed the man to the door.

Matisse stood waiting for the elevator, Blackberry in hand as he jotted down follow-up notes. So Dmitri Versakos ran a dating business. That alone set off warning bells in Matisse's world. Although adult pornography wasn't illegal, he'd spent time investigating the on-line sex trade world before the agency moved him to anti-terrorism to feel uneasy. This case just kept pulling up new stinking garbage.

Chapter Thirteen

Sex doesn't mean anything, even when it's good

Thursday Evening, July 14th

The shimmering heat waves hanging above the pavement like mirages all day disappeared, replaced by a faint aura of pale purple with the evening.

Miller squatted beside the rusty gold fender, gripping the lug wrench as though it might refuse to do its job and escape at any moment. With each twist of the wrench, she revisited last night and Milski's.

She looked up at the sound of a car turning into the alley. Matisse's black Lexus picked up a trail of dust in its wake as it headed her way. He pulled to a stop beside her and lowered the driver's side tinted window. Matisse leaned out, backlit by the last of the sun, turning him into a fallen saint. "Problem?"

"Someone slashed my tire last night. Had to take a cab to work this morning." She huffed between pulls on the wrench. She'd put in a ten-hour day at work and attacked the flat tire in semi-dark, the sun already having disappeared behind her gray slate roof.

Miller sat back on her heels and wiped away a drop of perspiration running down her nose. "Damn. Why is it when a man changes a tire, it looks easy? And what the heck do I have a degree in mechanical engineering for, if I can't even change a tire?"

She'd seen Matisse last at Milski's, bending over a woman who looked like she had walked off the cover of a female version of GQ. And here she was, still sweaty from working all day, fighting with a wrench, after spending last night babysitting a Hell's Angel wannabe.

"Looks like you've turned that lug nut into the enemy. Want a hand?"

She shook hair off her damp face and turned to give him a direct look, inexplicably annoyed at his offer. Why the hell were women always struggling when men came along? "I'm inclined to refuse, but I want to get this tire changed tonight, so I'm going to accept."

She stood up and stepped out of the way. He turned off his engine and stepped up to the job, reaching for the wrench. His back to her as he worked, she stared at his T-shirt stretched across a broad back. He wore some sort of fanny pack today, probably his weapon.

Fifteen minutes later, with the sparc in place, he'd put away her tools. "We'll go get you a new tire."

"You don't need to bother. I can handle it tomorrow morning."

He banged once on the top of her car, emphasizing his words. "I'll follow you this time. Let's go."

A sense of being taken care of, something only her dad had done for her, replaced her sense of helplessness, and she suppressed the urge to lean into him.

"I need to get my purse."

"Don't bother. You can pay me back later."

Who could have predicted the world of tires would bring Matisse and her together? Somehow it happened. The night at Milski's forgotten, subtle sexual attraction pulled at her over the tire display.

In the end she left her car in the garage, waiting for the new tire ordered from the distributor.

Miller stared out the window at the empty streets of Hammond as Matisse drove her back to Whiting, watching the last of the seniors scurrying home after early dinners.

Neither of them spoke until he pulled into her alley. "Got anything cold to drink?"

"Follow me."

He took her stairs two at a time, clearly more relaxed than she felt inviting him in for a social visit. She opened her door and stood back. Inside, a dim light burned over the sink. Miller dropped her backpack on its hook and moved quickly to fiddle with the window. She punched 'play' on her IPod and Billie Holiday *Come Rain or Come Shine* filled her kitchen. Immediately the level of intimacy in the room revved up a notch. *Hell.*

She stood there, uncertain, wanting to take back the action. An airless sense of anticipation filled her, the kind of expectation one had right before sex. The feeling seemed completely unjustified in this case, since he gave no indication of any move in that direction.

"Miller Abel listening to Billie Holiday?" His tone sounded light.

"You like the blues, Matisse? I'd have picked you out as a fusion jazz man. Or maybe opera."

"I like opera. I like jazz too. Where's that cold drink?"

"Take a seat."

She pulled out two sodas and popped the tabs. A Bozo the Clown plate on the table was piled high with pink and purple cookies. Apparently, Sparky's answer to a bad tire day.

Miller sank down opposite him and watched as he picked out a blue cookie.

"You bake these?"

She made a face. "No. I'm no baker. My downstairs neighbor left them on my landing."

He took a bite. "Tastes like Cheerios. And strawberries."

"You're probably right. I think the strawberries are from a pudding mix."

He nibbled at a corner. "Not bad." He glanced over at her. "So you had a date last night with Joe Sedlack?"

"Yes." Back to business, the sudden shift in subject pulled her out of her vague sexual fantasies into reality.

"He call you?"

She nodded. "Tuesday. I forgot to mention it the other night in the middle of my rescue."

"You set up the date as part of your work with me?"

"Sure." She made a face. "There's no way I'd normally date a kid like that. When he called and asked me out, I agreed."

"You get me anything from him?"

"A little. He mentioned again that he knew my brother, Jacob. And he made some vague references to the Lake Coalition group, which seemed a little odd."

"Why's that?"

"He's not the kind of kid to be into saving the earth, as far as I can tell."

"So do you recommend I dig deeper with him?"

"Not sure. It just seems strange he's suddenly so interested in me." She took a bite of cookie and stared out the window. "I gave it two hours before I found I couldn't take any more of him. He's a little scary."

"Scary?"

"Maybe creepy is the word. When he took me home, I was a little relieved to find Sparky in my yard, dashing any expectations he might have had for the end of the evening."

"Sparky? Your downstairs neighbor, right?" He motioned with his cookie. "I met her the other night."

"She's hard to miss. If she's around, she definitely makes her presence known."

"Just a reminder. You're not doing anything dangerous in my investigation. Just going about your life and paying attention. Okay?"

"That's what I'm doing."

"I never intended for you to feel obliged to go out with some bastard who scares the crap out of you."

"That I ran into him and he mentioned Jacob was an open invitation for me to see what he knows. And then he called and invited me out. I couldn't pass it up. Besides he doesn't really scare me–much. And if we hadn't been at Milski's last Saturday, he'd never have called. He saw me, remembered who I was, and asked me out. Normally I'd have said no, yet with his interest in the Lake Coalition Group, I couldn't pass up the obvious lead he might provide. I doubt if he bothers me again. My charms aren't that powerful."

"So apart from the few threads you mentioned, you've got nothing?"

"Next to nothing. The subject of the Lake Group came up and he implied some sort of mysterious knowledge he's got."

"Like you said, if that guy's an environmentalist, I'm a Bears' lineman." He rubbed his face and she followed the movement.

"I know. Yet he says he's been to a couple of meetings."

"Those meetings have a lot of North American employees showing up?"

"Yeah, although that's not unusual, since Wayne Cornell started the group a couple of years ago and he's a former EPA specialist at North American," she said. "Contrary to what one might assume, mill employees are no different than anyone else. They want to protect their lake. And in fact, have a vested interest in making sure they aren't directly responsible for doing damage to the environment.

"So, you have any thoughts around what Sedlack's real motives might be?"

"No. It could be we're trying to pigeonhole him. You know, a biker, tough talking, and all. My brother rode a bike too, yet he and his friends were into environmental things. Joe Sedlack could have a real interest, and I'm missing it."

"Your instinct says he's not connected?"

"No. I'm just trying to be fair, and he didn't strike me as someone who'd put the good of the world before his own interests so I couldn't guess why he's attended Coalition meetings. He did say he planned on meeting someone at the next meeting. Something about unfinished business."

Matisse leaned back in his chair, soda in hand. "That sounds promising. No idea who or what, though?"

"No." She watched him finish his drink and make a move to stand. "I was surprised to see you at Milski's again last night." The statement slipped out, although questioning him about his private life was the last thing she wanted to do. She didn't want him to leave.

"I like the feel of Milski's. Reminds me of my dad."

"It has its charms. A cop hang-out, so I've heard."

"Santos mentioned that." And that was that. No mention of the woman who'd made him look so relaxed sitting across from him. Instead, he flashed her a smile that turned her mouth dry. Her breathing turned shallow and all thoughts ceased as her focus shifted to the sensations in her body.

"Probably not a good idea between us, Miller."

The words took her by surprise, the straightforward acknowledgement of what was between them.

"There's nowhere to go with this, you know, if we cross that line."

She gazed at him, trying to read his desire behind the words. "Not everyone has a 'where' they want to go, Matisse." She wanted sex with him, more than she cared to admit, not as a destination, but rather as an event.

Before fear stopped her, she leaned forward and kissed him with parted lips. His own lips felt firm, the curve distinct. Moving as if in slow motion, he stood up and slipped out of his holster. He lay it on table and paused again, as if weighing his options. The white of his T-shirt glowed in the faint light of the kitchen. Perspiration sticking the cotton to his chest outlined the pattern of hair beneath. Pushing aside the table between them, he pulled her to him. She inhaled the mixture of laundry detergent and male. His body felt as solid as the thirty foot maple she'd hid behind on her way to school as a child.

He caught the back of her neck, sliding his cool fingers into her loose hair to cradle her head. "Miller."

The kiss felt as firm and steady as all his movements looked, and he tasted of Coke. She responded to the thrust of his tongue with her own. With trembling fingers she traced the lines of muscle on either side of his spine.

"I still this think is a bad idea," Matisse murmured against her lips. "You're sure?"

"I'm sure." Her whispered reply must have sounded otherwise since he pulled back and checked her face.

"No strings sex, is what we're talking here? Right?"

"Absolutely."

The move to the bedroom came easier than the kiss, a casual stroll down her dark hallway. The only indication of urgency was their quick breathing echoing off the walls. And her hammering heart. The entire scene played out as surreal as a Dali painting in black and white relief.

The single bedside lamp cast long shadows around the room. Standing beside the bed, they made a single outline against the far wall.

Matisse stepped back enough to peel off his shirt, revealing a mat of dark hair. At forty-five, the only indication of age was a heaviness of muscle over the chest.

He kept a hand on her as he reached out and peeled hers over her head as easily as his own.

She wore a plain white bra like all of her underwear these days, all frills tossed aside with everything from her former life.

He seemed not to notice or care about her lack of seductive devices. He turned her around with the slightest pressure on her arms and unfastened the bra. It slid to the floor, unnoticed.

The sound he uttered could have been her name as he caught hold of her shorts and pulled them down, dragging her panties with them.

In one move he swept her up, tossed back the bedspread, and dropped her on the bed. She lay naked, staring up at him. Her body generated a low hum that started at her throat and ran down to pool between her legs.

She'd had sex last three months ago with someone she'd considered as a possible long-term relationship. He'd disappeared the week of the murders and she'd written him off, along with any future relationships.

More important than how long it had been was how long since she'd felt anything except pain.

Matisse still wore his wrinkled khaki pants and she watched him shove them down. As he leaned over her, his pupils dilated, the kindness replaced by lust, she knew tonight would be far more than she could expect or predict.

Holding his body above hers, his arms on either side, he studied her with narrowed eyes, a feral animal in no hurry with his prey, breathing as loud as a runner midway through a marathon.

The room palpated with expectation. Her thoughts spun to a stop as her body took over. Completely naked, he lay down facing her, blocking the dim bedside light. She inhaled sharply as his jutting penis brushed her belly.

From then on it played out slow and deliberate. He caught hold of her hair and pulled her head down to watch. How ironic—the most erotic sexual encounter she'd ever had was with a man more fastidious than anyone she'd ever met. When she shuddered, he drew back, paused and moved forward again, this time entering her with a quick thrust.

He was formidable and it took her breath away. She let him roll her to her back as he moved up over her, beginning the dance in earnest now. Their bodies met, hard and fast, desperate and driven, no trace of civilized man or grief stricken woman. From then on, nothing was the same.

****

Matisse lay back, inhaling to a ten count, fighting for control. The sheets beneath him were twisted and damp. He crooked one arm over his face and shifted his head slowly. Miller lay inches from him, her head turned away, her breathing regular.

Her room was as barren as a nun's cell, as impersonal as a twenty-dollar motel. The small bedside lamp wore a pleaded shade the color of flesh, and it cast a strange apricot hue over the bed. There were no windows, leaving the room as dark and silent as a tomb.

He eased off his side of the bed. Standing naked in the dim light, he leaned down and picked up the pile of clothing. He separated hers and dropped them on a lone straight back chair, the soft swish echoing off the ceiling.

The bed moved slightly when he sat down. It was a double, large enough for tonight's romp. He pulled on his crumpled trousers and shirt, two hours since he'd pulled them off, a lifetime of feelings ago.

He turned to check her a last time, no movement. Using his feet, he searched for his shoes and worked them on. Without air conditioning, the room smelled slightly stale, but she'd burned incense earlier and it lingered, not too heavy, lending a sweet backdrop to the musky aroma of sex. A small fan whirred as it rotated back and forth on top of a dresser across the room.

He swiped at the sweat trickling down his face and shut his eyes to blot out the scene. What the hell had he been thinking? Nothing apparently, since his dick had been in charge for most of the past two hours.

Since his mother died, Matisse had worked hard to live a sane life. Tonight, with little more than a five second pause, he'd had unprotected sex with his inside source, knowing it was only about the sex and nothing else. *Damn it!*

He stood up, heaved a sigh, stepped out of the bedroom, and pulled her door closed. The light from the kitchen spilled faintly down the dark hall, pointing the way out. He followed the path, his mind a jumble of regret.

The kitchen looked the same, his jacket still hung over a chair kicked out of the way, now sitting at an awkward angle. The soda cans sat where left on the table.

He reached for his jacket, and thought about leaving a note. What the hell could he say?

"Sorry. Didn't mean to fuck you. Couldn't help myself.' That wasn't far off. He'd wanted her from the get-go, however much he tried to convince himself she wasn't his type. She was too young, too vulnerable, with too much pain. He'd wanted her anyway. Even worse, after two hours with her, he still wanted her.

Matisse let himself out, tested the lock on the door and made his way down her steps like a drunken sailor, into the darkness, humming with night noises. He eased into his car conscious of the lingering scent of her on his hands and face. Three miles later, he pulled into the motel parking lot, reached into his glove compartment for his car pack, and leaned back.

He lit the cigarette and took a quick drag, leaving it dangling from his swollen lips. He leaned back, too exhausted to go inside.

Sex. Not that he ran short on women to do it with, including Andy, the woman in his life for the past year. She'd told him where to find her while on assignment next door in Gary. Why the hell couldn't he have tapped down his libido until tomorrow when they'd plan to meet and discuss their mutual cases? That relationship made far more sense than he and Miller's. Andy and he shared work, similar lifestyles growing up in Evanston, the standards of the well-educated north shore families, and liked each other. Friends with benefits.

Matisse hated one-night stands, yet he sure as hell liked it tonight. Why the Abel woman? Too thin, too intense, and too young for him, along with all that baggage she dragged behind her right now.

He couldn't deny she'd lit a fire under him and who the hell knew why? And who cared? Nothing more than chemistry and the rest could go to hell.

Still, his lack of control gnawed at him. He shut his eyes and drew a deep drag, releasing the tension in his mind. With that came images as hard and fast as if he'd returned to her bedroom.

Despite the rough and ready nature of it, the sex still had been sweet. Scorching sweet sex. Picturing the scene from an aerial view of her bed, it had been about as sweet as two alley cats tangling on somebody's front lawn. What the hell was sweet about that? It was Miller herself, when she wasn't disappearing into the dark places of her mind to fight some battle.

She'd run her hands up the backs of his thighs and over his ass. He could feel her fingers trembling as he'd sprawled out over her, crying out soft words as she came. Despite the assault of body on body, he'd come away feeling tenderness.

What the hell was there to do about the unprotected sex? She must be sure of herself since she hadn't objected. He should at least ask her about the situation, when she'd last had a check-up, if she was on the pill. *Something, Goddammit.*

He smashed out the cigarette, shoved open the car door, and grabbed his holster. He'd left the room air conditioning running on high and the cold hit him like an icy shower. He slammed the door shut behind him, tossed down his stuff, and threw himself face down on his bed without removing his clothes. The lingering smell of sex drugged him and then pushed him over into dreamless sleep.

Chapter Fourteen

Adventures can be daring or merely escapes from reality

Friday, July 15th

With no car and exhausted from lack of sleep, Miller took the day off from work. Myron Kowalski woke her at eight to tell her she could pick up her car with a new tire and the spare back in the trunk. An offshore breeze filled her apartment with the scent of sweet clover from some farm far away.

She drank her coffee and thought about last night with Matisse in her bed. He'd gone off without waking her, leaving behind her clothes piled neatly on a chair beside the bed to remind her it was more than a fantasy. *Damn.* Had last night ruined all chance of continuing to work with him and get information? She didn't know a lot about him yet one thing was certain, he was a man of conscience. He'd probably call and apologize, and then coolly remove her from any part in his investigation.

By noon the lightness of being from a night with Matisse turned heavy, reminding her of her real usefulness to him. Miller trudged up her stairs, dragging groceries for the week. She stashed them automatically, bored and restless with the day.

She pulled out her laptop and unabashedly went over the list of names she'd pulled off Matisse's Blackberry last night as he dozed. Some of them clearly were significant, others surprised her. Joe Sedlack and Wayne Cornell were obvious. The rest, including Zelenin, left her wondering. A couple of the names were completely foreign to her.

Googling them was easy, the results unrewarding. Wayne Cornell's history was neither ominous nor suggestive of any illegal history. He finished his graduate research work in environmental science, along with a degree from the University of Michigan in metallurgical engineering. The man came from money and still lived in his parents' compound in the nicest part of Whiting. She found an article about the founding of The Lake Coalition Group on Wiki. Nothing shocking or even titillating in any of it.

In the digital world, Joe Sedlack could be called the invisible man. She found nothing on him, no Facebook entry, no Twitter account, no mention of him anywhere. If there was something in his past, it didn't show up on the Web, since arrest records weren't public. Unless he'd merited a small column in some newspaper, that part of his life was hidden.

Nothing. Somehow she'd have to get more from Matisse.

Miller punched in Jacob Abel. His picture popped up on the monitor, so large it felt as though he was in her kitchen. The sudden wrenching in her heart felt as physically real as if she'd taken a poison, hitting first her chest, followed by a punch to her solar plexus.

Jacob. The sobs erupted from a tiny cave of pain that slid out from behind her heart and pushed against her rib cage.

At last she leaned back, limp, head aching, dried up and empty, like a vacuum had sucked out her soul and left behind a rag doll of a body. Funny how emoting worked that way.

A noise, something like a cross between a gasp and a moan, slipped from her lips and she pushed herself up, dragging her body to the sink. She filled the kettle, rummaged around for anything edible and discovered a leftover bowl of tuna. Her fingers worked automatically, making a sandwich she didn't want, pouring tea, cleaning the counter.

She picked up the dishes with fingers as weak as an eighty-year-old woman and focused on moving to the table. The sun screaming in through the screen door drew her, and she pushed it open and crept out onto her landing. The heat felt like a hot shower, reviving her. She placed the dishes carefully down on the top step and lowered herself down beside them, resting her feet on the third step.

The first few bites took concentration to swallow past the lump of clay in her throat. After that, if she chewed slowly, it got easier. She drank the tea greedily, sucking in the lemon-ness of it, imagining it flowing through her veins and out into her limbs. Then she let herself think about Matisse again, steady and reliable. He even smelled reassuring, that indefinable scent reminding her of business suits and pressed shirts tinged faintly with tobacco, of important meetings. A man living in a man's world.

Unlike Jacob, who would never be a man. She swallowed hard and forced her heart to open up, letting herself feel. She could still love him, even in missing him. She could remember his funny words, his crazy jokes about her name, his endearing adolescent tricks, like slipping slimy pimentos into her running shoes, then standing in the door watching her slip into them.

She lost track of time, sitting in the sun, letting it heal her.

After a long time she stood up, piled up her dishes, and drifted inside. She pulled out her phone and stared at it. A call from Lexie, as usual. Faithful as an old dog, she'd call and leave a message once a week. Nothing urgent, her gentle requests were always the same—give me a call, I'll find a babysitter, and we'll go out for a drink. The weekly meetings they'd established over the years ended abruptly the week her family died. Miller stared at the number, debating and decided to call and ask Lexie to go to the Coalition meeting with her and Sparky. She'd be known there since one of her boyfriends was part of the group, and she'd love the idea if she knew they were investigating something for the FBI.

"Lexie. This is Miller."

"Miller," Lexie replied. "It's good to hear from you again so soon."

"Do you have a few minutes to talk?"

"Sure. Glad to. Anything to pull me out of that downward spiral of the gibberish of kindergarteners." A single mom, Lexie had two kids, ages four and five.

Where to go now? Apologize again for dropping out of her life for two months?

"You have no idea how much I appreciated your being there for me during the funerals and your calls, even if it didn't seem like I cared."

"I know, Miller."

The silence between them stretched out for Miller, filled with memories of Lexie in her life, hanging out at her house as a kid, even going on vacations together. Lexie had always been there. "I wanted to catch up on your life, Lexie, and I'm headed out tonight to a meeting and thought you might meet me there."

"What's the meeting?"

"The Lake Coalition Group. I'm planning on dropping by tonight. My neighbor's going with me. I know it's late notice, but I thought you might like to come along."

"Miller, I wish I could. My parents are taking my kids and me to a Cubs game tonight. Don't let this be the only invite I get. I promise if I get a day's notice, I'll rearrange my life to spend some time with you."

"I know you will. It's my fault. I just thought of asking you along and took a chance. I would love to see you. Any possibility of tomorrow night? Maybe Milski's for an hour?"

"Let me ask my parents. I think I may be able to swing loaning the kids out to them over the weekend and have tomorrow free."

"That's great, Lex. Leave me a message, if you can swing it. Let's say seven tomorrow night?"

"Good. I'll get back to you. What's all the interest with the Lake Coalition thing? I didn't think you were into movements."

"No. Let's just say I'm doing some research. Have you been to a meeting?"

"Nope. Remember Jerry Fedderer from high school? He's into it big time."

"Jerry? He's still around?"

"He's teaching these days, at Hammond High School. Weird, huh?"

"So are you dating him?" Lexie kept a hot and heavy dating life going, despite her focus on her two kids.

"Yup. Hard to imagine, isn't it? Me and the class nerd."

Jerry Fedderer, a kid who talked like a Methodist minister with the build of Chicago Bears tight end. "Is it serious?"

"Not yet although it could go that way. He's civil and polite. He loves kids and I matter to him," she said. "It won't stop me from going out and having fun with you though. And what about you, Miller? Any men around these days?" Their weekly girls' night outs always focused first on men—and sex.

"Not really. There is someone around. At least he was a couple of nights ago." Why the hell share it? Why the hell not? Lexie and she had few secrets, until two months ago when Miller slammed the door on everyone.

"So give. Who and what?"

"He's an FBI agent."

The pause was so long Miller thought she'd lost the signal. "Wow. Something to do with your family's case?"

"Sort of. He's here working with Lou Santos on a possible connection between his FBI case and my family's murders."

"I see. Interesting. You and an FBI guy. Is he staying around long?"

"A few weeks. I'm doing some digging for him, keeping an ear out for anything unusual. Like with the meeting tonight."

"You're not doing anything dangerous, are you?"

Now there was a question. Lexie knew her well, could guess at her emotional state without her family. She knew there'd be nothing to keep Miller from throwing herself over the edge of a volcano, if it solved the murders. "Lou Santos is overseeing this, so I'm sure no danger can come my way."

"What's the FBI like in bed?"

"Lexie."

"Come on, give."

"He's a very nice man. Older, sane, an adult."

"Hmmph. What's he like in bed?"

"Can't give you an accurate account. It was a one night stand."

"Well, have another one. You can never have too many one night stands, if it's good sex."

"Call and let me know if you can swing Milski's tomorrow night." Miller rang off and smiled. Lexie never changed.

****

Blackie's in Hammond turned out to be Milski's on a grander scale and crowded on a Friday night. The dartboard, pinball machines, and pool tables competed for the attention of environmental hipsters.

Miller spotted the Lake Coalition right away. A circle of twenty or so, strangely mismatched people occupied three tables crowded into one corner. She pulled up a chair in the circle.

She'd ended up bringing Sparky, who dressed herself up ultra-conservative tonight in fatigue-green pants and a strange, toad-colored T-shirt. Across her chest in sparkles sprawled the words "Save the Whale."

Wayne Cornell, an academic looking man in glasses and crew cut, in his mid forties, slight of build, and dressed in nondescript clothes stood in the center of the Coalition group. He nodded at her. "Miller. It's good to see you." Then turned and addressed the crowd. "One of our engineers from North American Steel has joined us." The words set off a simultaneous turning of heads towards Miller, who winced. She'd chosen to wear a beige T-shirt with tan shorts and flip-flops to avoid calling attention to herself. So much for keeping a low profile.

"Schlitz?" The waiter asked, wearing a T-shirt and jeans. He looked like he belonged in middle school, not taking orders in this place.

"Thanks." Miller pushed a bill into the kid's hand.

Wayne Cornell gave a low whistle to call their attention to him. "We won't do introductions here. When we take a break, mingle around, and network with others. We want to keep pushing the word out, so make sure you connect up. And make sure you follow the group on Twitter and our Facebook page."

He then delivered a mini-lecture on the lake that included a subtle chastisement of the capitalist system using a flow chart as his only prop. The discussion belonged to Cornell alone. The others, mostly young, listened to the dry facts about water contamination from industry with eager expressions. Cornell's conversation didn't offend, he didn't sound angry, didn't provoke reactions, and stayed focused. That in itself Miller found interesting when these days most causes were loud and argued a lot.

Twenty minutes later, he called a short break and people wandered up to her, introducing themselves. The names swam past, an almost even mix of men and women, many faces familiar, if not the names. Mill workers by far outnumbered the rest. There were a couple of students from the local two-year college, a priest, a couple of computer people, and some who said they ran their own businesses. She counted eight or ten who introduced themselves as steel mill employees.

Five minutes into the second half of the meeting, Joe Sedlack sauntered in. He slid into a seat at the back of the group as out of place in his black leather as a stripper at a priest's convention. He got no more than a glance from the group, nothing uncomfortable about their looks. Inclusion and diversity; this group walked the walk.

Sedlack scanned the room and locked in on Miller. He gave her a grin as he took a gulp of his beer.

The next thirty minutes Cornell focused on actions, public and/or political, that might be taken to point out water irregularities. They followed this with a fifteen minute brainstorming session and then set up the next meeting.

Miller watched cautiously as Joe Sedlack sidled towards her. However irrelevant she thought he was, he smoked with sexual energy tonight. That, or his blunted rage seemed to appeal to more than a few women following his stroll across the floor.

"Hey Miller. Good to see you."

"Hi Joe. You've met Sparky, my neighbor?" Miller said.

"Sure. I'm kind of surprised you showed up here tonight after turning down my invitation. You planning on getting involved?"

"I'm just sitting in tonight to get an idea of what they're doing. I'm not ready to commit."

"Sounds like you're not committing to much these days." He sounded insolent, as usual.

"No," she replied and stood up. "Want to head out, Sparky?"

Sparky, busy networking, turned. "Let me just jot down a couple of emails and I'm with you. Meet you at the car."

"See you, Joe." Miller waved and headed for the door, ignoring whatever he called after her.

Despite the fact that the most conscientious Lake Coalition people rode their bikes or took public transportation, cars still filled every space in Blackie's parking lot.

The hairs on the back of Miller's neck stood up as she crossed the hundred yards to her Honda. She glanced back at the door. No sign of Joe Sedlack, thank God.

Ping! Something glanced off the top of the Honda and whizzed past Miller's ear. She ducked, listened, then stood up and shoved her key into the lock. She climbed into the safety of the dark car adrenaline pumping, heart hammering. Trembling, she fought for the ignition in the dark, exhaled in relief when she found it, and shoved in the key.

She backed out of the tight spot as quickly as she could and made a sharp U-turn for the exit.

Crash!

The sound wasn't loud, more like the noise in her head when she crushed ice between her teeth. She glanced in her mirror and caught the last of hundreds of tiny pieces of glass falling in slow motion. It took less than five seconds and nothing remained where the rear window glass used to be.

She jammed her foot down on the gas pedal and skidded to a halt in front of Blackies' back door. Sparky came out the door of the bar, laughing, surrounded apparently by nun groupies. "Hurry, Sparky. Get in!"

Sparky waved, trotted over, and climbed into the Honda. "What's up?"

Miller sped out of the lot, ignoring the question. She glanced back. No one followed. Shaking with adrenaline, she loosened her grip on the steering wheel and eased up on the gas.

"Hey Miller!" Sparky looked back. "Whoooa! There's no back window now!"

"I know." Miller inhaled and let it out slowly. "I think someone just shot at me." She began to shake.

Sparky reached into her sequined bag and pulled out a phone.

"What are you doing?" Miller asked.

"We need to call the police."

"No."

"No? You can't just have someone take a shot at you and then just drive away." She flipped her phone open. "Give me the number of your FBI friend, then."

Miller slowed to a stop just shy of Lake Highway. "No. He already is nervous about my getting into trouble. I'm not going to tell him anything happened. If he finds out, he'll take me off his case."

"Can't you at least let me in on what we're up to?"

"I'm his inside source. I'm keeping my eyes and ears open for anything unusual going on around me."

"I know that, or suspected. What else is going on?"

Miller sighed. What was going on that she could tell this woman? She shifted gears and turned onto Lake Highway. "Look, Sparky. This is really important. What I'm doing while I work with the FBI is get whatever information I can get around my family's murders. No one's telling me anything about that case. And when

Matisse dropped into my lap saying he was doing a combined investigation with the Hammond Police, it seemed like fate. I could at least get some information so I don't have to sit around going crazy. I can't. Not anymore. I need to do something."

"So, you're using the FBI connection with both cases as an opportunity to do what neither Matisse or the Hammond cops want you to do, investigate the murders on your own."

Miller nodded.

"And the connection between the two cases is?"

"An email threat to my father that points to something going on with the water. Matisse is already working on a similar threat to Chicago's water and this fit right in. He's agreed to use me as long as I am good." Miller glanced over at Sparky. "Please don't call anyone. He found out that I'd been snooping around a warehouse where I didn't belong. He already warned me I wasn't going to get another chance. If I get into trouble again, I'm done as far as working with him is concerned."

"I see. Well, at least you're not alone. You've got me." She didn't even smile when she said it.

"Look, Sparky. I can't drag you into this any more than I already have. It could be dangerous."

"Too bad since I'm already in." She did grin this time. "You turn anything good up yet? And why the warehouse?"

"I found a reference to it in something I found at work. Then someone found me there and I ran. Matisse found out after I got stranded on the highway on my way back to Whiting and I had to call him."

"So now he doesn't trust you."

"I'd say so."

"And you're sleeping with him, right?"

Miller pulled up to a red light and stared at the woman. "What makes you say that?"

"Dunno. I saw him, or actually heard him, leaving last night. Like around two in the morning."

"You are too nosy," Miller said, "And too perceptive." Oh, what the hell? Sparky already guessed, so there was no point in constructing an elaborate lie for her.

Sparky shrugged. "No big deal. And pretty interesting. Like a novel."

"Yeah, some novel."

"So, let's go home and we won't report this. Just promise me, you'll be careful when you go anywhere after this. We don't know if someone took aim at you specifically or if this was just another Hammond drive-by."

They drove along in silence until they pulled up behind the duplex. "I'll get my window fixed tomorrow," Miller said. "And Matisse will never know."

Chapter Fourteen

Stability is an overrated state of being

Late Friday Night, July 15th

Matisse phoned Miller at eleven-thirty and he knocked on her door five minutes later.

"You were parked outside when you called me?" she said.

"Almost. I was turning into the alley behind Main."

He wore his shirt unbuttoned at the neck. His tie dangled from his suit pocket. He hesitated inside the door as she stepped back. Tonight, his former romance with the bottle showed on his tired face, a little puffiness around the eyes, a very slight sagging of jowls.

His eyes lingered on hers, a magnet drawing her to him and her feet took her where her mind resisted going—into his arms. The sense of coming home felt too good. Standing close enough to feel his breath on her face, she let herself enjoy the sensation for a few seconds. Then she stepped back, hands resting lightly on his arms as she searched his face. "Sorry."

He had no intention of going into what happened last night. Like most men, sex was something one participated in, like a sporting event, not an occasion for personal interrogation. She took a deep breath and jumped in anyway. "Are we going to just step over what happened last night, as if it never happened?"

He stopped and looked her in the eyes. "No. Although I've gotta admit I'm feeling a little awkward here."

The silence in the room didn't make it easier. She listened to the wind blowing off the lake and searched for something normal to say. "Have a seat, Matisse. Can I get you something?"

"No. I'm good. Just tired." He pulled out a chair and dropped into it. "How'd the Lake Coalition Meeting go tonight?"

"I'd say mildly interesting, I'm not sure how useful any of it is to you. Wayne Cornell runs a very orderly meeting. No incivility, no shouting out, or angry accusations. The organization seems focused on keeping watch to make sure the lake is protected, like their name indicates. I didn't hear any threats or any suggestion of taking illegal actions, and no unusual activities the group is focused on right now. They are doing rallies, which are perfectly normal for an environmental group, probably a few every year to keep public attention on the lake."

"You went to the meeting alone?"

"No. I was planning on it, and then Sparky offered to go along."

"Sparky."

"You remember. My downstairs neighbor. Mary Catherine Doherty. The former nun who dresses outrageously and is very nosey. She's looking for adventure and wants to be included in whatever I might have going in that line." Work moved the conversation into safe territory. "I like her."

"Good." He stopped. "Anything else you've got for me?"

She weighed her options here. Turning herself back into his case source was damned awkward enough, having spent time doing sweaty, noisy things to each other. It only made hiding things from him all that much more difficult. What could she leave out? The attack, for sure, since there was no proof that Sedlack had taken that shot at her.

"Two things. First, the rallies. They have two sched-uled. One for this Sunday at the Diamond Oil Facility, the other one next Wednesday at the Lee Hammond Water Treatment facility on Baseline Road."

He whistled soundlessly. "Hell, that's pretty interest-ing. Especially the water treatment site. Any discussion of why they picked those two sites?"

"The first is obvious. There's been a lot of local news lately about illegal dumping at Diamond, a lot of questions. Cornell said with the water treatment facility the point of media attention, the plan of the Coalition is to focus the public directly on possible threats to the water and the impact those threats have on ordinary citizens."

Matisse frowned. "So what do you think? Is it some-thing important?"

"I'm not sure. I'd definitely make a point of watch-ing the rallies and seeing if someone interesting turns up. I just don't see what this has to do with my dad's mur-der. He was as concerned about protecting the water supply as Cornell is."

"I'll send someone to each of the rallies."

"You don't want me to go? Since I've already put in an appearance, it wouldn't seem unnatural if I turned up."

"Let's wait and see. I'll let you know by Sunday morning. Will that work?"

"Yes." What else did someone like her with no life have to do?

"You mentioned there were two things you got from the meeting. What's the second?"

"Joe Sedlack. He showed up halfway through the meeting. He's not someone I'd pick out as a guy with a big interest in the environment. I think I told you he said he met my brother there, so he's attended at least one meeting before." Miller shrugged. "So I suppose it's not out of the question."

"Did you have any exchange with him?"

"A little. As I was leaving. The other night he mentioned, or maybe implied, he had something to do and was going to a Coalition meeting."

"Did he say anything during the meeting? Did he talk with anyone?"

"Not that I noticed."

She searched for something more to toss him like a bone. "You said you'd get back to me the other day with some more leads to follow?"

"Yeah. I've got a few things." He pulled out his Blackberry and tapped on it. "I'm emailing you a list. Nothing tricky. No bounty hunting." He grinned at her. "Just a few quiet questions to a couple of people I want to get back to without making them nervous the Feds are after them." He gave her a half smile that washed over her like a warm shower. "Good job, Miller. Have you ever considered doing detective work for real?"

"It's what I do, in a way. I gather information and figure out the puzzles in machines."

"Probably way more interesting, in general."

They exchanged mutual smiles this time.

He looked like he was going to get up. He surprised her by leaning forward. "Is there anything else you need to say to me?"

The question sounded lawyer-like. Then she remembered he was a lawyer. "You mean about us last night? Will you get into trouble with the FBI for having sex with your inside source?"

"No. It's pretty much 'don't ask, don't tell' when it comes to those kinds of activities. The FBI looks the other way. Like most companies, they pretend it doesn't happen, unless there's some problem that makes it public."

"Well, if you're worried about me, Matisse. Don't. I won't tell them. I'm not upset and I don't feel misused. I like sex. It was good last night. I'd be happy to do it again, if you're into it. If not, I'm a grown-up. I'll get over the rejection."

Now she'd surprised him. She saw it in his face.

"I don't know what to say."

"You don't have to say anything. When you leave, it's over. The only problem I have is we didn't get around to protection. Stupid of me."

"No. Stupid of me. I'd blame it on your taking me by surprise, except that's bullshit. You can count on it not happening again."

"Sex or unprotected sex?"

"Unprotected," he said. "Let's give it a rest for now, although if it happened again, I wouldn't complain. Working for me, following my rules, it's a little weird. And with what you've been through…" He lifted one shoulder. "As for your reasons, I'd guess it's got something to do with dulling pain."

"If I am dulling the pain, does it matter? You're not my therapist, Matisse."

He paused. "You're right. It's not my place to be your caretaker." He reached out and brushed her face with fingers that felt cool against her cheek. "I'll be in touch."

She moved to the window and watched him head down her stairs in the dim light. He turned at the bottom and waved. "Stay safe, Miller." He slipped out the gate, past her Honda with the back window shot out. He didn't spot it.

Chapter Sixteen

Escapes and other innocent pleasures

Late Friday night and Saturday

Miller watched the Lexus pull off and let out her breath. If he'd seen the damage to her car, he'd have turned around in a New York minute and been back at her door demanding an explanation. She stretched out her legs, fighting the feeling she'd been run over by a truck and left beside the road. She wasn't that out of practice with sex, just the kind they'd had last night.

She headed for the shower, stripped, and stepped in. The water hit her skin and she shivered at the image of his hands running over her thighs. God, was she actually falling for this guy?

Two minutes into the shower her cell rang. She thrust an arm out and fumbled for her phone. She squinted at the caller ID display. Matisse.

"Hello."

"Miller. What the hell happened to your car window?"

Holy Crap. "Not sure. Must have happened earlier this evening at Blackies."

"Damn it!" The words sounded strange coming from Matisse's mouth. "And you've got a bullet hole in your roof." He said it almost as an afterthought, but he clearly was pissed at her again.

She reached over and flipped off the water.

"Did you report it?" he asked.

"I've been a little busy, Matisse. I'll report it this morning."

"I don't suppose you'd like to tell me why you didn't bother to mention it tonight?"

"Because I planned on taking the car back to Myron's Garage in the morning. And I don't know that it has anything to do with your investigation."

Matisse didn't reply, probably working on his composure. Or preparing a lecture.

Miller waited and he didn't respond. "Look, Matisse, there are plenty of random shootings to go around in Hammond. There's no proof this had anything to do with me personally. I knew if I mentioned it, you'd be upset."

He grunted something she missed.

"Are you?" she asked.

"What? Upset? It doesn't matter now." She had no trouble hearing him now. "The bottom line is I don't believe in coincidences. One more incident and you're off my case."

Fine. That was that. Last warning. Next time he'd dump her. That fact moved up her timeline, nothing more. She had no plans on stopping what she was doing. "I get it. So what do you want me to do next?"

"I'm emailing you that list for follow-up. Remember. I don't want anything tricky and no bounty hunting. Just, for God's sake, ask a few last questions of a couple of people I want to get back to, and while you're at it, avoid making them nervous."

"All right."

"Remember, I want a police report on your car filed tomorrow."

"I will."

He'd hung up.

****

Miller set off for Myron Kowalski's after breakfast. A legend in the Region, the place was busy already. Myron had seen it all—cars stripped down for parts, battered trucks used in drunken parking lot bumper cars, damage from police chases. A bullet hole wouldn't make one more dent in his day, although even he got suspicious seeing her two days in a row. He straightened up from the open hood of an '82 Dodge Pick-up and jabbed a dirty finger at her Honda. "Drive by?"

Hell. "Don't know. Could be."

He took a quick glance back at her, then nodded, an exploding window no surprise to him. Normal people would probably be freaked out at someone shooting at them. Maybe as a lone survivor of a triple homicide, she reacted differently. She felt fear as almost separate from herself as if compartmentalized and unrelated to the horror of what she found in her parents' house. As for grief, who could predict that? Sometimes it stabbed at her. Mostly, she felt only a heavy, sad weight that rarely left her.

"Where'd this happen?" Myron was talking now. Asking a question.

"Sorry. What'd you say?"

"I said where'd this happen?"

"Blackie's parking lot."

He nodded as if that explained it all, even the bullet hole in the roof.

"When can I pick it up, Myron?"

He rubbed his weathered face as he considered the glass decorating her back seat. "Oh, give me a day. Should have it done late tonight. How's about I leave it parked out back with the key under the mat, seeing as we're closed tomorrow?"

"Thanks, Myron. I appreciate it."

He pulled off his White Sox's cap, wiped his sweaty forehead with the back of his hand, and replaced his cap on his balding head. "I'll get Harold out in the garage to give you a lift home."

Miller filled out a police report at Myron's with the barest of information she could provide and stood waiting for her ride, watching Myron take a tire off a pick-up. He tossed the old one on a six-foot high stack and wiped his hands on his overall. "I hear you moved to Whiting. Over there by the mud flats. Kind of a dangerous area, ain't it?"

"The damage happened to my car in Hammond, not Whiting."

"And gettin' your tire slashed? That Hammond or Whiting?"

She gave up. "Whiting."

A truck with 'Myron's' on the side backed out of the garage, pulled up in front of her and she climbed in.

"Well, watch yourself. Okay, Missy? You don't need any more bad news around you."

Miller stretched her face around her teeth with something as close to a smile as she could manage. "I'll be careful."

****

Restless and car-less Miller filled in the afternoon organizing the next steps in her investigation. She started with the email from Matisse that included the names of follow-ups. She printed it off and ran her eyes down the page, sorting items into significant and insignificant. The need for useful action pushed her forward, the fear of him removing her from his case too real, whether because he'd slept with his inside source or because he decided he didn't want to be hooked up to a loose cannon.

She slid her other list—the one she'd taken off Matisse's Blackberry—out of her backpack and studied the names. Greg Zelenin, Joe Sedlack, and Henry Winston. The list he'd emailed her was a limited version of the one she'd pilfered the other night as he dozed. She'd already started digging online into these guys and nothing special had turned up. Was there anything here that really mattered to Matisse? Or was he simply using her for his grunt work, eliminating those he knew were dead ends, leaving the good stuff for himself?

Her eyes moved slowly over the names. Some she recognized and dismissed, knowing their history much better than Matisse. She pulled out a pen and drew lines through these. The three remaining names were Jeffrey Owens, Wayne Cornell, and Dmitri Versakos. Jeffrey Owens , the CEO of North American Steel led the list. Of course. He gave the orders at the company and had the final say on what rules were kept—or broken. Matisse's notes read 'Check the man's history, problems with the mill, gossip going around.' And then there was Wayne Cornell. She knew what most people in Whiting knew about the man, all of it good. In a stretch he maybe could turn anarchist over some affront to the lake. There was no way she'd suspect him of murder.

Versakos. It stirred something in her, not feelings or thoughts, just a bunch of vague body sensations, a slight chill followed by an unfamiliar queasiness. She filed the name away for later and decided she'd start with Wayne Cornell, then Jeffrey Owens. The first step with him would be to find a way to search the employment records for other possible connections between North American Steel and Hammond Water. She couldn't do anything until she retrieved her car from Myron.

She got a call about the car a little before six. "I've got your Honda sitting nice and safe out behind the garage. Come by tonight or in the morning, whichever suits you. The key's under the mat. Just leave me a check in the door drop."

"I appreciate it, Myron. Thanks again for doing fast work. Both times."

Seconds after she flipped her phone shut, it rang again. Lexie.

"Hey."

"Well, I did it. Got a babysitter. My mom's going to bite the bullet and skip her bridge club so I can get a night out. You ready to party?"

Shit. She'd forgotten the promise to Lexie to go out tonight. She folded up her lists and piled them on top of the unanswered sympathy cards. So much for her investigation. "You got a car? Mine's at the garage."

"Sure. I'll zip by and pick you up and we're on our way. It'll be like the old days."

"Give me thirty to get myself into a dress."

"Gotcha."

****

Saturday nights Milski's hid the pool tables, brought in live music, and drew a bigger crowd. Tonight it rocked, the band from Jacob's world, not Miller's. The beat pulsed through the overheated room like a throbbing heart. Cops and factory workers who frequented Milski's on weekends jostled butt to butt on the dance floor and lined up three deep at the bar.

Lexie led the way, elbowing through the teeming humanity with the best of them. She captured a small table at the far end of the room as someone vacated it and motioned for Miller to follow. "You okay?" Lexie asked.

"I'm good." Who'd have thought she'd be spending another Saturday at Milski's, the third time in a week she'd been to the place?

They snagged a waitress and got their beers in hand before settling down for a serious talk. Lexie wore some sort of strapless mini-dress in black that turned her tiny-person daytime persona to sultry. Miller tugged at her skimpy yellow shirt that didn't quite meet the waistband of her skirt, both of them stuffed away forgotten. She felt as awkward in the get-up as a ten year old stepping on stage at her first piano recital. The males on the prowl in the room tonight glanced their way repeatedly.

Lexie leaned over her beer. "So, let's have it. I want the full story of your dealings with this FBI agent."

"It's not as exciting as you make it sound. He came to my door last week looking for Miller Abel. It was clear he had some sort of agenda in mind. Once he got over the surprise of finding a female 'Miller,' he gave me an abbreviated version of his investigation in conjunction with the Hammond cops. Just routine." *Yeah, right. Sorry, Lexie, I can't elaborate more for you.*

"Sounds pretty cool. What's the connection with you?"

"My dad's job. The police found an email warning my dad about a threat to the local water. Matisse is running some sort of investigation with similar concerns and they called him in. Like I said, no big deal. Just routine for him."

"Matisse. Cool name. What's he like?"

"Mid forties, nice looking in a buttoned-down, FBI kind of way. Overall, I'd have to say a nice guy. Not what I'd expect when someone says FBI."

"You like him."

Miller shrugged. "I do like him." She slanted her gaze away from Lexie to the crowd. What happened in her bed last night had nothing to do with like.

"You slept with him?"

Miller pulled her gaze back to Lexie. "How'd you pick that one out of the air?"

"I've known you a long time, and I know that look when you're thinking about sex."

"Oh."

"Miller, I think it's great. You've been hiding out up there in your little prison for weeks. I can't even imagine how you're dealing with everything, and I think it's great you've found yourself some comfort with this guy."

"It's only been one night. The important fact is that he's giving me access to some leads in my family's murders, something I couldn't get close to with the Hammond cops."

"You're tracking the killer yourself? First, I'm shocked that you're putting yourself in that much danger." She looked horrified, all right. "Second, I am amazed some FBI agent would be willing to share information with you."

"I can't sit around, Lexie, and be depressed. I spent six weeks doing that. Matisse showing up at my door gave me something to do around investigating the murders. And second, he gives me small tidbits of nothing to do—like go to a Lake Coalition meeting and see if I hear anything useful. Or sends me off to have conversations with a couple of people he wants to eliminate from his list. It's not much, but I've managed to expand it."

"Sounds tricky. Especially since you've slept with this guy. More important, isn't it dangerous to be tracking a murderer yourself?"

"Yeah." She paused. Lexie wasn't anybody's idiot. "I'm careful."

"Yeah, right. Don't get yourself hurt, okay, Miller? Promise me?"

"I can say I won't, but I'm not real big these days on believing life doesn't hurt. I definitely don't want to get myself into trouble. I might have a few weeks ago, but hey, it must be the healing properties of sex. I'm going to keep searching for the murderer, but I don't really want to die doing it."

Lexie's bottle stopped half way to her mouth as someone tapped her on the shoulder. Above her a guy flashed a smile that lit up his plain face.

"Wanna dance?"

Lexie turned. "You mind, Miller?"

"No. Knock yourself out. We came out to have some fun. Go ahead."

Miller followed Lexie in the crowd for a while, then leaned back. She closed her eyes and listened to the music, something else she didn't recognize with a heavy beat, good for dancing. She let it sweep her some place far away, so far off she almost missed the tap on her shoulder.

"Miller."

She looked up into Matisse's eyes. It took two beats to tap down the surprise at seeing him. "What's up?"

"Wanna dance?"

Another surprise bringing on another pause. "Sure, if you're game, I am."

He held out a hand.

Miller took his hand and stood up, knocking back the chair.

Two minutes out on the dance floor, the music slowed and he pulled her into his arms. He wore jeans and a T-shirt tonight. It made him look younger, accentuating the body she now knew well. "What are you doing here?" she asked.

"Having a night out. Santos mentioned some of his cops come here and suggested I stop by, get to know them a little, maybe make my investigation a little easier."

Miller rubbed her nose on the cotton shirt. He smelled good. Why did men who smelled good always smell like laundry? They moved silently, alone in the crowd, alone with their own separate thoughts. The song ended and she glanced up at him, not finding his eyes in the glare of overhead light, although his mouth looked set.

"You want to stay or can I drive you home?"

"Let's go," she said. The inevitable bad ending with him could wait until tomorrow.

Lexie returned to the table, the same smiling guy still hanging over her.

"Lex, this is Matisse. He's offered to take me home. If you want me to stay, I will."

"Nah." Lexie motioned up at her friend. "Luke, you'll keep me company here a while longer?"

"No problem there." The guy had a drawl that could only be an Indiana country accent.

"You sure you'll be okay driving home by yourself?" Miller said.

"No problem. I'm a big girl. How about if I get Luke here to follow me and make sure I get there safe?"

"Good. Sorry I'm checking out so soon."

"It's all good, Miller. I'm really glad we got to hang out. Let's make it a regular Saturday night thing."

They didn't touch as they strode to the far end of the parking lot and found his car. Matisse drove fast, his eyes on the road. The silence between them felt more like expectation than real tension. He glanced over at her as he pulled up in her alley.

"Parking in plain sight tonight?" she asked.

"Sure. No point in playing silly spy games now since everyone saw us together at Milski's."

She climbed out and watched as he locked up his car. Whatever this was between them, it didn't feel like dating.

Chapter Seventeen

In this strange land—bare of natives

Saturday Night Late, July 16th

Matisse came around the car, bent his head and touched his mouth to hers, phantom-like at first, then firmer as he moved closer. She opened her lips, finding the edges of his, tasting him. She inhaled, taking in the smells of his day and his world.

She moved in tight between his legs feeling his erection through his jeans prod at her bare belly where her top parted from the skirt.

"Do you want me to stay?"

"Yes," she replied without hesitating.

"Then let's get upstairs before your friend, Sparky, sticks her head out her door and asks us in for tea."

She took his hand and led him up her steps. Inside, she headed straight down the dark hallway to the bedroom. He dropped his coat on a kitchen chair and followed.

The only light came from the bathroom. She switched on the bedside lamp and turned, the room airless and stifling. He didn't move towards her. Instead, he stood by the bed and watched, letting her lead.

She pulled his belt free and eased the jeans off, nudging him down onto her bed. She carefully removed his T-shirt, the simple action such a conventional prelude to greedy sex.

He watched her with his nostrils flared, his pupils dilated to pinpoints. His bare skin burned her palms. She stopped and searched his eyes for any other emotion besides desire. She saw nothing else there. She pulled off her clothes and stopped again, feeling as awkward as the first time she'd undressed in front of a man. "Sorry. I'm making this ridiculously difficult. The whole thing is starting to feel like a scene from a low budget sex film."

"Not to me," he said. "Want some help?"

She laughed aloud and the tension in the room eased. "I'd appreciate it."

He took hold of her hand again, and slid it down over his chest. She felt his heart kick up beneath the mat of thick hair.

He didn't hesitate before he pulled her up and over him, forcing her leg between his outstretched ones. He pressed her knee up against his scrotum. Her hand slid lower, down his belly, and encircled his penis. She moved her hand lightly up the shaft, her fingers gliding across the tip and down again.

He made a savage, unintelligible sound, out of place in the small room. Shoving back the sheet, his thighs quivering, he replicated her movements with his own hand making small circles on her back. Slowly he stroked lower, over her buttocks, down her thighs, and up again, probing, searching until he found what he wanted, and plunged a finger into her.

"Humph!" The sound exploded out of her and she tightened her grip on his penis, squeezing rhythmically.

He shifted her up on top of him, holding her in position for a few seconds before lowering her down onto him. He arched up and filled her.

"God!" She felt her climax building already, and she began to move, pushing against his shoulders, as he levered her up before going deeper. She fumbled for the cool, iron bed frame and caught hold, pulling herself forward and up, where she paused and came down onto him.

He loomed up beneath her, his face drawn back, the mask of the hunter sighting his prey.

"Matisse!"

His body arched, jerked, and he bucked one last time, rolling her over and under him. A low scream, drawn out like a siren, met his, echoing off her walls.

She fell back at last, her legs splayed, her body taking his weight.

The sense of release lasted a long time and she let it consume her, unwilling to look at him. The physical presence of him beside her felt fiercely at odds with the contained man he presented to the world. It confused her. She kept her eyes shut tight, unwilling to confront what she might see in his eyes.

At last, he withdrew from her, the ripping apart of the two bodies, bound together by sweat and sex. She felt him roll away and only then did she open her eyes, his movements feeling like an assault both on her body and her psyche.

Why did sex always come to this? Great for relieving tension and inevitably followed by uncertainty that seemed to last long after the act itself. Reminding herself of the ridiculous posturing of human beings mating didn't save her from feeling an emotional letdown and sense of doubt that always assailed her after the sex act. It was no different tonight, even with no attachment to the outcome. She glanced over at Matisse. He looked happy enough, with his eyes closed, and a slight smirk on his face.

Unexpected laughter erupted from her. The bark sounded rusty with disuse and it made her laugh again.

Matisse opened his eyes, looking surprised, but he laughed back at her, giving her a full blown bellow of laughter. "Well, that was something," he said. "Or maybe something else, since the first time was something."

****

"So what happened to you, Matisse? You never talk about your past." They were still lying in the dark room. She'd aimed the small fan on the drawer across the room directly at them, making it almost comfortable. The small light beside the bed still burned.

"You're talking about my drinking?"

"Yeah, that." Shadows played about them and she shifted her pillow beneath her head, pushing herself up against the back wall. She shifted under the light sheet, moving her leg inches away from his, giving him space.

He lay on his back, looking years younger. When he reached up and rubbed a hand down his face, she felt a small rush of tenderness for him so powerful it almost hurt.

"Want the short or the long version of my story?" he asked.

"Long."

This time he turned slightly and gave her a half grin. "You asked for it. It's pretty simple, actually. I liked booze. I always liked booze. In college, while the other kids were doing dope, I bought beer. In law school I graduated to hard liquor, Scotch mostly, and turned into a great social drinker." He looked straight ahead. "I know it's hard to picture, yet twenty years ago when I got my law degree, people still went to cocktail parties. Even socially conscious companies like Logan Group. Right out of law school, I loved the scene."

"Impressive, and hard to imagine. You don't seem corporate. Or FBI, for that matter."

"Yeah, well my dad's a successful lawyer, as is my sister. I grew up in Evanston, with lots of contacts. I'm not saying I didn't have some consciousness going on. My mom did environmental work and five years on the job, a spot opened up at Logan, so I moved from patents to environmental law. Did a lot of traveling back and forth to Europe setting up EU contracts. I never drank alone, never drank in the morning. As the years passed, I found myself drinking every day."

She sighed. Hell, no one, not even this sane man, escaped struggling with life.

"Then my mother died, killed by an off-duty drunk cop heading home from a promotion celebration. It stopped me cold. I took six months off, re-evaluated things, joined AA, and went back to school for my Master's Degree in Environmental Science."

The personal information surprised her, or maybe the vulnerable nature of the information. She'd never have considered that anyone who looked so calmly competent could have something to hide.

"I gave up alcohol along with corporate law and applied to Quantico." She could feel his eyes on her, gauging her response.

"It's counterintuitive, isn't it? Becoming a cop when your mom was killed by one?" she asked.

"You think I haven't considered that? Only on paper are humans logical. I became the good cop, the nice guy out to prove law enforcement has integrity. Out to show that justice works, especially when it comes to the environment."

She reached out and placed her palm against his cheek, his skin unexpectedly cool, his beard prickly. He caught her hand and turned the palm. It tingled at the touch of his lips. "Enough of my story. What are we doing here?"

"Looks like sex to me, Matisse."

"The best damned sex I've ever had, for sure." He gave her a half grin. "My question—second time I've asked it. Do I need to regret what happened here? Is this going to further complicate us working together later?"

"No." She didn't hesitate. There'd be no later. No need to consider collateral damage, since within a day or two at most, she'd take whatever steps she needed, legal or not, to hunt out a killer. And Matisse would not hesitate to kick her out the door of his life for running her own agenda. "We live in separate worlds. It's unlikely our paths will cross once you're through with your investigation. So I'm good, Matisse. If you are."

He hesitated, his face looking uncertain. "I am," he said after a moment. "Although what makes you so certain our worlds can't meet again?"

"The Region is a million miles from Chicago. Or Evanston. You probably have season opera tickets, even. The opera, for God's sake, is as foreign in Whiting as sumo wrestling."

"Opera puts you off?"

She blew damp hair off her forehead. "That's not the point. You and I have one real connection. This investigation."

His leg brushed up against hers under the thin sheet. "Looks to me like we've got another one now." He punched her arm lightly. "For now, right? In any case, opera or sex, you're right. The point is moot since the last couple of nights are an anomaly, the fantasy of a lonely man. I'm too old for you, kid." He brushed his knuckle against her damp hair falling across her eyes. "Let's leave it at that."

"Are you staying tonight?"

"It's tempting, but I need to get some better rest."

"We can manage that." She turned her back and nudged up against his chest, pressing her back against his belly.

He groaned and pulled her tighter. "What the hell? I can live on a few hours of sleep."

Matisse left at four, tossing on clothes as he made for the door.

Miller stood at her window and watched one more time as his Lexus pulled away.

She shoved up her window and leaned out. The night air felt like velvet against her face, quiet, lacking the usual frantic sounds of night creatures. A breeze caught at the sheet wrapped around her and the scent of sex rose up. Something stirred in her chest, distinct from the sharp pain of loss she'd suffered for two months. It felt unfamiliar, like the bittersweet sense of a relationship that could have been something. He knew it and she knew it. Her future was inevitable, catch a killer, even if it meant destroying her own life. That she could even care a little about what she could never have with Matisse surprised her. Whatever happened between Matisse and her, he'd awakened her frozen heart.

Right now, she needed a good eight hours of sleep, not the three she'd allowed herself. First, she needed a shower to wash off the distracting scent of Matisse.

Chapter Eighteen

The expectation of danger always brings danger

Sunday morning and night, July 17th

Matisse's instructions popped into her mail midday. Miller rolled her eyes and scanned down the page.

She mentally arranged the items he'd requested she take action on, or rather Matisse's list of useless actions for her to take. Talk with the men, do some Google searching on them and see if she could find any link to anything he was doing, even after he'd done the initial interview and found nothing. None of the tasks seemed more than a few notches above routine. The same three names he'd sent her in the email: Greg Zelenin, Wayne Cornell, Joe Sedlack. Was the murderer one of them? She needed a daring action to take today, before he took her off his investigation. It was clearly only a matter of time when either his conscience ate him up over sleeping with his source or he took her off his case because she was a pain in the ass, also known as Whiting's best example of a loose cannon.

She ran her fingers over the signature on the bottom of the email; Robert Matisse, Federal Agent, Chicago Office. *Hell.* It occurred to her that she was falling in love with the man, at the worst time in her life and with someone who would be gone in three weeks with no more than a 'thank you ma'am' called back over his shoulder.

She pulled out Matisse's real list and studied them.

There it was again, that name staring at her—Dmitri Versakos.

Unexpectedly, she began to shake.

Dmitri Versakos? The name brought a chill to her body. Who was he and why was he on Matisse's list? And why did the name terrify her?

She pushed the name away into the back of her mind for later and skipped down to the last name–Jeffrey Owens. After the name Matisse had penciled in "Business/money problems?" All she had to do was wait until dark, and she could easily look into that question.

****

Miller had picked up her car at Myron's before heading to North American. She waited patiently until she saw the janitorial truck pull out of the lot, then strode quickly across the parking lot up to the west door. She punched in the security code with unsteady fingers and slid her key card into her pocket. Nothing illegal about her needing to be in the building at night, since she often got called in on emergencies. Tonight, technically, she had no emergency, and especially no need to be in the executive suite, where she was headed. She hesitated at the receptionist's desk that guarded the four offices of the administrative suite. Aside from a small light shining over the desk, the entire suite was lifeless and silent. No one worked Sunday night except the cleaning staff and one night guard.

The employee files were kept in the personnel office, the last room in the executive suite. She turned the knob and eased the door open. With no exterior windows, the room felt airless in the darkness.

She slid out her penlight and moved quietly about the room. Behind the slick reception area and executive director's office lay the real North American Steel, hidden from view with its rusty file cabinets and utilitarian furniture sixty years outdated. The personnel cabinets lined the far wall of the small room like robots, within reach of the bulky desk belonging to Marjorie Latham. She was on the wrong side of seventy and still headed up Human Resources. Despite years of hands fumbling over folders, she kept those files meticulously updated, without question more accurate than the computer employee database. The only reason the files were digital at all lay at the feet of the US Department of Labor's AHTD standards, requiring all employee files be computer accessible to fulfill OSHA requirements.

Miller propped her penlight so that it lit up the file area, took a deep breath, and started pulling folders. Her heart thudding, she fumbled through paper after paper, without a clue what she wanted to find.

She narrowed her search down to the male employees tonight, and only those who had managerial level jobs, which eliminated two-thirds of the two hundred plus men employed by North American.

She'd been working an hour and just pulled out Jeffrey Owens's folder when she heard the sound of a door shutting somewhere beyond her in the darkness. She pressed the folder against her chest to listen. Except for the thudding of her heart, the silence seemed complete. A minute passed, then another. She could explain being in the machinery rooms well enough. Getting caught in the executive suite could get her fired.

She sank down to the floor where the perpetual burnt metal smell from the steel ovens had even seeped into the plush carpeting. Pulling out her phone, she reached for her small pile of personnel folders of interest and systematically photographed each page.

After the first few files, she got faster, managing the maneuvers in the dark without dropping pages, the click-click of her camera the only sound. Saving money these days, the company shut off the AC at night even in the executive suite and her T-shirt stuck to her back with sweat. She ignored the perspiration running down her nose and kept clicking, pausing between files to listen. Nothing, no sound, no doors opening. She didn't expect anyone here at night but who knew? One of the administrative staff could have stayed late or thought of some emergency himself to handle tonight. She stood up on trembling legs and made her way back to the file cabinet, carefully replacing every folder one by one.

Stashing the penlight, she opened the door and stuck her head out. The hallway lay in silence. She stepped out and nudged the door closed, her fingers trembling as she reached for her keys. Her heart pounded now, speeding up with every moment. From this view she could make out the twin emergency exit lights glowing red on either side of the door, a long stroll through purgatory to freedom, if she needed to escape.

A swish of air behind her, a brief sense of someone there gave her little warning. She began to run. The blow took her down five steps from the exit. Blackness engulfed her.

****

Miller's nose twitched at the stench of garbage wafting about her. She jerked her head back and was assaulted by a wave of nausea so powerful she gagged. She clawed with desperate fingers at something that tightened about her neck, panic rising in her throat. She pulled and tore at it until at last she ripped it loose— plastic wrap. Another wave of nausea passed over her, and she retched once more, sank back, and waited limply for the sickness to pass.

She forced her eyes open and squinted up at into harsh light streaming in through a dirty pane above her. Daylight. Her head pounded with pain. Her whole body ached as if she'd been run over. Carefully she moved her head, paused to let the world stop spinning, and looked about her. The room had an enormous ceiling with windows too high to see out, the walls looked like reinforced steel, and there was no door in sight.

Where the hell am I?

Something sticky trickled down her face, and she reached up and touched it. Blood. The acrid smell of it mingled with the stink of garbage.

Shifting about one leg, then the other, she slowly rolled her head to her side and waited for the dizziness to subside. She carefully traced the scene about her, searching in her mind for some reason for her to be here.

Bags, garbage bags, lay in a circle about her body. The first thing she recognized was the sign on the wall beyond. It read 'No recyclables in the dumpsters. For trash only.'

Someone had tossed her into a dumpster in the recycle room of North American Steel.

She shut her eyes tight. What the hell happened? The last thing she could remember was a hall glowing red.

A file cabinet. The personnel room.

She pushed her focus from inside her head down her body, sucked in oxygen, and rolled over onto her stomach. She levered herself up onto her knees which worked well, except it left her nose pressed against a bag of rotting food.

A door opened somewhere nearby, echoing like a bell ringing inside her head. She opened her mouth to scream and swallowed it back.

"Anyone here?" The faint accent sounded familiar. "Whoever is here, come out or I'll sound the alarm."

This time she recognized the voice and something like a squeak came out her mouth. She felt a hand reach out and catch hold of her arm. "Miller!"

She looked up into the face of Jerry Hayworth, the night watchman, peering over the edge of the dumpster.

"Help me!" She moaned.

"Right away. Right away! You lay still, okay?" He disappeared and she lay back, shutting her eyes, trying to hold her breath against the nauseous smells.

What seemed like a long time later Jerry was back and with much fumbling and swearing, he pulled her over the edge, holding tight as he fought his way down a ladder.

The watchman propped her up on the deck and she lay shivering, her vision swirling. Her clothes felt wet, clinging to her was that stench of garbage. She swallowed reflectively, pushing away the urge to vomit.

Minutes later she heard anxious voices a long way off. Hands lifted her, followed by more voices, and a siren. She must have passed out again. Her eyes were forced open and a woman in white held a small light that blinded her.

"You'll do."

Someone tucked in a blanket around her and she felt blessed warmth. They lifted her then and began moving her, jostling her head.

"Lie still. You're heading for the hospital. We'll get you there just fine." The voice was a phantom, someone beside her, an EMS maybe.

She didn't bother arguing. Her head hurt too much to make an effort. She woke again, this time to the jolting of a gurney as they rolled her down a hallway with more lights that seared her eyeballs.

Doors opened and closed, hands reaching for her. "We're going to remove your clothes."

Something smelling of laundry soap, rough and warm, slid over her arms and she sank back.

"Okay now?"

"Yes." The mumble response came out a moan.

Miller kept her eyes closed, watching her brain grow more sluggish, the fear dissipating now, followed by a calm that felt almost giddy.

She slept again, this time waking to more voices and movements. She was in a hospital now. She felt herself rolled past people, their voices mingling, and then brought to a stop and hands lifted her again.

She opened her eyes and saw hands pulling a white curtain around her bed.

From then on, people came and went. They wheeled her to x-ray, lifting her head, and putting her into some sort of machine. Then back again to her white curtained cubicle, where they poked her with needles and other pointed instruments.

There she lay with eyes shut.

"Miller Abel?" A voice she knew, Matisse.

She opened her eyes and rearranged the jagged edges of reality. His fingers reached around the white curtain before he appeared. His hair looked damp, as if they'd caught him mid-shower. He wore a blue T-shirt and khakis, no suit and tie today.

"Miller."

She stared up into his eyes. "Matisse." Sudden tears formed behind her eyes and she shut them quickly. "Damn, Matisse."

"Damn? You're damning me?"

"No. Just damn that you always catch me in my weakest moments."

"If you're talking about your illegal activities, you deserve to be caught in your weakest moments."

She expected his scorn. She didn't expect how useless it made her feel.

A cop wearing blues stepped into the cubicle behind Matisse. He looked young, not much older than Jacob. "I'm Lieutenant Pollen." He flashed a badge for her. "I'd like a word with you, if you're up to it?"

"I'm afraid someone's beat you to it." Miller nodded at Matisse. "This is the FBI, and they got here first."

Matisse stepped up and flashed his badge back, two gorillas sizing each other up. "I'm not investigating the attack on Miller Abel. I'm here because she's been working for me on an investigation."

"And that had something to do with the assault?"

"That's what I'm considering. We haven't gotten that far yet."

Lieutenant Pollen nodded and turned to Miller. "Can you tell me what you were doing in the mill late at night?"

"I'm an employee, a mechanical engineer. I get called in a lot at night for emergencies."

"And you got called in last night?"

And so the shit hits the fan. "No, not in this case. I was doing a little investigation on the side for Special Agent Matisse. I used my access to North American to do that." And whether the local law considered that illegal was anybody's guess.

"Officer, I can vouch for this being part of my investigation, if that helps."

Miller let go of a small sigh. Despite his obvious disgust with her, he'd taken her side.

"Okay. In that case, I'll need to get a little more information from both of you. I'm not here to charge you. Your employer declined to file charges."

"And what about her attacker?"

"We don't have much right now. No signs of forced entry, and nothing from the night watchman who found her."

Matisse stepped back and shoved his hands into his pockets.

"You were found in the recycling section of shipping and receiving. Can you tell me if that's where you were when you were attacked?" Pollen said.

"No."

"Which office?"

"Personnel." Matisse stared at her and this time she ignored him. "I must have been dragged down to Shipping and Receiving. The last thing I remember is stepping into the dark hallway."

"Can you tell me about what time you arrived and what time you estimate you were attacked?"

"I got there around midnight, so it was probably between one and two when I came out into the hallway." She glanced up at Matisse who looked even more unhappy.

"Anything else you can remember about that? Anything at all?"

"No. The last thing I remember is pulling the door closed behind me." She envisioned the hallway with its faint red light. "I think I heard something. Just a step, or maybe a feeling of someone nearby. That's all."

"And what about when you came to?"

"A terrible stink of the garbage I was lying in and a lot of pain in my head."

"We'll need to get a statement from you. Can you come down to the station or should I send an officer to you?"

"I'll come down if it can wait until tomorrow. I'm not sure I'm even being released today."

"The doctor told me they're not going to keep you overnight."

"Okay. Give me a day, and I'll be happy to come in and give a statement. The Whiting police department?"

"Yes."

"Keep me in the loop on whatever you find, will you, Lieutenant?" Matisse said.

"Of course."

Only when he'd gone, did Matisse turn back to her, his face stone.

Chapter Nineteen

Barely begun, barely ended

Early Monday, July 18th

"I'll take you home," Matisse said.

"I'll take a cab."

"Don't be crazy. I'll drive you."

Not the first time she'd seen him seriously annoyed, the odds were this wouldn't be the last.

He gripped her arm lightly as he escorted her out the ER door and into his Lexus. Thank God he'd stopped somewhere and picked up clothes for her and she didn't have to wear her own stinking of blood and garbage. Inside his car, she sank back against black leather that cradled her like a baby.

"Thanks for getting some clothes for me, Matisse. Did you buy them?"

"No. I stopped by and asked Sparky if she had something you could wear." He slipped his key into the ignition. "Fasten your seat belt."

The overcast sky seemed like a metaphor for his mood. To the west, bolts of electricity split the black clouds. Thunder, the kind that rumbled across the sky like a mile-long freight train, followed seconds later, indicating the storm must be only minutes away.

"Lean back and shut your eyes. I'll have you home soon."

She rested her head against the cushion and sank into the feel of the leather. Her life before the murders hadn't been that different from Matisse's, with all the predictable pleasures and comforts most Americans expected. A sense of regret washed over her that very soon all of it would be gone. She knew she was close to the killer now, she could feel it. And once she found him, it would all end. Either she'd be in jail for murder or she'd be dead herself. Damn Matisse for bringing her back to feeling something and for making her care.

Matisse flipped a knob and the cool air blew across her face, as soothing as a walk by a mountain stream.

"So what the hell are you up to, Miller? If I wanted to see their records, I could have probably found a reason for getting a subpoena."

He wiped a hand over his face and a sharp pang of guilt and regret shot through her. For the first time she got a glimpse into what his world must be like and the problem she'd become. "I'm sorry, Matisse. I'm definitely way more trouble than I'm worth."

"Yeah. I'd almost agree. Almost." His face softened. "What *were* you doing in there?"

"Like I said, taking a look at the files."

"Which files?"

"Those of anyone who was fired or anyone on the inside who registered complaints about the water runoff."

He jerked the car sharply around a corner and onto Seeley Avenue, his normal calm gone. "You could have suggested the idea to me, you know, and I'd go about it through legal channels." He slowed the car down. "And what did you find?"

"Nothing much. Do we need to have this conversation right now? I'm feeling a little sick. I can't even make sense of my own words with all the pain meds in me."

He sighed and made the last turn onto Main Street, heading towards the lake. "Okay. Eventually though I've got to have answers, Miller. And I want a promise from you there'll be no more investigating on your own."

Her turn to sigh. What the hell could she say? "I'm not promising that, Robert. I'm a private citizen. You don't have a say over what I do or don't do." Her words sounded ragged to her, like a crazed woman.

He must have thought so, too, since he didn't bother to reply. He pulled up in her alley, turned off the engine, walked around to the passenger side, and helped her out, more gently than she deserved. Someone had brought her car home from the mill and parked it as usual.

Mourning doves cooed nearby, drowned out by the harsher cries of excited gulls who warned of the coming storm. She made it to her first landing leaning on Matisse, when Sparky's door opened.

"Miller," she yelled up. "What's happened to you now?"

"I was mugged. At work."

"Need any help?"

"We're fine," Matisse said.

Sparky ignored him as efficiently as if he were a seven year old in her catechism class and followed them up the stairs. On the second landing, a gust of wind caught the bag of meds Miller clutched and flipped it out of her hands.

"I'll get it." Sparky scuttled down the steps and picked up the sack. Miller smiled. The woman was incorrigible.

"Keys?" He held out his hand.

Miller passed them over to Matisse. The dark apartment felt stuffier than usual, taking her breath away. She limped to a chair and lowered herself into it, Sparky not far behind.

"Whew. It's really hot in these upstairs apartments. That's why I asked for a lower one." She dropped the paper sack on the table and pulled up a window.

Miller shut her eyes, ignoring both of them, waiting for the swirling to pass. A small breeze off the lake blew across her face, one of the benefits of living upstairs, despite the heat.

"You should get to bed," Matisse said. Obedient, she let him lead her down the dark hallway, Sparky on her other side.

She sank back on her bed, refusing to remove her clothes. Someone took her shoes, someone turned on her fan, and she let herself sink into the darkness behind her eyes, a drugged sort of slipping away.

"I'll be right downstairs if you need me." Sparky's rusty voice faded away.

"I'll call you later tonight.' Matisse's words were muffled. The last thing she heard was the soft shuffle of footsteps down her hallway.

****

Miller squinted in the dim darkness. Someone had placed a cup and plate with a sorry piece of toast beside the bed, probably Sparky being Sparky. It must be night, although it was hard to tell in the windowless room.

The night continued with a cast of bizarre characters coming and going–the cable man at her door morphing into her attacker, the bodies of her family rising up in a macabre dance, Matisse pointing his finger at her as he slammed a door in her face. The last image, a replay of the scene in Hammond with herself lying in a pool of blood, pushed her up and out of bed. It seemed likely most people suffer dark nights of the soul from time to time, even people with normal lives. Whatever a normal life might be.

She pulled the twisted sheets off her body and stumbled into the bathroom. Dark smudges decorated her eyes, accompanied by swollen lids. Her hair lay in a tangle, sticking out around her head like a wet mop. *God, what a freak!* Was this what Matisse said goodbye to a few hours ago?

Holding onto the sink with one hand she leaned down and flipped cold water on her face, letting the water run down her neck until the front of her nightshirt clung to her chest. If Matisse could see her now, he'd wonder why he ever wanted her.

She turned off the water, peeled off her sodden shirt, and leaned forward to stare at her naked body in the mirror, turning slowly. Black and blue marks decorated her buttocks, her shoulders, both arms, spattered here and there with bits of dry blood like sprinkles on a cake.

It took all of her energy to step into the shower. Ten minutes later she shut it off and climbed out, shivering. She draped a pale blue towel about her like a ghetto Venus.

Her head throbbed, although not enough to be tempted by the bottle of Percocet on the dresser. If she succumbed, she'd be too disoriented to plan.

The kitchen, lit by the faint dawn, seemed too sweet for her lingering nightmares. Outside, she listened to the sounds of the morning. In the distance she heard a child's voice, sing-song, probably calling out to her mother to get her up. The high pitched sound of it made her heart hurt just a little.

She sank down at her table and felt despair engulf her. She'd found a way to dispel it when working for Matisse, but here it was again, feeling like someone strung a sack of cement about her neck and she was sinking into a morass of hopelessness and loss. Who wouldn't be in despair after what she'd seen? But it was more than that. There was something else. She'd been happy most of her life, hadn't she? Images nagged at her, a queasy sense of a thought that wouldn't go away, pressing her forward toward the real terror.

She heaved her body up, resisting the pain that shot up the back of her neck, like a large hand squeezing her brain.

Today she felt twenty-five years older than yesterday.

****

"Hey, Miller. You up?"

Sparky's trucker's voice penetrated the closed inner door.

Miller opened the door and stood back to let her in.

Sparky held a bright red mug. She always brought her own, probably preferring a world of color to Miller's anemic one. In her other hand she held a plate with a muffin atop sunny eggs. "Breakfast for you."

Miller shuddered. "Maybe after I've had some coffee."

"No problem." Sparky set the plate down and picked up the tea kettle. "Have a seat before you fall down."

Miller took her first look outside. Rain, a steady, gentle patter, an insult to any good Midwest storm. The drops hit the tin roof with a constant ping.

"Sparky, have you ever noticed how life can change in an instant, for no reason? One morning it feels like the end of the world, the next morning you wake up with a sense of the newness of it all?

"Yeah, it's like that, isn't it?" Sparky grinned and set one of Miller's white mugs on the table in front of her. "Who's to predict what makes us happy, right? Or unhappy. What's so good—and bad—about life is that it is so unpredictable."

"Sparky, the guru," Miller said. She picked up the mug and sucked in enough coffee to shift her mind from low to overdrive. "Yesterday felt like one of those times when life can't get any worse or better and there's nothing to do and nowhere to escape. Today I am actually feeling like I can manage, whatever happens. What's really weird is that I'm pretty sure I'm off Matisse's case. He didn't say anything last night, just goodbye. "

"You're talking about your working agreement, right?"

"I guess." Miller stared at Sparky in her strange green jumpsuit. The woman either was completely insane or was really an amazing individualist. "I got a last warning about my putting myself into danger and even illegal situation the other night after the incident where someone shot out my window."

"He seemed worried about you last night."

"Of course he was. He's a very nice man. I think he's mostly worried I'll ruin evidence for his own case, or worse, get him into trouble if I get arrested since he was the one who asked me to investigate for him. As far as the personal stuff goes, it's all about sex. Nothing else. He might feel some guilt for sleeping with his inside source, someone who he'd never meet in his normal life, although I even doubt that. Men have a way of justifying sex. He's just worried I may run after him or demand more than he wants to give. It's pretty clear our worlds don't mesh." She smiled. It didn't even hurt much saying it. "I've probably lost my only information pipeline, if he's really dumped me from his case. I'm not going to let that stop me from finding my family's killer."

Sparky grinned, looking a little uncertain. "Okay, so you've got a game plan for us?"

"I've got leads on a couple of people Matisse is focused on. One of them very likely is the murderer of my family."

Sparky stayed for an hour, sitting across the table from Miller and listened intently to Miller's plans for catching a killer. Sparky said no more than a few words.

****

Matisse phoned twice during the morning. Miller ignored both calls. A little after eleven she heard footsteps on her stairs and Matisse knocked on her door. She studied his face through the window. He looked as uncertain as she felt.

Opening the outer door, she stood behind the screen, meeting his eyes, not inviting him in. He looked back at her, not speaking.

"How are you?" he asked.

"Not too bad, despite all the bumps and bruises covering my body."

"Good." Another pause. "May I come in?"

Miller reluctantly opened the screen and stepped back. She avoided touching him.

"Want something? Iced tea, maybe?"

"I'll take some."

He wore a raincoat, the kind men wore in big cities. He slipped out of it and tossed it across the back of a chair. He wore his gun.

"Sit down," she said.

Silence fell between them, wider than the lake out beyond the mud flats. Miller set his glass of tea on the table and pushed the sugar bowl towards him.

"Thanks."

The first night he'd come to her door there'd been rain too, a storm more typical of the lakes. Today's was the all-day kind of rain, weather for poetry—and making love. She knew he hadn't stopped by for that. By the look on his face, he meant business.

"Miller, we need to talk."

"All right." She could play this.

"I think you know what I have to say. I warned you a couple of days ago that if there was one more incident where you got yourself into trouble, I'd have to remove you from my investigation." He wore a flat, unreadable expression on his face. "I can't use you anymore. You're too unpredictable. You attract danger. I've given it more time than I would have with anyone else because I care about you, Miller. But we're done here."

She nodded, feeling nothing except regret. There was nothing more to say. He got to his feet and stood looking at her, his face still impassive. He'd pushed whatever he felt for her far back behind his eyes.

He reached for his coat and went out her door. He left his iced tea on her table, untouched. Miller reached for it and took a taste, then poured the rest down the drain. It was time to find a killer.

Chapter Twenty

Murder is never respectable

Monday, July 18th

Matisse pushed loose papers around his desk with an idle finger. All quiet today in cop land. He had the place pretty much to himself, except for a couple of uniforms sharing a newspaper who were sitting at a desk across the fifty-foot room. Thank God for small favors, since his office had been confiscated by the duty officer this morning to house a perp causing trouble. He took a taste of the coffee and grimaced. Not bothering to stop at Starbuck's, he'd resigned himself to Mr. Coffee sitting against the back wall surrounded by lonely cracked mugs. Nothing like the sour taste of boiled coffee.

Matisse's day only got worse. Thirty-six hours without sleep didn't help. Nor did the rain that turned Hammond a dull gray and reflected inside his head with a vague, sense of hopelessness.

He cursed it all. Two hours ago he'd walked out of Miller's life. Any fool could have predicted the brief interlude with her would be nothing more than a speed bump in his life. So why the hell did he feel like someone had carved a hole in his chest?

He'd punched autodial ten times in the past two hours, hanging up before she could catch his caller ID. Their relationship was over. He'd said his goodbye. Why the fuck drag it out? He was pretty damned sure the last goodbye only meant no more easy information for Miller. Mind numbing sex didn't a relationship make.

The raw feeling didn't stop hurting just because he poured reason into the mix. It kept throbbing away, like an infected tooth. She'd showed no emotions when he told her he was taking her off his case.

He pulled himself back to his list of suspects and continued to weed whack his way through the dead brush of names.

A quiet anxiety prodded at the back of his brain, so subtle most people would ignore it. Except he wasn't a man prone to worry. That, in itself, made him uneasy. It hung there, ominous, running in the background.

He picked up his pen and rewrote the names on the yellow legal pad, pausing after each to see if it could be the source of his nerves. It was no use. He couldn't ignore the hairs standing up on the back of his neck. He knew the source—Miller and her own private agenda. Less than two weeks around Miller and he could guess her next steps. He'd bet his red Corvette sitting safe in an Evanston garage that she ignored his warning and even with a concussion, was already working on another plan to find a killer.

Matisse didn't doubt Miller's ability to get what she wanted, with or without him, whatever the hell it was she wanted. Despite the picture she presented to the world of a woman struggling to hold on, her unswerving focus on pursuing her own agenda turned her into a liability for his own case.

He squinted at the names again, gritting his teeth searching for what she'd spot. He shook off the notion that her plan was to catch a killer at any cost, even with her own life. She might fantasize she was investigating murder, yet he wouldn't let himself believe she'd be crazy enough to confront him herself.

At least she didn't have the whole list. He'd given her just the names of people he'd ruled out having any connection to the murders. None of the men on her list had any motive to kill an entire family.

As for the longer list, she'd never find a way to those names.

He slumped back in his chair and sighed. Gregory Zelenin, Henry Winston, Jeffrey Owens, Dmitri Versakos, Wayne Cornell, and Joe Sedlack. His own investigation was getting close to being concluded. He had nothing on any of these men, just vague suspicions and some connection they all had to the water department. Not much to go on. And it felt too pat. His instincts told him there were too many connections in his case.

He stood up and loosened his tie. Taking some deep breaths usually helped. He willed his mind to slow down and let his mind land somewhere, trusting his instincts.

Wayne Cornell. A scribbled note beside his name indicated he'd called Friday, asking for Matisse. Hell, too many distractions. He needed to find out what the man wanted.

He pulled out his phone, checked the number again and punched it in. "Mr. Cornell? This is Special Agent Matisse returning your call. What can I do for you?"

"Agent Matisse. I was wondering if you'd care to meet me. Today if you will? I have information I think you're looking for."

"You know what I'm investigating?"

"Vaguely. You're with the FBI anti-terrorist division, and you've been focused on North American Steel and water runoff. That said, I have something I'm sure you'll find useful."

"I'd be happy to meet with you. Can you give me some idea of what it's about?"

"I'm sure you know that I run an environmental activist group called the Lake Coalition Group."

"I'm aware of that, Mr. Cornell."

"I'm sure you're also aware that I worked at North American Steel for quite a few years, took early retirement, and what I have to say is problematic for me. I don't want to cause problems for friends who still work at North American."

"I can understand, Mr. Cornell." Matisse drummed on the desk with his pen.

"I've done some research around some of North America's policies." Cornell paused. "I decided it's time to pass my research on to you. Especially since I got threatening calls, two of them in the last couple of days, and I think it's time to get the authorities involved"

"What were the specifics of the threatening calls, Mr. Cornell?"

"Some melodramatic low breathing and a few unin telligible words the first time. Then the second call got specific. The caller warned me to stay out of North American's business-or else."

"Did you mention what you were working on at the meeting?"

"No. Not specifically. I usually keep our discussions general, although I had a side conversation with someone I know I can trust."

"And who might that be?"

"Greg Zelenin. We didn't go into much detail there, though."

"Then how'd the caller know you had something?"

"Don't know. Someone broke into my car that night. Maybe he found some information in my car."

"Did you report the break-in?"

"No. Nothing was taken as far as I could tell. All my files were there. I had my laptop with me inside."

"You got any idea who might want to threaten you?"

"Well, obviously anyone with a vested interest in keeping the water pollution problem quieted. So someone from North American or the water department."

Matisse glanced down at the names on his legal pad. Henry Winston, Jeffrey Owens, and of course, Greg Zelenin, two of the three connected to North American. "Since you're calling the FBI, I take it you're putting a stop to a side investigation of your own?"

There was a long pause, "I'm not sure." Cornell paused a second time. "Look, Agent Matisse, I'd rather talk in person. I'm at home right now on my land line, and I don't feel real comfortable talking on it."

"All right, Mr. Cornell. Where and when? I don't suppose you want to come downtown to the Hammond Police Department?"

"Somewhere less obvious. There's a small pub not far from the police department, by the name of Flytrap's. Know where it is?"

"I'll find it."

"Where are you right now?"

"At the station."

"Just ask anyone there. They'll point you towards it."

"Fine. Say in thirty minutes?"

"Make it an hour. I have to do something first."

"All right. Three o'clock at Flytrap's, is it?"

"Sure thing. See you then."

****

Flytrap's lived up to its name on the outside at least—a hole in the wall kind of place with a scarred, blood-colored marble facade. Matisse walked inside and blinked three times in the pitch dark. Once his eyes got used to the gloom, he saw the inside looked better than expected. A long homey bar ran down the entire left side with a large ornate mirror hung above it, reminding him of places he'd only heard about in New York City, drinking joints where they called alcohol 'booze' and the likes of Frank Sinatra and his Rat Pack hung out.

The bartender also was a surprise, a good-looking woman in her mid thirties, who glanced up from her dishwashing to give him the once-over, then go back to a soapy mug, more interested in its shape than his.

He found a seat deep in the belly of the place, dark and silent. No loud music intruded here, no pool table junkies, no loud drunks. Serious drinkers or people with serious lives only allowed.

The bartender sauntered over and he glanced at her face.

"Lexie, right?"

"Miller's FBI agent. Matisse, right?"

"Yeah, that's me." The sense of embarrassment he felt was crazy. He didn't owe Miller's friends explanations about their relationship.

"What'll you have?"

"Club soda, with lime."

A grin almost tipped up her mouth but evaporated before it managed the move. He liked her coolness without obvious judgment showing on her face, that kind of energy small women often carry off well, quick, clever, and no nonsense. Probably the way Miller had been until eight weeks ago.

Why had Miller gotten his attention? She was a secretive, scarred woman whose real motives had nothing to do with what she felt for an FBI agent who had dropped into her life on a rainy night to throw out the red carpet for her revenge fantasies. The words to some poem he'd forgotten years ago did a circuit of his brain: 'You dance inside my chest where no one sees you.'

"Anything to eat?"

"What have you got?"

"We do a mean steak burger with fries."

"Sure, I'll give it a try." His stomach did a brief hurrah. The last solid food his belly had seen was about twenty hours ago.

"Gotcha." She gave him a full tilt grin this time and headed for the bar.

The food turned out to be far better than it should for any restaurant in Hammond. He kept one eye on the fluorescent clock over the bar as he chewed.

By three-thirty, there was still no sign of Dr. Wayne Cornell.

Shoving aside his plate, he reached for his phone. He dialed Cornell's cell number. It rang six times before Verizon informed him service was unavailable. *Shit!* Where the hell was the man and what was so urgent if he hadn't bothered to turn up here?

He piled up dishes and bussed them over to Lexie at the bar.

"Thanks. I appreciate it."

"Can I ask a favor?"

"You can ask."

"I'm waiting for someone, a 'no-show.' I'd like to leave my contact information in case he turns up here?"

She wiped her dripping hands. "All right. Shoot."

He slid a card across the bar to her. "If someone comes in asking for Special Agent Matisse, give him this number."

"Will do." She took his card

Matisse searched for some small talk to blunt the impersonal exchange with her. "Have you known Miller a long time?"

"Yeah. Since junior high. We were best friends through high school and beyond." She gave him a look that could be read as hostile. "You're not gonna do anything to make her life worse right now, are you?"

The direct comment set him back. Make her life worse was what he already had done by giving her the impetus to go on a hunt for a killer. "I'm doing my best to not hurt her. And to make sure no one else does."

She shrugged. "Just checking."

He hesitated. "She had a run-in last night at her work and ended up in the ER. If you're a close friend, you might call and check up on her."

"Is she okay?"

"She's got a mild concussion. They sent her home. She'll probably be laid up for a day or two."

"Hell, Miller's life is a disaster. This is only one more thing." She stopped to glare at him. "Is she still working for you?"

"No. She's not part of my investigation anymore."

"Because she's in danger?"

"Whatever danger Miller's in is of her own making." Matisse checked his phone. No messages. "I've gotta go. Like I said, give her a call. She can use a friend right now."

She tucked his card it into her pocket. "I'll call her."

Blinding sunlight met Matisse at the door. What the hell happened to Wayne Cornell, he wondered?

****

Chief Santos' door stood open when Matisse dragged himself up the Hammond Police Department steps and into the squad room.

Santos was scowling at his computer screen, punching the keyboard with two fingers as though it was a rotten carcass on his desk. He looked up.

Matisse took a deep breath and plunged in. "You know about Miller being attacked last night at North American?"

Santos pointed to the chair opposite. "Take a seat."

Matisse sank down in the chair, inhaling the frigid air. Even with the door open, Santos' office was fifteen degrees cooler than the squad room, and still Matisse was sweating.

"So I wanna hear your side of it. What happened?" There'd be no playing nice now between the FBI and the Hammond police.

"She took it upon herself to do some unauthorized investigating in the middle of the night at the mill. Someone caught her unaware, knocked her out, and tossed her into the garbage bin."

"Christ!" Santos said. "What the hell sort of investigation?"

Matisse skimmed over the bare facts he knew about Miller's separate investigation.

"Shit."

"Exactly. I took her off my investigation."

Santos rubbed the back of his neck with one hand as the other hand reached for his dish of butter mints. He didn't offer one to Matisse. Instead he shot a look across his desk that would have made a rookie blanch. Matisse steeled himself for what was coming.

"You started this. What are you gonna do to stop her from going off half cocked and getting herself killed?"

Matisse hesitated. He had someone in place and didn't want to blow the cover yet. "I've got someone watching her."

The scowl didn't leave Santos' face. "So, you're giving me a promise nothing is going to happen to that girl, right?"

"You have my word."

Matisse could hear the man exhale. "Okay. I'm gonna take your word."

Neither of them spoke, letting the silence stretch between them.

"So where is she now? Hospital or home?" Santos asked finally.

"Home. They released her last night."

Santos thought it over a moment. "Humph. I'll put in a call to Miller."

"Chief, go easy on her. I took her off my case, so she's been warned."

Santos pushed away his mint dish. "Hell, Matisse, I hate this. Hate that we don't have anything on the Abel murders. That Miller's out there doing what I'm sure she thinks we should be doing. She's alone and I hate the whole damned thing."

"I know."

Santos narrowed his eyes at Matisse. "Is there something personal between you and Miller? And don't tell me it's none of my business, Matisse. I'm asking as a friend of the family, not a cop."

Matisse lifted a hand to loosen his tie. "I care about her, if that's what you mean. I'm on her side, so yeah, it is personal in that way."

"You married? Or involved with someone?"

The question spoke clearly the man's era, and Matisse almost laughed aloud. No sex for sex's sake in this guy's world. It was a fair question. "No. Was married when I was 25 for a year. We went our separate ways."

Santos expression was unreadable. Did the man want to have Matisse hook up with Miller? Or not? "You'll keep an eye on her for me, even if she's not part of your investigation?"

"I'll make sure she's safe."

"You're not looking for a wife? A family?"

Matisse heaved a sigh. *Jesus, the guy wouldn't let up.* This conversation would never happen in Chicago, whatever era the man came out of. "I'd like a wife and kids. Someday. It sort of passed me by while I wasted ten years on binges. You know how it is. Time slips away when you're busy getting drunk every weekend."

Santos turned to juggle a clear green glass paper-weight as though weighing Matisse in his hands. "So, you're sober these days?"

"Four years now. A drunk driver, an off-duty cop killed my mother. That sort of sobered me up over-night."

Santos nodded, letting the paperweight slip from his fingers. Alcoholism was a common problem for a lot of people, whatever culture they came from. "As far as time slipping away goes, I've got two kids, grown, married. One lives in Wyoming, the other in Japan. Who'd have thought it would all go so fast? I remember their births like it was last night." He pushed his glasses back up on his bridge. "Ah-hem. Now, what was it you wanted? Some police business I can do for you?"

Matisse reached for his notepad. "I've got some thoughts about our mutual cases I'd like to toss at you. And a question or two." He reviewed his list with Santos, leaving the two most important names for last. "I've got a couple of questions for you. First Dmitri Versakos?

"Yeah? What about him?"

"You know him?"

"Yeah."

"And don't like him?"

"I haven't seen him in some twenty years, although once a slime ball, always a slime ball. I know he moved back to the Region a couple of years ago. Runs some sort of Internet business over in Gary."

"Can you give me any specifics? Aside from being a sleazebag?"

"He got caught up in porn stuff back in the 80s, pre-Internet. Took off and left his wife and kid with nothing except the house. The wife filed for dissolution, took whatever money she could get, and split." Santos cocked his head. "Got something on him?"

"He showed up on your list, looks like from Charlie Abel's address book. I'm just operating on cop gut right now. I don't have anything, just a feeling. And his name is still on that list, not crossed off. I went over to Gary and had a quick meeting with him at his office. His set-up stinks, reeks of something illegal. And he was nervous."

"Maybe he's back in the porn business. Or maybe he never left it. FBI could make him very nervous."

"Yeah. I thought of that. And there's something more. I just can't put my finger on it."

"So, what do ya' need from me? All I can tell you is that he used to be the head of the water department."

"Is there any other connection to Charlie Abel? Anything recent?"

"Nope. Not that we found. I'll check around and see if any of my men know something else."

"That'd help. I also need someone to do a few hours research, find out what he's been up to for the past twenty years. And what that Internet company of his is up to. I'd do it myself or get my office to do it, except I think it looks better coming from Hammond PD. Less likely to make him nervous. Concoct some sort of story about his owing back city taxes or something."

"We can manage that. I've got a kid, a young girl, eighteen years old, who's a whiz digging up shit for us. Stringy kind of girl, hair, legs, even clothes. She sure is hell on wheels on the keyboard."

"Thanks. I'd like to get this thing pinned down and get my investigation wrapped up in seven days. Think she can come up with something in the next couple of days?

"Sure. Just give me a day or two to get her set up, then call her, say Tuesday or Wednesday." He swiveled his chair, sighed, and did a one finger tap dance on his keyboard. Swinging back to face Matisse, he read off Thea Bender's contact info.

Matisse took it down and didn't budge.

"Something else?" Santos said.

"Wayne Cornell. I had a meeting set up with him this afternoon down the street. He called me. Said he had some information. Something to do with North American Steel." Matisse shrugged his shoulders. "He never showed. And his cell's shut off."

Santos reached for his phone. "He's that Lake Coalition character, right? Used to work for North American Steel? Smart guy? I'll have someone track him down."

Matisse watched Santos put a call in to Dispatch. The request for the license and car always sounded the same in cop jargon everywhere. It took five minutes for the duty officer to get back with the make and model. Santos punched in more numbers and put out a BOLO for Cornell's car. "Shouldn't take too long to spot the car, if he's out and about. It's one of those new Volvo sedans. How the hell does a guy who used to spend his days measuring dirty water get enough cash to buy a car like that?" Santos didn't wait for an answer but pushed a note over with the make and model, along with an address. "Here's the guy's local address."

Matisse stood up. "Thanks, Lou."

Santos nodded. "I appreciate your taking Miller off your case. And your keeping an eye on her too."

"No problem." Now not only was his own conscience biting him in the ass, this man's confidence in him was as well. Too bad he didn't drink any more. Booze sure as hell took the edge off things, like people depending on you.

"At some point her world's going to straighten around. Until then, I'm going to make sure she survives." Santos turned back to his database, having gotten in the last word.

Twenty minutes later Santos stuck his head out of his office. "Wayne Cornell's car turned up off the service ramp at I-94 and Hammond Avenue. I've got some uniforms on it. You wanna get over there and find out what the hell's happened to Cornell?"

"Yeah." Matisse automatically snatched up his holster. Cornell's abandoned car gave him a nasty feeling. "What's the fastest way over there?"

"Go up Main Street four blocks till you get to Hammond Avenue, then head north fifteen blocks. The service drive is just beyond the entrance to the freeway. I'll give my guys a heads-up the Feds are on their way."

Matisse grabbed his laptop as an afterthought and headed out the door, exhaustion pushed aside by the rush of adrenaline pumping through him. A break? Or a breakdown?

****

A Blue with his hat in hand stood by a white Volvo, as spotless as the day it came off the assembly line. The vehicle couldn't have been parked in this abandoned part of Hammond for more than an hour or two at most. Otherwise, the car would be stripped bare, sitting on its chrome Azuka rims. Or maybe even rimless, if someone figured out how to get the high-end wheels off the car.

A younger cop, female, red hair sticking to the back of her thin neck, leaned over the passenger side and gave him a quick glare, hand going to her holster. Matisse badged her and she stood up, flashing him a stone face. Santos must have called ahead since both officers immediately stepped back, whatever their faces said. He climbed slowly out of the cool dark of his Lexus into searing midday heat. He pulled on a pair of rubber gloves, slipped on his shades, and began a stroll around the car. He eased open the driver's side door.

Ignoring the Blues, Matisse went to work with his camera, aiming, snapping, aiming, snapping. The female stood closest to him, ready to challenge the thin blue line drawn between the FBI and the Hammond PD.

Matisse focused on the clean car, the lack of any sign of struggle or blood. Five minutes passed, then ten. He'd lost the attention of the Blues now. They'd taken up his route, prowling about the car, showing a semblance of business, without actually doing anything. This was his territory.

A cell phone rang and the male cop picked up. "Yeah. Sure. Sure. He's here. No. Yeah, Got it."

"You check out the trunk yet? Or the backseat?" Matisse asked.

"Nope. We were getting to it, but the Chief called and put the brakes on our CSI."

"Anyone else around when you turned up?"

"No one," the man replied. Maybe in his early thirties, he had a face as smooth as a newborn baby's butt. The sneer decorating it looked strange, like a Hell's Angel's tattoo on an infant.

"How'd you find his car? Cruising?" Matisse asked.

"Coincidence mostly. We got the BOLO ten minutes before we spotted the car."

Matisse squatted down beside at the driver's side and put his tweezers to work. The interior looked showroom clean. He glanced over his shoulder. "Got a name, Officer?"

"Hyatt."

"Officer Hyatt, I'm looking for something specific. Give me ten more minutes and you can call in your CSI team."

Matisse popped the trunk open. He'd made it halfway when the stench of death swept past him, hitting his nostrils like a sledgehammer. It never got any better and he never got used to it.

Inside the trunk a pair of unseeing eyes stared up at Matisse. A plastic bag was pulled tight over a man's head turning him into a monster. In fact, the entire body had been shrink wrapped in thick plastic like a prime cut of meat. While the car definitely belonged to Wayne Cornell, it was too soon to jump to the conclusion this was the man himself.

"Officers. Get yourselves back here."

Hyatt looked down into the trunk and blanched although he managed to keep his expression impassive. Officer Lee's face turned as white as the man's inside the trunk. She shook herself twice, like a wet dog, ran for sparse bushes decorating the sidewalk and repeatedly heaved.

"When you're finished, Officer, put in a call to homicide."

Matisse leaned closer, holding his breath. The mixture of smells—feces, urine and blood cooked in the hundred-degree-plus trunk challenged his own stomach. The burger he'd eaten at Flytrap's threatened to reverse on him.

Matisse looked down again. The expressionless face gave no clues to what had happened to the man. The man's pale blue eyes stared up at nothing, his expression surprised, as if he'd been caught in the middle of a question. His long, thin legs were doubled back under him like a Gumby doll. His hands were not visible. What the hell had he been about to disclose?

Matisse patted down the man's soiled suit coat. In one pocket he found a wallet and flipped it open. Wayne Cornell would never pass on his information now, at least not in person. Holding the wallet between two gloved fingers, he dropped it into the evidence bag.

Stepping back from the trunk, Matisse sucked in the clean lake air like a long distance swimmer and dove back in. He worked his way down the rest of the body. At the legs he pulled out another wallet, nearly hidden beneath one bent knee, as if the killer had obligingly left it behind for the cops.

Matisse gingerly held up the wallet, dark and soggy with blood. He flipped it open with a fingertip. Inside, sharp dark eyes stared at him, the head tipped to one side, the grin challenging. The wolf-like face belonged to Joe Sedlack.

Matisse passed the evidence bag over to the Blues, as the CSI team pulled to a stop two feet from the front of the car. Ignoring them in their yellow slickers and gloves, he reached back into the trunk, shifted the body up carefully and looked underneath. He almost missed the manila folder, pushed under the spare tire chamber, a tiny corner of pale tan sticking out.

He eased the limp leg away from the folder and wagged a finger at the lead investigator of the CSI unit. "Get some photos of this, please."

"You the Fed?" The man asked as he snapped away with his camera. He spoke like a seasoned veteran, his face as bored as a man sitting through Sunday mass.

"Special Agent Matisse. Need to see some ID?"

"Naw. I had a call from the Chief. Just leave our scene nice and clean, and we'll be happy."

Matisse pointed at the folder with his index finger. "I'll need to retrieve that folder stuck under the tire. Wanna photograph the contents first?"

"Give me a couple of minutes, and it's all yours."

'You got it. Here's my card. When you're done, copy me on all those photos ASAP." Matisse backed away, wishing for a cold drink to wash away the lingering corpse smell. He sauntered over to join the lead who was busy instructing his three-man team.

Fifteen minutes later, Matisse held the folder, Crawford's card, and a promise from him they'd forward their findings and ME results.

The papers inside the manila folder were dry. No body fluids had found their way under the tire to soil them. Put there before the body? Probably. By Wayne Cornell himself? Most likely. And not found by the murderer? Obviously.

Three sheets, single-spaced, each with six columns giving dates, percentages, and rows of numbers unfamiliar to Matisse. On the top the title read North American Steel. With any luck, this file had something to do with why Cornell called for a meeting today.

Chapter Twenty-one

Is it safe to know in life?

Monday Late Afternoon and Evening, July 18th

Miller made the decision to go with her gut and pursue the unknown Dmitri Versakos from the list. There'd been no question about Sparky going along on the adventure. Since Matisse tossed Miller off his case, the woman refused to leave Miller alone for more than thirty minutes. There'd be no way to stop the woman from running out and climbing into the Honda now.

A little after nine with the daylight gone, Miller set out for Gary, Indiana, and Versakos office. Sparky peered out the side window of Miller's vehicle at the dirty limestone building trimmed in green marble and tarnished chrome. *The Meyers Building* was etched in the marble above the enormous double doors. Inside, it was possible to make out a hallway with elevators on either side.

"Well, the place looks all right," Sparky said. She spoke into the air, not looking at Miller. "What's next?"

"We wait." Miller turned off the motor, slipped down low in the seat, and pulled her baseball cap down over her face. Sparky mimicked all the movements right down to tugging on her rhinestone-studded black cap with the words 'Mustang Ranch' sprawled across it. A nun wearing a cap with the infamous insignia seemed totally appropriate in Sparky's world.

"So is this a good time to tell me why we're interested in this guy?"

"His name is Dmitri Versakos, and I'm not sure why I'm sitting here waiting outside his building, except he's on a list of possible suspects Matisse is investigating."

Sparky looked over at her. "So? You're off Matisse's case, so why is this guy important enough to make a trip all the way to Gary tonight?"

"I don't know. I'm operating on instinct. He was on Matisse's list, not the one Matisse gave me. He was my dad's boss twenty years ago at Hammond Water and a neighbor of ours. He's been gone all these years, and he came back a year or so ago. I did some checking on the Internet and found out he's been living in Florida."

"I understand he knew your dad. What else makes him a suspect?"

"I don't know. I don't even know why he was on Matisse's list. Just a feeling I have when I saw his name."

"What kind of feeling?"

Two people came out the door opposite, a girl about twenty with a man about the same age. Neither of them glanced at the car, heading north up the street in the middle of an argument.

"I have a bad feeling about the man. Nothing specific, just a weird queasy feeling in the pit of my stomach."

"Okay, I'll go with that. I trust those things. More people ought to trust them. How do you know he's up there in his office and that he'll be leaving soon?"

"I tracked down a home address. He lives in a gated community. I'm about to leave a message from the guard there on his office number that someone has broken into his house."

Sparky stared at her. "I'm feeling a new admiration here, Miller. Way to take the bull by the horns. The suspect by the balls."

Miller punched in *67 followed by Versakos office number on her cell phone and held her breath. Lexie had taught her the trick of blocking caller ID a few years ago when she'd been checking up on her ex-husband. It was simple enough as a temporary fix.

"Patriot Internet Services."

"This is Janice Dunn with Winchester Place Management calling. Does a Mr. Dmitri Versakos work at this number?"

"Yes."

"May I speak with him, please? This is regarding a possible break-in at his home."

The silence on the other end lasted so long, Miller wondered briefly if the girl had hung up. "Hold on. I'll see if he's around."

Then, "Dmitri Versakos here."

"Mr. Versakos. I'm sorry to bother you. This is Janice Dunn at Winchester Place Management Office. Your house security alarm went off a few minutes ago, and it's our policy to call and let you know. The cameras inside the house show no motion."

Miller hoped to God he had cameras inside.

"So far we haven't been able to verify an actual break-in. However, it would be best if you came by and checked out your residence to make sure things are in order."

"Okay." Versakos didn't sound happy. "I'm on my way. Give me fifteen minutes to get there, will you? Just have someone keep an eye on the place till I arrive."

Miller flipped her phone shut and grinned at Sparky. "How was that?"

"You sound like the real deal. Done this before?"

"I've seen it done on TV."

Sparky laughed. "What next?"

"We wait till he leaves. Wait a bit and make sure he's gone. Then see if we can get in and do a quick search of his office."

Sparky craned her head and stared at Miller, squinting inside the dark interior of the car. "Now I know why Matisse isn't using you. Here I thought you were a nice girl in a horrible situation. Instead, I find out you're a walking time bomb."

"What do I have to lose?"

"Well, I can think of a few things. Our freedom with our fannies sitting in the local jail. Or worse, our lives."

"Sparky, you didn't need to come along and it's too late to take you home. Just stay in the car and you'll be safe."

"No way. You're not leaving me out. I'm in." Her eyes narrowed at Miller. "You've changed, you know. You're not the Miller Abel I met a few days ago. You're one scary broad, tonight, Abel. I'm not complaining since I like a tough woman myself, so it's not a bad thing."

Miller kept her gaze fixed on the doorway.

"Have you thought about walking into his office and introducing yourself?" Sparky said. "Seems way simpler. We could tell him we need to use his Internet services."

"His Internet services are limited to fulfilling sexual fantasies and sex toys. Which would we ask about?"

"Well, probably the sex toys would be all right. I'm not quite up to sexual fantasies yet myself," Sparky said.

"Let's try my way first."

"You sure you're up for this?"

"It's fine."

"Since we're hanging out here waiting, what's up with Matisse and you?"

Miller made a face at Sparky. "The breaking and entering didn't suit him."

"Well of course not. Aside from that, what about you and him? Or is that too nosey? He seems like a good guy. You could do worse, even if he is the law."

"He is and I could, if I was looking for a long-term relationship, which I'm not. It was just sex."

"In other words, mind my own business, right?"

"You can ask whatever you want. I don't care."

"Okay. Let's say I've got a fascination with law enforcement men. What's he like? Is he for real?"

"How about FBI meets GQ?"

Miller refused to reminisce over Matisse's character with Sparky like a love-struck adolescent dumped by her first real crush. Just focus on what he'd inadvertently given her—a road map to find a killer. So why the hell did she feel so bad?

Sparky fiddled first with her tube top, then the radio, then the brim of her cap. They'd parked across the four-lane road from Versakos' building, far enough away to obscure a direct view of the two of them when Versakos came out of the building.

"Okay, we're good to go then. All we need is for Versakos to leave."

Five minutes later, a man and a woman emerged through the bronze trimmed doors. The man, dressed casually in white polo shirt and dark trousers was accompanied by a woman who from a distance could pass for being in her mid twenties. As they came closer, it was clear she was closer to her late thirties, dressed in a bright yellow, two-piece tube top and mini-skirt that showed off multiple naval rings decorating five inches of bare midriff. Miller stared at Versakos, a twenty year older version of the photo she'd found of him online. He looked like a man who was run by vanity. Neither he nor the woman looked in a particular hurry.

"Love her outfit," Sparky said.

"Hmmm. That's our man with her." Her heart accelerated and she pressed down harder on her reactions.

"Not bad if you like 'em slick. A little lounge lizardy looking, but still passable." Sparky said.

"His Internet images flatter him. Except for the bottled hair, since he's gotta be in his late fifties or even his sixties."

Dmitri Versakos raised his head as if he'd heard her, craned his neck like a raptor, and took a bead on Miller's car.

The girl saved the day, snatching at his arm, causing him to turn back to her.

Miller watched the unlikely couple amble down the empty street, two mismatched lovers out for a summer stroll.

She started her car and crept along with her lights off, watching Dmitri and the girl dash across the street into an open parking lot. Three minutes later, a black BMW shot out the drive exit and turned east, high beams hitting Miller directly in the eyes.

"Get down!" Miller reached across to shove Sparky below the dash, crouching over the steering wheel with bent head.

"Yikes!"

They waited in the car for ten minutes to see if Versakos would return. Sparky fiddled with her cap again, glancing out the window from time to time. "What do you think about that woman he has with him?" she asked.

"I don't want to think about her." Miller replied.

"Not his daughter."

"Probably not."

Miller checked the time, made a U-turn and headed back to the Meyers Building. She parked a block down and in five minutes she and Sparky were standing at the bank of elevators. They both stared at the doors, then up at the floor indicator light, and then over their shoulders in unison. One indicator had stopped on four, another at twelve. The third elevator's indicator moved slowly down the numbers towards one. Miller's heart pounded irrationally. There was no reason to expect Versakos to come back, but there was the security guard to deal with. Commercial properties in Gary ran on low maintenance these days, so this place probably had no more than one rent-a-cop for the entire building. Since he hadn't stopped them at the entrance, he could be anywhere.

Miller took a quick glance at the glass-covered directory of tenants and found Patriot Internet Services. Third floor. "Let's use the stairs and hope that's the night watchman traveling by elevator," Miller said.

"Right."

Miller pulled open the heavy door under the exit sign and stepped into a dim, red-tinted stairwell smelling of bleach. The cleaning service. More people to avoid.

"Got your flashlight?"

"Yes, ma'am." Sparky whipped out a man-sized light from under her black jacket. She wore matching black tights making her skinny legs look like a spider's climbing the steps in front of Miller.

They took the steps fast, pausing at each landing to listen. At the third floor they opened the door and stepped into a hallway that shone red with emergency lighting. They followed the light Sparky shone in front of them over wood floors that were an uneven, dull gray in the center, worn away by thousands of feet shuffling reluctantly to a doctor or dentist appointment over the past fifty years when Gary was a thriving community and the medical community kept downtown offices.

Glass paneled doors lined the hallway but most of the offices looked abandoned, the floors inside white with dust when Sparky shone a light through the glass paneled doors. They moved along the long hall, finding three offices with newly painted signs. Jay's Cleaning Services. Harmani's Accounting. Mosiers Temporary Agency.

Patriot Internet Services turned out to be the last door, at the end of the hallway. The sign looked carelessly put up, pasted over the name of some long-gone dentist, the D.D.S. still clearly visible.

"Wow. This place is a throwback to the beginning of the last century. It gives me the creeps to see all these empty places," Sparky whispered.

Miller ignored her and tried the doorknob of Patriot. Locked. She pulled out a credit card and slipped it into the crack in the door. She worked at it for five minutes, sweat forming on the back of her neck in the airless hallway as she worked.

At last the lock clicked twice and she turned the doorknob. She took a deep breath and pushed the door open an inch.

"Eureka!" Sparky hissed out the word.

Miller took a step into the office, dimly lit by Sparky's flashlight.

The inner door stood open. The room was furnished with a desk and two computers. On the floor were scattered many boxes, some open, most sealed.

"What's your plan, Miller?"

"You go through the boxes and drawers. I'll work on getting into his computer. There's a reason Versakos is on Matisse's list. I'll see if I can find out why."

"Damn." That was all Sparky said, as she turned to attack the boxes.

Miller reached over and touched the space bar on each of the computers humming along in the dark. Their screens sprung to life, casting the room a startling blue. Thank God no passwords were needed here.

Sparky worked silently, scuttling between stacks of boxes, each one stamped 'Patriot' with no other distinguishing marks. Miller watched her work, systematically pulling open each box and digging through it like a dog after a bone before she set it aside.

"Just cords and computer type things here so far," she announced.

Miller turned back to the computers. The man either was very stupid or very sure of himself, since he'd put no passwords on his systems.

"Lookie here!" Sparky held up rubber hosing in pale pink, about a foot and a half long. "What in the heck is this stuff used for?"

"I don't think I want to know." Miller turned quickly back to the computer, focusing on the email. She tried to ignore Sparky as she pulled more and more strange paraphernalia out of the boxes.

Sparky made a raspberry sound. She extracted a grotesque red rubber tongue the size of a half-dozen normal tongues with a blue plastic battery pack attached by a thin wire. "Now this I think I can figure out."

Miller clicked an icon on the newer PC. The second one seemed to be a mirror to the first. An identical twin. There were ten unanswered emails. Skipping past them, she opened the sent mail folder. A hundred and twelve emails. Order after order with product names like Twila's Twin Titillator and Christal's Hard Day. Ugh.

"Man," Sparky said. "This is real sleazebag stuff. That guy should be arrested just for promoting this crap."

Miller kept opening file after file. She checked the time between each file. Twenty minutes gone. Did they risk more time? Versakos could come back or the security guard could spot the lights and open the door. Even the cleaning people were a risk.

She scanned down an invoice from a company by the name of Netmark, Internet account. He'd renewed a domain name with them, the name *The Play Yard*. Miller read through the text of the message; a request to upgrade his account, a login page link, the username, no password.

She clicked on the link and the browser opened to the ISP's login page. She held her breath. His username and password magically appeared. He'd used a feature in Mozilla to manage stored passwords. Fantastic!

She pressed Enter and his file manager and FTP managers displayed. She opened the file manager link and watched a long list of files appear. Systematically, she sent each page to her own laptop.

"Damn! Sorry, but can't be helped. This guy is a snake." Sparky held a DVD case in her hands. Attached to it was a sheet of paper. "Listen to this," she said. *"1 DVD 'Little Girls Blue.' Girls from 5 to 10 years of age."* Sparky's face took on an unfamiliar, very serious expression in the dim light. "Can you pop this into his computer? We need to at least check one out to see what nastiness he's up to." She pursed her lips. "Or we could steal it."

Miller checked her watch again. "We'll need to take it with us. You okay with that? We can mail it back, if your conscience bothers you."

"I don't think I'll have a problem. I'll do a couple of visitations to Westville for penance."

Miller grinned. The image of Sparky traipsing into the Northern Indiana Federal penitentiary to clear her conscience was just funny.

"Cover up that hole you made."

"Okay. I'll stuff some paper in the bottom and it'll look as good as new. Until someone unpacks the box."

Miller clicked through the remaining pages of the FTP files, opened another browser, and sent all of them to her G-mail account. "I think I'm done here." Miller moved to Preferences in each computer, clicked on the desktop, and sent them both off to sleep.

"Good, Let's get the heck out of this place. I'm feeling my hair stand on end."

She'd only gotten the last word half way out when the clank of something hitting glass stopped her.

"Under the desk!" Miller threw herself under the desk, pushing up against Sparky. Her heart beat in her ears like a time bomb.

The lights from the outer office flashed, flooding the inner office with light as well. Someone moved around, pushing aside boxes. A click immediately was followed by the inner door opening.

Whoever it was stopped just at the door, accompanied by a hard rock beat vibrating through the room, the intruder's cell phone.

"Yeah?" A pause. "Naw. I'm just doing room checks." Another longer pause. "All right. Shit."

Miller exhaled sharply. She'd reached thirty-two in her mental counting. She sucked more air into her fluttering chest. Whatever the hell the guy was up to, the phone call had put a stop to it. The inner door to the office closed with a bang, the light disappeared, leaving them under the desk in the dark. Another sharp bang followed by silence.

Long minutes passed.

Miller felt the sweat again trickling down her back and stopped by the elastic of her waist band.

Sparky shifted slightly, the first move she'd made. "Who was that?"

"Security."

"Well, can we get out of this hell on earth now then?" Even Sparky was afraid.

"Let's go."

Chapter Twenty-two

When all else fails, fall back on routine

Late Monday, July 18th and Tuesday dawn, July 19th

Matisse wasted an hour and a half with the CSI team, sharing background info, followed by another hour filling out evidence records before he could focus on the actual murder. And how that connected up with his case.

The dark of night with poor overhead lighting brought some mercy to the squad room, obscuring the dirty windows and scarred tables. Matisse leaned an elbow on the worn table and stared down at the ME's preliminary report. Wayne Cornell had been shot twice and died of the obvious—a bullet to the back of the head, execution style. It took very little imagination to picture the scene. Sensing danger, Cornell probably leapt from his car and started running. The first bullet sent him sprawling on the weed-infested highway island. The second bullet drilled a hole through the back of his skull, killing him.

Matisse read through the report one more time and shoved it aside. The stench of police detention, the cheap booze, even cheaper perfume, and dirty bodies never made it into his consciousness, except in a subliminal longing for a cigarette. Drunks, prostitutes and pimps covered every available space along the back wall, their voices a cacophony of moans, screeches, and insults as they waited to get booked into the Hammond lock-up for the night. He picked up the pages he'd retrieved from Cornell's trunk and studied them. Columns headed water quality level, mineral content, and then more columns of toxins found—lead, mercury, and on and on. Nothing leaped out at him. Until he got to the last page.

Cornell, or someone, had scribbled a note at the bottom: "Owens approved—see emails."

Matisse switched to Google Earth and pinpointed Cornell's house. He lived in Whiting overlooking Wolf Lake facing Lake Michigan. A very high rent district for an environmental geek.

A background check on Cornell turned up more than enough money to support the neighborhood and fancy car. He had been the recipient of a legacy from his family who'd been the first owners of North American Steel back in 1900, then called Cornell Ltd. Five million from his mother in a trust the man came into at thirty-five. So he'd either worked for the fun of it or his passion for the environment drove him. An environmentalist by avocation.

Cornell started The Lake Coalition three years ago, prior to his leaving North American Steel. He'd been their environmental scientist in charge of EPA regulations for five years when he suddenly retired late this last year and Greg Zelenin got hired. From all signs, the abrupt exit stemmed from some sort of disagreement Cornell had with management. Over water filtering inconsistencies?

Who could say what drove a great grandson of a robber baron to turn against the source of his own comforts. Guilt about inheriting dirty money, literally, from back when no one knew or cared about what humans might be doing to their beautiful lake? There were plenty of examples of this phenomenon happening many times in the past. Look at some of the tobacco dynasty who'd set out on anti-smoking campaigns and given away all their wealth.

It also explained his job. Had North American Steel hired him to keep him in line, knowing he had a 'save the lake' ax to grind? Or had it been a positive image move. "We still have some of the old guard working for us" PR crap.

Matisse didn't dismiss blackmail as a motive for Cornell's murder. He'd seen too many people killed over greed. In Cornell's case, it seemed unlikely with all that family cash that the man would stoop to blackmail. Sticking his nose in places where he'd get in too deep, and he apparently had, sounded more like a man with an altruistic bend. Especially with what he knew of Cornell so far and his Lake Coalition group. Much less likely seemed to be assigning this as a random act of violence by some stranger strung out on life's highs.

Matisse pulled out the evidence bag with Joe Sedlack's wallet inside. What the hell did that dirt bag have to do with all this? There was no way the guy wasn't involved in this murder. His background check turned up a couple of traffic complaints. Digging deeper, there were two restraining orders on Sedlack, one by a former girlfriend who was the mother of his child and more recently one by a blackjack dealer where he worked.

The squad room was the last place he wanted to be right now, especially at midnight. He forced himself to stay another hour, swallowing down acrid coffee as he reviewed and uploaded the evidence the Hammond SCI team had passed him.

Santos would probably have the search warrant for Cornell's place by morning. As he filled out reports, Matisse debated about getting a jump on the warrant and searching Cornell's house tonight. It was inside the law to do it without the warrant, just barely, if he pleaded the exigent circumstance argument, to forestall destruction of possible evidence in a homicide case. The last thing he wanted was to alienate Santos, so he put in the time instead, reviewing the CSI evidence until after one in the morning.

At last, with a sigh he dragged his body out the door heading to his motel for a couple of hours of sleep. The wind had changed its direction sometime mid afternoon and now blew in off Lake Michigan, as if expressing all its pent-up frustrations Matisse felt in one long blow. He crossed the parking lot and unlocked his car.

He decided to take the interstate. When he spotted the Whiting exit, he changed his mind and took the off-ramp at high speed.

The streets of Whiting were empty this time of night, except near Milski's where activity hummed. Matisse drove five blocks past the bar, turned left on Main, drove two blocks down and made a sharp turn into Miller's alley. With his parking beams on, he made for her gate and switched off his engine.

A faint light glowed upstairs, probably from the fixture over the kitchen sink. Her car was missing. He stared up at her dark apartment window. Where the hell was she, and what could she be doing out this late after her visit to the ER? His guess was she had to be busy sticking her nose into murder. A little thing like a concussion would never stop her.

He fiddled with a cigarette, lit it, and took five puffs, the last one a deep drag, then flipped the butt out the window into the dirt.

"Shit!" Matisse yanked the gearshift into first, shot down the dark alley, and punched on his lights as he hit the street.

Chapter Twenty-three

The truth too late is a matter of life and death

Tuesday, July 19th

Returning to work turned out to be the best part of Miller's day. With the lingering effects of a concussion pounding inside her skull and a sleepless night, she downed two espressos, and gritted her teeth through the day.

At five o'clock she checked her watch and shut down her computer with a deep sigh. Before the murders, she'd happily worked fifty or sixty hours a week, out-manning every man in the place. Now she was avoiding going home to a desolate apartment with nothing except memories to comfort her. Since Matisse turned up with his case, her entire focus had shifted to finding a killer. Today, that looked as far from possible as it had the day she buried her family.

Dark clouds chased her home, lightning pushing her inside her door. She shut it reluctantly and stepped into her dreadful kitchen. With no work to distract her, no offices to burgle, and her only connection to revenge stepped back from her life, she stared miserably at the white walls of her solitary confinement. Sinking into the morass of it all felt like a slow death by quicksand.

Miller forced herself to stand. She roamed over to the refrigerator and reflectively opened it. All it held were two bottles of soda, a loaf of bread she'd thrust in there this morning in hopes of avoiding mold, and a chunk of week-old cheese.

She wandered down the dark hall into the bathroom, glanced at her raccoon eyes, and turned away. In the bedroom, she dropped to the bed and sniffed at the bed covers in hope of finding some lingering reminder of Matisse. The sheets merely smelled stale.

Her eyes moved from object to object in the room, landing at last on the chest of drawers. The single piece of contraband from her parent's house, the dresser, dark oak with three drawers had first belonged to her father's mother, who'd passed it on to Charlie Abel, the favored son. At the time of the murders, the chest had belonged to Jacob. Now it kept her company each night on her journey through sadness.

Miller leaned over and ran one finger along the smooth front, worn away by sixty years of use. The wood felt almost warm, like touching her mother's face. Or Jacob's.

Last night she'd had a visitation from the night voices. They didn't come every night, not even every week, and rarely they'd speak two nights in a row. And they never manifested more than once in a night. Did other people have these moments when, heart pounding, you get startled awake in the darkness by a voice from somewhere? You sit up, working to identify where the voices are coming from. By then the voice is no more than an echo in your head, having just missed whatever it was they were trying to tell you. Last night had been Jacob's voice.

She'd awakened as usual, heart pounding. *It's just a dream.* Who wouldn't have voices with her life? She'd gotten up, used the bathroom, taken an ibuprofen and gone back to sleep, grateful for the distraction of pain.

Now tonight she lay on her bed in the silence of the dark room and considered Jacob. She could hear his voice now, hanging hollow in the air, like a smile lingering in the emptiness. The unfamiliar feeling about her heart startled her, an aching softening. Tears streamed on her cheeks. She shut her eyes and felt him there with her, for the first time since that horrific day.

She must have dozed off. When she wakened she still lay in the dark bedroom, the small light still gleaming by the bed. Words, like something left inside her mind, echoed. "Miller." "Love." "Search" "Danger." The words made no sense, yet in her mind she heard them as clearly as if Jacob stood beside her bed speaking to her. The words were alarming, even as his presence was reassuring. Jacob loved her, and he knew she loved him.

She focused on the chest of drawers, hunched there in the corner of her room like a faithful dog. The drawers held only her clothes, not even her old clothes, but those soulless ones she'd purchased after the murders. She had kept almost nothing in the way of large objects from her past life, especially nothing to remind her of Jacob, except the chest.

She studied the dark hulk in the gloom, trying to recall when she'd brought it into the apartment. What she'd done when she'd had it moved from Jacob's room. Those days were filled with empty actions and little memory. Lexie had helped her with the move, asked if Miller wanted to keep something. After rejecting various things with too much pain attached, she'd decided to keep the chest.

They'd pushed it into the bed of a borrowed truck and unloaded it along with a few household items from the Goodwill. The house went up on the market while an estate sale got rid of the rest of her parents' life, all sold to the highest bidder.

Miller squinted at the chest, trying to recall if there was something else. She reached over slowly and opened a drawer. Inside, she'd neatly folded her three T-shirts, gray, beige, and off white. No black was allowed. She denied herself the role of only mourner left.

In a second drawer, she flipped through her three pairs of jeans and two pairs of khaki cargo pants. Sweatpants with matching hoodies made up the third pile in the drawer, one set of gray, another of navy. She fingered the clothes, feeling around one side for a small cardboard box hidden there.

The box felt as warm as the wooden chest and it reminded her again of Jacob. He'd covered the box with pictures of himself and his friends in a collage of smiling faces. With trembling fingers she clutched at it and moved slowly down the hall into the kitchen.

Miller took a seat facing the window and placed the box in front of her. The pounding of her heart felt ridiculous in the safe room. She shut her eyes and listened, opened them, and lifted the lid off the box. Jacob had covered the inside with strange, wonderful drawings from his life, memories that ended at nineteen.

She picked out each treasure, the memorabilia of Jacob's world, as though each was made of cobwebs. She unfolded sheets of thin paper that held notes, some from girls, some guys. There were small, white shells, and dried seaweed. She raised smooth pieces of sea glass and stared through the blue world. He'd kept bottle caps, a Harley-Davidson label, and metal screws from something.

Miller ignored the tears running down her face and laid out each item carefully on the table until only one item remained. She reached into the bottom of the box and pulled out a folded sheet of paper. She opened it slowly and spread it out.

Ten-year-old Miller Abel stared up at her, ashen looking, fear and confusion written on her face. She stood naked, her legs apart, staring into the camera.

Spots danced in front of Miller's eyes, the pounding in her chest moving to her head, accelerating the headache.

She stood up and shoved back the chair. It fell backwards and hit the floor with a thump. She stumbled to the sink, leaned over, and vomited into the pristine white.

Her body heaved and shook. Waves of heat vibrated through her, and she slid to the floor. Instinctively she pulled her body up tight in a fetal position and wrapped her arms about her legs, barely aware of the cold refrigerator at her back. Her mind leapt about frantically, searching for answers. Matisse had mentioned a picture he'd found in her dad's safety deposit box. This must be the picture.

Her chest heaved with sobs. Somehow she'd caused the murders.

****

Miller curled up in Sparky's overstuffed, pink damask chair, still hugging her shaking legs. Sparky handed her a mug of hot tea. "Ready to talk about what's going on?" she asked.

"Yes."

"Just tell me what you can. It'll all come eventually."

Miller inhaled slowly.

"A picture. I found a picture today. It was in a little box Jacob kept things in. I couldn't face opening it, so I stuck it under clothes in the chest."

"So?"

Miller swallowed, her throat dry. "Near the bottom of the box, I found a folded sheet of paper. It was a picture of me when I was little. A nude picture."

Sparky stared. The only obvious reaction was those caterpillar eyebrows rising a half inch. "Go on."

"I…" She stopped, hating the words she needed to say. "It happened when I was ten. I don't know why I never told anyone. I was probably too embarrassed. And then I forgot about it. Or suppressed all the memory maybe."

"It wouldn't be weird for a kid to suppress the memory of something that traumatic."

"It was Versakos."

"The creep's office we broke into? You mean he took the picture?"

Miller nodded. "He was our neighbor. He took a lot of them."

"Go on. Give me the rest."

"I stayed over at their house sometimes. The family had a son my age. That first day I remember, it was summer. His wife had gone off to pick up their son from baseball practice. I'd been dropped off by my parents while they went somewhere. They'd do that sometimes since I liked the boy, Seth. That day the father was alone when I got there. He invited me to wait in this white room, his office I think.'

The room pulsed with expectation, the warm silence deafening.

"I waited and when he came back he had a small Kodak camera, the kind everyone owned twenty years ago."

A wave of nausea swept over Miller, imagining the man's hands on her. Not rape, not even sexual molestation. Something far more widespread and viral and she had no way to prove it happened. As a little girl she'd had no understanding of what had taken place in his fancy house. Just that he'd paid attention to her, and she'd liked it.

"He told me he wanted to take some pictures of me, and he'd give me some ice cream if I let him."

"What about the son? Was he in the pictures?"

"No. Just me. Seth was gone. I remember I felt weird, like it was bad somehow, yet it seemed exciting. And I wanted the ice cream. So I said okay."

"He asked you to get nude?"

"No. Not at first. At first it was just some snaps of me, standing by the chair, eating the ice cream. It wasn't just that one day. He asked me to do it again. I don't remember how often. Each time he asked for more." She shivered. "I remember it seemed exciting, in an evil sort of way."

"Go on."

"He pulled out a doll, a Barbie Doll, dressed in a prom dress. I remember it was pink. He said I could have it, if I would take off my T-shirt and let him take some pictures of me like that."

She'd hesitated only a few minutes before ripping off the halter top she wore. She'd been undeveloped, her small chest flat with no evidence of the beginnings of a woman. He'd smiled at her, kind, no threat. He hadn't touched her, just snapped pictures. Three, maybe four. He promised he wouldn't touch me."

"Did he?"

"Touch me? No."

She thought about it. Had he? No, she had no memory of him even being interested. It seemed as sterile as a doctor's visit. She'd undressed, he'd snapped pictures, and then she'd get dressed. Except she'd enjoyed it. She remembered the feelings, the first stirring in her young life of something sexual, unfamiliar, and wrong. Just a few pictures and she could have a toy or a candy bar. She'd desperately wanted those things. He'd kept offering her more things, and she'd agreed to let him take some pictures with the small camera. A few pictures, that was all.

"Go on Miller."

She'd refused to take off her panties, and he'd switched to threats. He was going to show the pictures to her mother. She was going to be in trouble. If she did what he asked, he promised he wouldn't touch her but just take a few picture and that would be all.

Miller forced herself to look up, focusing on Sparky' face. She saw nothing there except compassion.

"After that it happened at least a few more times, each time I got something from him. The last time I had to pose nude and do things to my body. Me, not him."

"What kind of things?"

Miller cringed, embarrassed even now at the question. "Feel myself. Lay down and spread my legs. Rub things between my legs. Stuff like that." This time she couldn't look at Sparky. "He took a picture or two. He pushed a box over and told her to put one foot up on it. I knew doing that was wrong, showing my private place. I did it anyway." She remembered his smile, how he'd moved closer, placing the camera down low a foot or so away, clicking again and again, upward. She flushed and shut her eyes.

"I wanted the toys. I liked how it felt to have pictures taken of me. I was always the good girl. It was fun being bad for once."

"The last time, he said 'put your clothes on now, sweetheart. You've been a good girl. You can have all the doll things.' Then he warned me again and made me promise not to tell anyone we took pictures together. It would get my dad into a lot of trouble, if people knew I took off my clothes. And he'd tell the priest at church and my mother. She remembered nodding numbly, putting on her shorts, stuffing her panties into a pocket with shaking fingers. She'd taken the doll things.

He'd driven her home and she'd gotten out of his car before she reached her street, found a trash can sitting by the street, and tossed the doll from that day into the can and run home crying. Neither her mother nor her father had been home. She'd hidden in her room and locked the door, weeping until she'd heard them come in. She'd come out then, not looking at her parents, and run outside to play in the yard.

"So he kept you from telling anyone with threats?"

"Yes. He said it was our secret." She stopped. "I liked having a secret with a grown-up."

"Why did it stop?" Sparky asked.

"One day I went over and his wife was home. She said they were moving. That was that. I never saw any of them again."

She'd never told anyone about Dmitri Versakos and those afternoons.

"What's the connection with Jacob? How did it get into his keepsake box?"

The silence weighed a thousand pounds, pressing down on her like a vice grip, crushing her, leaving her feeling like that bad child again.

"I'm not sure," she whispered. "The sheet looks like it came off an Internet site. It has a web address on the bottom. I think somehow Jacob stumbled on the picture and recognized me."

Sparky sipped at her tea. "Well, that makes some sense with what we found last night. All that kiddie porn stuff." She leaned forward. "But what's the connection between the web site and the murders?"

"I don't know. I never saw Versakos again after he took photos of me. It just seems too weird that the picture turned up now. And that he came back to town before my family died. And who knows why Matisse has him on the list of suspects." Miller shrugged. "Maybe it's simply because my dad worked for him at the water department."

"That seems unlikely since it was so long ago."

"I agree."

"So you're trying to make a connection between these memories you have and the murders?"

"Yes." The word came stubbornly. "I know there's a connection. I feel it." She sighed and sank back, staring at Sparky's movie poster from Star Wars.

"Miller, you can't know that. Why would a man risk committing three murders for the sake of some pictures of a nude child twenty years ago."

"I don't know." Miller said.

"What is it?" Sparky asked.

Miller's mind tripped over thoughts of her dad, of Jacob's secret box.

"Miller, what is it?"

"I think Jacob found Versakos' pornography web site. And connected it up to the picture of me he had."

"Why would a twenty-year old picture of a little girl be used on the Internet?"

"Why not? He probably has a whole library of pictures of lots of little girls. He's had twenty years to compile them. Maybe he was selling them privately back then. Now with it so easy to upload pornography on the Internet, he could use all his pictures. Especially older ones that would be almost impossible to trace."

"Even if your dad and your brother did track him down, why would the man care if he was exposed? I mean it's illegal but there's so much of it, I think the authorities find it pretty hard to prosecute. There's lots of porn stuff out there. Lots of pictures of children. What could your dad have said that would cause this man to murder your entire family?"

Miller shook her head. "I don't know. I need to check the laws, find out what this man is doing now. Where he's been and why he left twenty years ago. And I need to see him."

This time Sparky shook her head. "You're not doing this alone. I'll help you all I can. Promise me you won't go after this man alone. Either tell Matisse or the police. Don't try and take him down yourself."

Miller smiled. Sparky, the Cold Case officer, discussing taking down an unsub.

"Thanks, Sparky." She reached over and put her arms around the woman's thin shoulders. The hug she got back reminded her of her mother's. "I'm going back upstairs and start digging."

"Okay. I'll be around all evening. Keep me updated on what you find, will you? I want to be part of this thing."

"I will." She pushed herself up, her legs remarkably weak, like a new colt or a baby bird. She didn't let herself think too far into motive. It would only put her as the source of something too horrible to consider.

"Take your pain meds for that head and don't over-do it."

"I won't, Mother!"

"Mother. Now there's the key. I thought I wanted to be Mother Superior. What I really wanted was to just be a mother. Looks like I might get to be a substitute one, if you'll let me."

"Sure. I can use one these days." She leaned in and kissed the woman's dry cheek. It smelled of something exotic with a name like Obsession or Midnight Passion. "I'll call you when I find something."

Chapter Twenty-four

The source of misery is often hope shrouding confusion

Wednesday morning, July 20th

The next morning with only four hours of sleep Matisse stumbled to his car. He stared up at the low clouds, feeling as gray as the sky overhead.

His motel was downtown, too close to the interstate and crime. Last night someone paid his Lexus a visit in the night, leaving the door ajar. They'd spread his glove compartment detritus out over the seat and stolen his battery, leaving a hole where it should have been. "Shit!"

Triple A Towing arrived thirty minutes later, looking leery, probably having been mugged there too many times themselves. They popped in a new battery and Matisse headed out for Hammond. He called ahead for word on Santos who was expected at ten.

By the time Matisse picked up his coffee, the threatening storm had abandoned the area, probably taking aim at Kalamazoo on its way to the Motor City. The day left behind was perfectly clear, pushing aside imminent worries over global warming. The air smelled as sweet as country hay, tantalizing the locals with dreams of many such days to come.

Lou Santos glanced up. He put aside the newspaper, and stirred the coffee in a mug that read *My Grandfather's a Cop—Watch out!*

"How's it going, Robert?" Santos' smile stretched across his round face.

"Having a good morning?"

"Yeah. I just became a grandfather—again. Great feeling. Sixth time, first girl."

"Congratulations." Matisse took a seat opposite with his coffee cup in hand.

"You don't have kids yet, right?" Santos asked.

"No." A sigh escaped before Matisse could clamp down his lips and ward it off. "I'm not sure I ever will at my age. Or whether it's even a good thing for me."

"Why say that? Kids are great. Grandkids are even better."

"I'm probably getting too old to deal with all those problems, watching the struggles my sister goes through with hers."

"It's worth it, believe me." Santos reached for a mint.

Matisse shrugged. "I'll have to get going, if I'm going to take it on."

"How old are you? Mid-forties, right? You've got some time."

Matisse rubbed his eyes and let a smile slip out. "I'll consider it, Lou, one of these days." He pulled out his files. "Anything new this morning on Cornell's murder?"

Santos' good mood dissolved. He shook his head. "Still waiting on the ME's report."

"Anything turn up on Sedlack?"

"Petty crime. A couple of restraining orders. Nothing major. The family owns a bunch of pawn shops in the area. My guys pulled him in late last night for questioning. He's sitting in a holding cell right now, while we wait for prints on the weapon. You got any ideas on connection to your case? Or the vic?"

"Sedlack's a punk. My best guess is someone hired him to take Cornell out. The question is why? And since he was spotted at a Lake Coalition meeting last week, I've gotta assume it could be connected to my case. Got anything on the gun yet?"

Santos shook his head. Thirty years in law enforcement had taught him to listen more than speak. "Hell. This is a fucking mess. And right back where we started. Our cases are stuck together like glue."

"The whole thing stinks," Matisse replied.

"You've got that right. It stinks like last week's garbage. And Miller being connected in any way is one more piece of trash I don't wanna even think about." He slung himself back in his chair, tilting it back so far Matisse stopped himself from reaching across the desk to save him from falling. "What about Sedlack's day job? Aside from petty crime, does he do any legitimate work?"

"Sporadic stuff, a go-for at the casinos, not much else. Just punk-for-hire, as far as I can tell."

"And the search warrant for Cornell's place?" Matisse asked.

"Yeah, they're already over there this morning," Santos said.

"I'll stop by in a while and see what I can see."

"Yeah, okay." Santos agreed. "What else you need from me?"

"North American Steel. I need a search warrant to take a gander at Owens' files. Maybe subpoena his hard drive."

"As CEO of the only solid job-creating business in the Region, Owens swings a big bat." he said. "Bring me more evidence that he had something directly to do with Cornell's murder, and I'll get that subpoena."

"I'll get over to Owens' office again and see if I can push him a little further towards that warrant," Matisse said.

"All right. Just keep me updated on what you find out and make sure you don't shove him right out of the country," he said.

Matisse stood up.

"So what about Miller? You gave me a promise she'd be safe," Santos said.

"She's not listening to me now, since I took her off my investigation. In fact, as it turned out, she wasn't really listening to me from the beginning. I'll keep an eye on her."

"Use your charms, Matisse. I can see you've got 'em," Santos said.

Matisse shrugged. "I'll stick around a couple of hours here in case you get something back from the ME or the prints. Any suggestions on how I can get inside Jeffrey Owens private finances?"

"Try First National. Ask for Bill Weber. He handles all the North American stuff. You might even get lucky and find they handle his personal accounts as well."

"Thanks, Lou." Matisse shoved his coffee cup into the trash.

"Yeah, okay." Santos nodded.

Matisse set up a meeting with Bill Weber at First National and spent the next thirty minutes signing off on duty reports. Santos assistant, Arlene, came by and dropped a copy of the ballistics report in front of Matisse. No surprises there. Cause of death-gunshot to the head from a double action SIG .45.

****

Arlene came back as Matisse was getting ready to head out. "Chief Santos wants you to you sit in on Joe Sedlack's interrogation." She steered Matisse down a narrow hall to a small room. Inside Santos nursed his grandfather mug, staring through a one-way mirror at the blank walls of the interrogation room.

"Take a seat, Agent Matisse. I thought you'd like to watch." He shoved a chair over with one toe and Matisse caught it. Two other officers, detectives, one a good looking black woman, the other a seasoned looking, forty-year-old man, stood leaning against the wall.

"These are Detectives Flora Banks and Jake Summerhill. They're going to interrogate Sedlack." He didn't bother turning. "Detectives, this is Special Agent Matisse of the FBI Anti-Terrorist Division."

They exchanged nods with Matisse, neither smiling.

"Sedlack claims someone stole his SIG from his apartment three days ago. We also got the results on the prints. They belong to the kid" Santos made a motion to a cop at the door. "Tell 'em to bring the kid in."

Detectives Banks and Summerhill slipped out the door.

Joe Sedlack, looking small and wiry in orange jail fatigues came into the windowless interrogation room followed by the two detectives.

"State your name." It was Banks doing the questioning.

"Joe Sedlack."

Matisse leaned forward to make out the tinny voice through the small speaker.

"Address?" Banks asked.

The officer was in her mid thirties, smooth cheeked, her manner a mix of a female Jesse Jackson and Oprah. She ignored Sedlack's insolence as she questioned him. "Where were you yesterday between ten and two?"

"You think I keep a journal of my every move? I was probably at a bar that time of night."

"I'm talking ten to two daytime yesterday."

Sedlack shrugged. "Sleeping?"

"Alone?"

"Who knows? I don't keep track of every minute of my life."

The questioning went on for two hours. Sedlack grew more and more sullen.

Feeling as frustrated as hell, Matisse gave up and went back to the squad room. He pushed his duty reports into a tidy pile and took off. He switched his order of business for the day to include a stop at First National on his way to do a thorough toss of Wayne Cornell's place, followed by another visit to Owens at North American for a try at some arm twisting.

At First National, Bill Weber came out to greet Matisse. The man almost looked too much like a banker to be one, rotund, balding, and smiling. He also looked astute, like a man who knew every financial secret of the world, and chose to run this small bank in Hammond as a joke on the big boys. He held out a beefy palm to Matisse and shook hands with the force of a Bank of New York VP.

"Come on into my office. Lou Santos called to clear the way for you. He's an old poker buddy of mine," he said. "There's no way I'd have seen you otherwise. You owe the man tickets to the White Sox, by the way."

"Thanks, Mr. Weber. I promise not to take up much of your time. Just a few questions and we're done."

Matisse stepped into the man's office and stopped, overwhelmed by blue. The entire room glowed with the color from the wall to desk to computer. Marine paraphernalia covered every available spot in the room, as if tumbled there at low tide.

Eighteen-foot high single paned windows looked out on the bank parking lot, also painted sea blue. Matisse took a chair facing the windows.

"Surprised you, huh?" The man pointed to a lounge chair with psychedelic fish swimming over it. "I'm a fisherman," he went on, "I love water, whatever form it takes. What do you think? Too much?"

Matisse blinked and shook his head. He hoped the guy didn't get insulted.

"That's okay. Some people find it a little over the top. I don't mind. It brings in a lot of interest in my bank, from curious people mostly. Good PR for the place."

Matisse pulled out his Blackberry.

"Mr. Weber, I'm with the FBI Special Anti-Terrorist Task Force out of Chicago, following up on a case."

"Yeah, Lou mentioned something about that."

"I'm looking between my case and North American Steel. In that regard, I'd like to look at the company's account and ask you a few questions about financial dealings."

Weber's happy expression turned dour. "I'm sorry. Without an injunction, I can't tell you anything about North American's banking activities. Have you talked with Jeffrey Owens? He'd be the one to discuss this with."

"I've talked to Mr. Owens. He assures me everything is in order at his company, and yet I have reason to believe otherwise." He paused, searching for a way past the man's Midwest integrity. "I'm going to have to insist you tell me what you know about both North American Steel and Jeffrey Owens' financial dealings."

"So, is this an official FBI investigation?"

"Yes."

"I'll need you to give me a written statement to that effect," he said. "Don't want to get my bank into some lawsuit."

"I understand. I'll give you whatever authorization you need."

"All right, shoot."

"Is North American Steel in debt? If so, to what extent and does the bank have a lien on any of the company's property?"

Weber took out a handkerchief and wiped at his brow. "I've got your word this won't go any further than this room?"

"You do. If we need to use what you say in court, it will be a closed grand jury hearing or separate statement."

"All right. Just be sure it goes no further than between us. My words, I mean."

Matisse nodded and waited.

"North American Steel is in hock up to its gills. Bottom line, the bank owns the property. We could call in
the loans they have with us at any time. We won't
because we don't want to lose our shirts on this. And
with the mill a major employer in Hammond, it would
put hundreds of people out of work. So we're holding on
taking any such action right now, keeping our lure in the
water."

"And Jeffrey Owens?"

"He's CEO, he owns a big chunk of stock, and he's
in as deep as he can get. He banks with us also." He
paused, wiping a thin line of sweat off his upper lip.
"Not only does he have North American Steel to worry
about. He's also got a loan out on a three-million-dollar
house over on the lake in Michigan City that's about to
get repossessed."

Matisse's brain did a back flip. Ka-chink. "How
much time are you giving him?"

"About three more months to get things straightened out with NAS."

"Or then what?"

Weber shrugged. "Repossession, and the bank takes
over the North American Steel property as well. We'll
probably sell it off, hopefully, not to someone who's
going to deep six the business, since it supports a lot of
people in the Region."

Matisse tapped notes into his Blackberry.

Weber shifted about on his chair, clearly uncomfortable. "Can you tell me what this investigation is
about? Something to do with misappropriation of funds?
Nothing on the scale of anything violent, is it?"

"I can't say more right now, Mr. Weber. There may
be no connection to our investigation. If it turns out

otherwise, you'll be getting a subpoena from the FBI for a grand jury hearing in a matter of weeks."

"Hell." Weber looked like he'd just sucked up a can of his fishing worms. "Does this have anything to do with Wayne Cornell's murder?"

"You know the man?"

"Yeah. This is a small town. Everyone knows his family and his story. He inherited a big chunk of cash, when his parents got killed in an airport bombing ten years or so ago." He puffed out his cheeks. "Saw it in the morning papers. Jesus Christ." He glanced up. "You say you're with the Anti-Terrorist Division? Then you're investigating some kind of foreign terrorist thing having to do with NAS? Like Al Qaida?"

"Not foreign, home grown terrorism."

"Well hell. I don't see what any of this has to do with North American Steel."

"Right now we're looking at motive. First money, second revenge, any related affiliations. Any chance I can have copies of last month's statements. Both for North American Steel and Jeffrey Owens?"

Weber stood up slowly. "Give me a few minutes. And while you're waiting, I'll need in writing from you that you're not going to go public with this."

"I can't guarantee that, Mr. Weber. I can promise it will only be used for corroboration right now. If there is a grand jury hearing, it will be private." He paused to let the next words sink in. "The murder is another issue. If some connection is found to the murder of Cornell, I can't promise you won't be called in on that to give evidence."

"Jeffrey Owens never appealed to me personally. Too smooth. Yet I've never heard anything about him doing anything illegal."

Fifteen minutes later, Weber's secretary—a flat-chested woman close to forty, with a hairdo so sedate a nun would be ashamed to call it her own–came in and handed Weber a folder. He passed it across his desk to Matisse who stood up. "We'll be in touch. Thank you, Mr. Weber." He shook the man's sweaty hand and sighed as he exited the cool blue room. Splashes of blue lingered in his field of vision for the next few minutes as he headed for Whiting.

****

Cornell's house stood silent, guarded by a lone uniform standing at the door. Matisse flashed his badge and ducked under the CSI tape.

The house felt cool and Matisse silently blessed the time when a house like this would be built to take advantage of the lake across the street. He searched through the rooms until he found Cornell's office.

Cornell was no man's fool. He'd stashed a hard copy of all sensitive material relating to his personal investigation in his bottom locked drawer. Feeling no compunction, Matisse jimmied it and pulled out the file. Inside were copies of the water records, marked with red for those days that registered above average toxins. They had occurred every Friday for the past six months. Three sheets near the back were copies of North American's finances, with red circles around amounts taken out in $20,000 lump sums, the initials 'JO' written beside each withdrawal. Matisse took out the corroborating statements he'd gotten from Weber for the last month and confirmed all withdrawals for the month of June.

Slipped into the back of Cornell's file lay a single sheet with the words *Greg Zelenin* sprawled across it in long hand. Matisse stared, frowned at the name and pictured the face.

It took him two hours to search, catalog, and photograph computer files before he stepped back out into the quiet street and late midday heat. He smiled at the officer sitting on the step.

Matisse opened all the windows of his car to let in the offshore breeze and leaned back to study the files. Everything here pointed to North American Steel and specifically Jeffrey Owens being in deep shit. And it looked like Cornell had dug up the shit that proved Owens was subsidizing his income and paying his overdue personal expenses by fudging the water department dispersals and EPA filtering requirements without actually spending the bucks to do it. He'd save at least $100,000 every six months bypassing the filtering process even just once a week. The question was what was Greg Zelenin's role in all this? Did the man hold a major piece in the game himself? Had Cornell found out Zelenin's part in this mess?

He reviewed the key players again in his case. Jeffrey Owens, Wayne Cornell, Greg Zelenin. And of course, Joe Sedlack. Who else? What about Miller's other friends? How did they figure?

He pulled at his collar rubbing the back of his neck, a constant irritation. Like Miller Abel. *Fuck*. He had to get his investigation wrapped up and get the hell out of the Region.

And where did Dmitri Versakos fit into all this? He'd done some research on the man who turned out to be running a website selling sex toys. And maybe even sex. The man was beetle dung, and yet being the scum of the earth was no crime. There'd been no evidence connecting anything environmental to the man, except he'd been water department director years ago. And he'd been in Charlie Abel's address book. He wrote off Versakos as a bad lead.

Before heading back to Hammond, he put in three quick calls to his father, his sister, and his Chicago office. And then he called North American Steel, "I'd like to speak with Mr. Owen," he said.

"Sorry. He's gone for the day," the woman replied.

Matisse checked the time—five-ten. *Shit.* "All right. Thanks." He debated about eating in Hammond and opted for Chinese food in Whiting. He found a small table at the window and spent a quiet hour reviewing more water quality reports from Cornell's computer.

It was a little after seven when he placed the last record back in the folder. He was too beat to look at one more number. He got into his car, thought about going back to the squad room in Hammond and instead made his way to Miller's alley. He crept down it and shut off his engine. Her car was gone again tonight. Maybe at work. Maybe out causing trouble. He lit up his daily cigarette.

Five minutes later Matisse tossed his butt out into the weeds and headed for the Motel Six.

Chapter Twenty-five

Avoiding danger is no safer in the long run than outright exposure
—Helen Keller

Wednesday, July 20th

The wonders of the Internet didn't fail Miller. Again, the answers were there. The puzzle pieces, that is. All she needed to do was fit them together and discover what was missing. Tracing Dmitri proved to be fairly simple. The divorce proceedings were public record and Miller got to them with no more than one call and a visit by Sparky to the County Clerk's office on Monday.

Dmitri Versakos' forwarding address when he'd left the Region still occupied a folder in a water department file cabinet along with a reference check and a stamped copy of a reference letter in the files, the antiquated system inherited from the previous secretary fifteen years departed. Gladys sounded thrilled to forward copies. Thank God for the old days where secretarial jobs were blessings and diligence was a prerequisite.

Miller studied Versakos' Florida address: 2695 Fox Glove Lane, St. Petersburg. Another of those pretentious street names that fulfilled the dreams of many middleclass American families, dreaming of suburban affluence.

Miller tracked the address down online and got a phone number. An Eldon C. Blake was listed at the address. She debated over what could be gained by calling the place. Maybe she would get a lead on the man's life, and what he'd been up to in the past twenty years? Maybe find something to connect him to her dad? Miller punched in *67 to override caller ID and then the number.

"Hello. This is Detective Morris with the Chicago Police Department. Is this the Blake residence?"

"Yes?" The voice sounded over sixty and frightened. "This is Mrs. Blake."

"I'm sorry to bother you, Mrs. Blake. It's nothing serious, just a few questions," Miller replied. "Is this 2965 Fox Glove, St. Petersburg?"

"Yes, it is."

"We're looking for someone who lived at that address twenty years ago. A Mr. Dmitri Versakos Do you recognize that name?"

"No. We've only owned this house for sixteen years."

"Can you tell me who you purchased it from?"

"Well, let's see. I think it was a woman, nice looking, pleasant, a bit abrupt. You know, like a business woman."

"You don't happen to remember her name, do you?"

"Well, no, I don't."

"What about the realtor who sold you the house?"

"Well I should, since it was my husband's business. Palmetto Realty. He sold it when he got sick five years ago."

"I'd appreciate the phone number, if you have it at hand."

"Just a minute, let me look. My husband's passed. Two years ago. Hold on a second while I find it." A yappy bark, something small sounding, like a Pekinese filled the silence until she returned. "Here it is. 204-5967."

"Thank you very much, Mrs. Blake. The Chicago Police Department appreciates it." Miller hung up and wiped her wet forehead. It must get easier, conning people, the more one did it.

She keyed in the new numbers.

"Palmetto Realty, Deborah speaking."

"This is Detective Morris with the Chicago Police Department. We're working a cold case, and I need some information on a house you sold."

"I'll do my best."

"It was twenty years ago. Do you keep records going back that far?"

"I'm sorry, we don't."

Miller sighed, the letdown physical. "I believe the house now belongs to the former owner of your company," Miller added.

"Oh yes, that would be Mr. Blake. That could make it easier. I'll pull the title if you want to wait. It will take a while."

"Never mind. Thanks anyway."

Thirty minutes of Google searches on Dmitri Versakos' name turned up nothing much. Then she tried Seth Versakos, the little boy who'd been her friend, and came up with five results. On the fourth try she found the son.

"I'd like to speak to Seth Versakos, please."

"Speaking."

"Seth, I don't know if you remember me. My name is Miller Abel. We used to play together as kids. In Hammond."

"Miller. Yeah, I remember. How long ago was it? Fifteen years or so?"

"More than twenty."

"Oh. Yeah. Of course. We left there in '89."

"You live in San Mateo now?"

"Yeah. I run a small auto supply store. I can't seem to shake the Midwest steel belt mentality. How about you?"

"I still live in the Region. I work at North American Steel. It used to be Calumet and Northern Steel back when you lived here."

"Right. Well, how about that?" She could hear his thought almost as if he said it aloud. *Enough with the small talk. What the hell could you want from me?*

"Is your mother well?"

"She's doing all right. A few health issues. She remarried and lives in Santa Clara. What about your family? They all well?"

Silence. She swallowed and jumped in with both feet. "My family was murdered two months ago." She waited for him to absorb it and utter the usual awkward condolences. He did. "I was calling because I'm doing some family history things. I wondered if it would be possible to get in touch with your mother."

"Family history, like ancestry stuff?"

"Sort of. I'm putting together a history of my family, and I wanted some reminiscences from friends over the years." The explanation sounded pathetic or maybe not, since he bit. "Sure. I can give you her number. She's just out of the hospital a week and recuperating. Her name's Edith Andes now. Got something to write on?"

She took down the information.

"I'm really sorry about your family, Miller. Were you an only child?"

"No. I had a brother. He died also." Twenty years put a deep silence hole between them. Who wanted to reminisce about someone's murdered family? He made no mention of his father.

Miller dialed. "Mrs. Andes?"

"Yes?"

"This is Miller Abel. You knew my family twenty years ago in Hammond. Your husband was my dad's boss."

"Oh." She said. "Yes. I remember you. How are your parents?"

"They've both passed on."

"Oh dear. I'm so sorry. It's so sad that we're all getting up there in years." She trailed off. Miller held back about murder. The woman sounded too weak to handle anything that traumatic.

"I'm compiling a history of my parents' lives, and I was looking for information or any memories. I was hoping you could tell me some things." The explanation sounder lamer out loud than it had when Miller first formulated it in her mind. Miller pressed on, constructing vague questions on the spot. The replies she got surprised her, the stories tugging at her heart.

The twenty-minute mark passed when Miller threw in a question about the woman's ex-husband. "By the way, Mrs. Andes. You don't happen to have your ex-husband's address or know where he is? I'd like to ask him some questions about his memories of my dad."

"We divorced under very difficult circumstances. I have no information on him."

"I'm sorry."

"Well, it's been a long time now. Some things are better forgotten," she said. This was followed by a five minute diatribe on her ex, ending with "He was a very bad man."

"He ran around on you?"

"Yes and much worse. He, well, he liked younger women."

Miller clutched her phone. The woman couldn't even bring herself to say 'little girls.'

"It was very difficult to keep it quiet during the divorce. I tried my best for my son's sake."

"I can understand that."

"Well, it wasn't easy, especially with all those piles of terrible pictures."

"I'm sorry to bring these things up for you."

"Yes, well, he was very difficult, at any rate, pictures or not. I don't mind telling you he had a very violent temper and used to do things to me that would be considered abuse these days. I'm just happy I got away with my son and the bit of money I was able to salvage from the divorce."

For the next fifteen minutes she ambled through happier tales of her new husband and life in California. Miller finally got rid of the poor woman who'd been married to a sexual predator turned big-time child pornography dealer.

Miller went back to the computer and searched for other sites that pulled up Versakos' name related to sex or any litigation connected with him. She turned up nothing. Whatever the man had done in Florida and wherever he headed next, the police hadn't pursued him for anything major. If he'd run a child pornography site in Florida, he'd escaped without getting caught and slipped away into another darker hole.

Miller shivered. Her stairs creaked twice, followed by thuds as someone slowly made their way up to the landing.

"Miller?" The voice came from down below. "You okay?"

She sighed, pushing aside her computer keyboard and rising. "I'm all right. Come on up, Sparky."

Sparky pushed the screen door open and came in. "What's new?"

"Quite a bit actually."

"Good. Fill me in." Sparky pulled up a straight back chair. "By the way, how's the head?"

"Still aches. I think I'll live though." She smiled at the woman, glad to have the bulldog in her here right now. The woman almost made her want to give up solitude. "I've found out quite a lot about Dmitri Versakos. Basically, he's a snake."

"Well, we'd figured that out yesterday. What else is new?"

"I found his ex-wife and got background information on the man." Miller said.

"Where do we go next?"

"I'm sick of circling him. I'm going to go for the direct approach. I'm heading back to his office and waiting for him to show up."

"At this time of night?"

"No. I'll wait for morning."

"Then what?"

"I'll figure it out when I get there. Confront him. Ask him directly about how the picture of me got online. Accuse him of murder, even, and see how he responds."

"Of course he'll deny it."

"I don't care at this point. I'm tired of waiting around."

****

Wednesday morning Miller pulled on navy cargo pants and a worn T-shirt. She retrieved a pair of dark running shoes from her closet and slid her feet into them. She slipped into a light cotton jacket to hide her .38.

The cold air came from the offshore breeze. It flicked tendrils of hair in her face, and she pushed the stray strands up under her baseball cap. She breathed in the first cold air in weeks and felt her pulses shift into third gear. At last, a shift in the wind.

They took the freeway to Gary, making the trip in a record ten minutes during rush hour. From time to time, Miller glanced over at Sparky, who was looking rested and once more eager to go. She'd debated about refusing to let the woman come along, but how dangerous could it be midmorning in downtown Gary?

They parked in an off-street lot in an alley that reeked of urine. Versakos' building was a monolith to better times.

Miller and Sparky crossed the street, avoiding the sparse morning traffic. Miller pushed open the Meyer's Building front door. A lone guard looked up, did a quick nod, and returned to the newspaper sitting in his lap. They looked conventional enough in today's world of tattoos and piercings. He clearly felt no danger from them or anyone, no need to question who they were, or what they were up to. Who'd expect a middle aged woman and a slightly younger friend to be hauling heat in broad daylight? Even if they were carrying, no one gave a damn in Gary, since almost everyone felt obliged to tote a weapon for protection.

They proceeded to the bank of elevators and took the nearest one. The ride moved fast, screeching to a halt on the third floor. The outer office of Patriot was empty. Behind the inner door they could hear high-pitched laughter interspersed with squeals.

Sparky took a quick sideways glance at Miller. "I think we're interrupting a filming for his website," she whispered.

Miller ignored her and moved to the inner door. She knocked sharply three times. Silence followed something close to a moan. They waited, listening to scurrying sounds behind the door, like mice caught at midnight.

Miller turned the knob and pushed. The door opened slowly revealing the girl from the night before, kneeling on the floor in front of Versakos. The man hurriedly zipped up his trousers.

A tripod stood close by his chair, with a small video camera sitting atop. He leaned over, pushed a red button on the side, and tossed Miller and Sparky a false smile. "May I help you?"

"I'd like to have a few words with you, Mr. Versakos. Alone."

"Ronny, move your butt out and give us some privacy."

The girl stood up and turned. Her spaghetti straps hung down, revealing the tops of small round breasts, pink and glistening.

"Excuse me." The girl moved past them, pulling at her straps. Just a normal day at Patriot Internet Services.

The door shut quietly and Versakos motioned at them to take seats. "How can I help you?"

He didn't remember her. Of course not. She'd been a child with waist length hair a pale blonde, the color only seen in children. Now her honey brown hair was stuffed under a baseball cap and her too-thin face replaced the round pinked-cheeked one of childhood.

"My name is Miller Abel." She stopped, leaving the words hanging in the air like a frozen breath.

"Abel?" His expression didn't change, although a hint of color turned the mottled skin of his neck a shade darker.

"You knew my father. You used to be his boss twenty years ago."

"Oh, yes, of course. Miller. I'd never have recognized you." He flashed her his business smile.

"I'm here about the photos of me on your website." She paused again, giving him time to track the direction she was headed. "You took them when I was ten. They were illegal back then. They're illegal now."

His eyes did a quick dance towards the door, moved back to his desk, before returning to her face. "What do you want?"

"You had no right to take those pictures of me twenty years ago, and you have no right to have them up on a porn site now."

"You have no proof I posted photos of you."

"You deny you posted them?"

"Yes."

"And you deny you took them?"

"No, of course not. You were a cute little girl, and you let me take some harmless photos of you."

"I was nude!"

"I don't know anything about any photos of you on a web site."

"I think you do. And I think you know something about the murders of my family as well." The words shot from her mouth, smoking hot in the cold room. Sparky caught hold of her arm. She pushed it away and rose.

He stood up as well, matching her move for move. "I don't have to listen to this. Get out of here right now before I call the police!"

"Don't worry. We'll leave, but this isn't over. I'm notifying the police of what I've found and that you're involved. I've seen your websites."

"What the hell right do you have coming in here and making accusations? You've got no evidence against me."

"I've got plenty of evidence. There are hundreds and hundreds of illegal pictures of children on your websites. The last time I heard, it was illegal to post pictures of children performing illicit acts or having them done to them."

He reached into his desk drawer. The gun he pulled out was aimed at her chest. "I said get the hell out of here! And if I hear you've taken any of your stories to the police, you'll be sorry you messed with me."

Miller swayed as spots formed in front of her eyes.

"Let's go, Miller." Sparky pulled at her arm again with a quaking hand. "The guy's insane. Let's go."

"I'll show you what insane is, if I see or hear anything more from you." He shook the gun at them. "Now get out of here and don't come back."

Miller let Sparky drag her from the office, down the hall and into the elevator. The door clanked shut, leaving them facing the ornate chrome doors. Sparky's face shone white in the bleak sparse elevator light.

"You okay?"

"No." Miller wiped her hand across her mouth, surprised to find spittle there. She leaned back drunkenly against the chrome bar circling the sides of the elevator. "Thanks, Sparky. I'm okay. Look, I'm sorry I dragged you into this. I should have warned you hanging out with me has its drawbacks. Next time stay home and be my backup from there."

"Miller, dear, I'm not going to let you do this alone."

"Yes you are. I'm not taking you with me again."

"So you're not going to leave it like he said? You're going to keep pursuing this guy?"

"Of course."

"Until he's in jail?"

"Or he's dead."

Chapter Twenty-six

Revenge is poison to the soul

Thursday, July 21st

Miller sat at her desk staring at the picture of Jacob. She'd brought it to work a week after the murders, but this was the first time she could bear to set it out. Her brother stared into the camera, as if laughing at her as he tossed a football to someone.

The day dragged on as usual with new parts to catalog, work orders to write, calls from frantic floor managers with machine problems to handle. No one would ever suspect the plan she was working on as she calmly took care of mill business. And yet coming up with a plan to trap Dmitri Versakos was more difficult than Miller imagined. Even as she turned bolts and oiled the parts of heavy machinery, she wrote out scenarios that would entice him to meet her. All of them she crumpled up and tossed into the wastebasket.

Going over possible actions, she decided the simplest, most direct method was best. She would place a call to his office at the end of the day and tell him she was going to the police tomorrow. If he wanted to talk, she'd be home.

Then she sealed up a plain brown envelope addressed to Matisse at the Chicago FBI field office and dropped it into the mail. A second envelope she addressed to Santos. The originals she placed in a folder, ready to be dropped in a safety deposit box at the bank on her way home from work.

What about Sparky? Shouldn't she get some sort of letter to better explain what Miller was doing and why she was leaving Sparky out? Carefully, Miller hand wrote a letter, using stationary as plain as Sparky's former life. She kept the note brief, just a declaration of her intention to trap Versakos in case she failed.

A sharp pain stabbed her in the chest, so powerful it caught at her breath. She had to kill the man. Kill the man. The words sounded crazy. She didn't care. She'd already committed herself.

At four-forty-five she took a deep breath and dialed Versakos. When his lizardy voicemail came up, she flipped the phone shut. She called two more times with the same result before she left her message.

"This is Miller Abel. I told you I know what you did. If you don't meet me, I'm going to contact the FBI and tell them everything I know. Special Agent Matisse is already aware of you, and I'm sure he'll be eager to talk to you. If you want to avoid the FBI, leave me a message where we can meet." Then she hung up.

Her hope—and fear—was that Versakos would break into her apartment where she'd be waiting, gun drawn. She'd shoot him before she had second thoughts.

Her cell rang as she walked to her car. It rang four times and she let it go to voicemail.

Driving fast, she opened all the car windows and let searing heat rush past her face. Tonight had to be the night. She could wait no longer. Versakos had to come. It had to be tonight.

The alley looked empty. No errant kids, no cars. She pulled to a stop beside her gate and leapt out. She had things to prepare.

The red sun hung directly above her building, about to cast the first shadow of the evening as it eased past the roof. The heat felt like a giant hand pressing down on her bare head. She took the steps two at a time, adrenaline running wild. Something was wrong. Her screen was shut but the inside door stood wide open. She halted, peering in, listening.

Versakos? Had he beaten her here and was waiting inside, gun in hand?

She reached for her bag and pulled out her S&W. Thank God she'd pushed it into her sack this morning. In the past weeks with Matisse around, she'd often leave the gun home. Today she brought it to work with her.

Miller took a deep breath, pulled open the screen, and stepped into her kitchen.

Her table lay on its side, the few dishes she owned smashed on the floor, as if someone had purposely stomped on them. Food from the fridge decorated the walls.

Her heart raced like a runaway train. She turned to her computer. It lay on the floor, along with loose paper and books.

With the gun muzzle pointed dead ahead, she pushed the safety off and took a tentative step down her dark hall, then another.

Flipping on the bedroom light, her breath caught at the destruction. Her mattress was slashed, all her drawers emptied, and her clothes were tossed everywhere, most of them in shreds.

Versakos searching for evidence? He hadn't had time to come to her apartment, since she called him with the threat of exposure. He had tossed her place because of her visit yesterday. Thank God she'd made copies of the photo and stashed the original where no one could find it.

She checked the bathroom. The shower curtain hung like a limp body. Her few cosmetics lay scattered and broken in the shower stall. The roll of toilet paper had been dumped into the bowl.

Moving automatically now, she went back to the kitchen and turned a chair upright. Trembling, she dropped into the seat, gun pointed at the door, waiting for Versakos to burst through.

She debated about calling the police and nixed the idea. They'd want answers she didn't want to give. And they'd be here for hours, keeping Versakos away.

At ten-thirty she flipped on the safety and shoved the gun into her pocket. She stood up, reached for the table and tipped it upright. Avoiding the cheese and soda on the floor, she made her way to her computer, picked it up, and set it on the table. She found the cord, plugged it in, and holding her breath, pressed the 'on' button.

Seconds later the blue screen appeared. She waited, praying for a miracle. It happened when the OS icon popped up followed by her password menu.

The desktop came up and she began opening files. Everything worked. Either he was sure she would never leave what he was after on her computer or in the end only wanted to terrorize her.

****

For two hours Miller checked and rechecked computer data, a stupid exercise in futility as she passed the time waiting for Versakos to show himself.

At last she staggered back to her bedroom, feeling as if she'd already battled with Versakos and lost. She shoved the torn mattress up on its frame and turned it over to the side with fewer slashes. Without bothering to find an undamaged sheet she threw herself down. What the hell difference did it make if she lay in a room that resembled the garbage bin she's been tossed into the day before yesterday? What did any of it matter at this point? It was too late to turn back. Sadness pressed down on her. Too late. The only thing that mattered was getting through tonight and tomorrow, she'd go find Versakos and kill him.

Sleep came quicker than she thought. She woke up in surprise to the jarring ring of her cell phone near her head. She fumbled for the light, switched it on, and blinked at the chaos in the room, remembering last night.

"Hello?"

"Miller?"

"Yes."

"This is Jerry Hayworth, the night guard at the Mill." He hesitated. "Sorry to wake you up. I didn't know who else to call."

"It's okay, Jerry. What's the problem?"

"Mr. Zelenin came in a few minutes ago and ordered me to leave. He said if I didn't, he'd have me fired. I can't reach Mr. Owens, and I don't know what to do. I can't leave my post. I'm the only man on tonight."

"Did he say what was up?"

"Something about evacuating the building. He asked if anyone else was here. I told him no. It seems nutty to me that he even asked. He knows we don't have anyone on the night shift these days, except me. And what's he doing here at night? He's never done that before."

"Do you know where he went?"

"Last I saw him he was going into Foundry Four."

Miller reached for the bedside light. The ovens ran twenty-four/seven, unless one was down for maintenance. Oven Four had its maintenance a month ago and would be running tonight as usual. "Did he say anything about how long you were to leave?"

"Nope. Just said get out, wait three hours, and then call the EPA."

Miller shivered. What was Zelenin up to? Why would he want Jerry to call the EPA? A variety of possible reasons went through her mind, none of them good. Had he found some problem that was about to become a major environmental event? If so, why go in alone?

"All right, Jerry," she said. "I'm on my way. I'll be there in ten, fifteen minutes tops. Tell me where you'll be, and I'll meet you there?"

"I'll be at the first west-side entrance, the one closest to Foundry Four."

"All right. And for God's sake, stay out of his way."

She struggled to her feet, finding her way around the shambles of her room and down the hall. No need to dress since she'd thrown herself on the bed fully clothed. She checked her watch—her confrontation with Versakos had been twenty-four hours and a lifetime ago.

She reached for her backpack, stashed her flashlight and cell phone in it, and shoved the Smith & Wesson in her jacket pocket. She found her keys and did a final scan of her kitchen. Without pausing to let in the fear, she locked the door behind her, and ran down her steps.

She ignored the urge to pound on Sparky's door and beg her to be backup, especially since there was no light coming from Sparky's place. She was probably sound asleep in her king-sized bed.

The Honda engine caught hold on the second try. She eased into first and took the alley slowly, breathing deep to slow her racing pulse.

She glanced in her rearview mirror—Versakos could easily be hiding in the backseat. She was alone.

She drove fast, faster than her normal run to the mill for a machine emergency. Otherwise, it might have been just another late night job. The tension riding with her felt ridiculous, yet refused to abate. It reassured her that the .38 lay deep in her pocket like an old friend.

As she drove down the lake highway, deserted at two in the morning, she rolled down her window and listened to the night noises, constant and reassuring. How many more of these night trips would she be making? One more? An occasional truck passed her, hauling today's last load of steel or petroleum towards the rail yard.

She flipped on her radio. Nina Simone cried out her love for Porgy from an all-night, Chicago blues station. She turned up the volume, letting the music soothe her. She thought about Matisse and the look in his eyes when she'd last seen him, disappointed in her again. She moved on to thinking about sex, picturing his bare chest as he lay beside her, tracing the line of her torso with trembling fingers.

Swallowing, she felt the sting of tears. Not for the loss of Matisse. Rather for the loss of opportunity. For her family and for herself, no marriage, no children. No parents to welcome grandchildren into the world. No future, no future, no future. The words echoed the pounding of her wheels over the road.

Nothing, nothing, nothing.

She ignored the tears and kept driving.

She picked up her cell and punched in Matisse's number, reason overtaken by the urge to hear his voice. Just once more.

"Matisse here." His voice was thick and rusty.

She punched 'End' quickly. Stupid. He'd call her back right away, seeing her number on the caller ID.

She shut down her phone and buried it in her sack. In the distance she saw the lights of North American Steel lighting up the dark, and she shivered.

Chapter Twenty-seven

Morality is often blind belief disguised as good deeds

Friday, After Midnight, July 21

The factory loomed in front of Miller, macabre at night with its monstrous doors. She pulled around to the west entrance and the night watchman stepped out of the shadows. Miller pulled to a stop beside him and climbed out. "Jerry?"

"Miller. Shit. I'm glad you're here." He wiped a hand across his shirt. "Something don't feel right to me."

"It's okay. I'll take it from here. You stay outside. If you see anything funny, call the Whiting cops. And then the Hammond police."

"Hammond PD won't come over here. Out of their jurisdiction."

"They'll come. They're working a case with the FBI related to North American. If anything out of the ordinary happens, don't wait for my okay. Just call them."

"What's this about?"

"Can't say for sure. You have your gun?"

"Yeah."

"Ever used it?"

"Nope."

"Well, don't use it on me if I come out in a hurry. Or anyone else, unless there's a gun pointed at you. Okay?"

"Sure. Just make sure you identify yourself coming out, will you?"

"Yes."

Jerry unlocked a small emergency exit inside the huge foundry door, and Miller stepped silently into the enormous dimly-lit foundry. Her hand rested on her gun in her pocket.

Miller knew every twist and turn of every room, from the slant of the floor to every piece of machinery. She made her way quickly along the hundred yards that led to the eight-foot wide hallway towards the fourth furnace nicknamed "Henry" She pulled the small steel door open with a yank and stepped inside. The furnace lay smoldering, a sleeping giant from metal hell. The groans and heavy thuds echoed around the massive five hundred square foot foundry room as through an ogre resided inside the chamber, protesting against idle days.

Foundry Four lay in almost complete darkness, except for the orange glow from Henry casting shadows. The emergency lights ran at a premium and were set to every third one, along two walls, barely discernible as light.

She moved slowly, ambivalence like a dead weight dragging at her. Instinct warned her she was about to stumble into something very bad, but the idea that Greg Zelenin might be the source of that seemed crazy. And yet Zelenin had warned Jerry off. Why? Whatever happened in North American might involve Matisse's case; however, it was too late to contact him now since inside the foundry itself, the thick lead walls prevented any phone signal from getting through.

Miller moved within five feet of the oven door, the only light source in the shadowy room. Her knapsack hung loosely off her shoulders, the bottom bumping into her butt. A faint scraping sound hit her ears as unfamiliar in the face of Henry's usual grunts and groans. She stood at attention, acutely aware of someone moving in the dark. She exhaled quickly, held her breath, and strained to hear over the pounding of her heart.

She heard the scratching again. It sounded like a piece of metal being dragged over something. She knew what the sound was. Someone had just come into Foundry Four through the far door.

Hidden in deep shadow, someone crossed the floor, a slight squeak with each step.

Miller squinted into the darkness from her side of the enormous room. The figure came out of the shadows in front of her, looking small, his size dwarfed by the thirty-foot ceilings looming above them.

She waited, her heart thundering so loud it seemed as though whoever stood there must hear it. She kept a hand on the gun in her pocket.

"Miller!" The man stepped into the light cast by the oven, close enough for her to make out his face. Greg Zelenin.

She took a step to the side, sensing something threatening about him. "Greg. What's going on?"

"What are you doing here?"

"Jerry called me. He was worried."

"Fucking A! Can't the man obey instructions for once?"

"He was doing his job, Greg." She glanced at the bag he held in his hands and inexplicable fear rushed in, filling her nostrils. She felt for her weapon with fingers slick with perspiration. "What's up?"

"Nothing. I'm doing some late night inspections. Nothing to concern you. Why don't you go back home and get some sleep. There's nothing you need to be here for."

She smelled his fear, a metallic odor mixed with wild animal, and she clutched the pistol tighter. It was easy to recognize deadly intention, her own dangling before her eyes at every moment. Greg looked beyond talking, beyond reasoning, like herself.

"Stop!" The word, maybe fifty feet off, echoed around the walls. "Don't move!"

She knew that voice. Versakos.

Somewhere across the foundry floor she heard shuffling footsteps, moving towards Zelenin and her who were clearly outlined in the light. "Don't move or you're both dead."

"Who the hell are you?" Zelenin called out.

"Dmitri Versakos. Who the hell are you?"

"Greg Zelenin, I work here. Environmental specialist."

"Well, Mr. Environmental Specialist, you've wandered into something you don't want to be a part of. My business is with her. I'm sorry to see you here, buddy, since that's going to complicate things a bit."

The hairs on Miller's head stood up as the voice moved closer. She pushed her hand deeper into her jacket pocket, and the cool metal of the Smith and Wesson hit her palm.

Versakos stepped into the light cast by the furnace. In his hand he held a large gun. He'd have no problem killing them both, before they could do more than take two steps.

"I don't know what the hell you're up to, but before you use it, you'd better think about what I've got." Zelenin held out the baggie containing something white. "This is ricin. Ever heard of it?"

"No, and I don't give a fuck, whatever it is. Don't make another goddamned move or you're dead where you stand."

Miller clutched the pistol tighter, feeling for the safety with trembling fingers. She flipped it off.

The shadows in the room swirled around them and her eyes shifted in and out of focus. Versakos took a step forward, then another. At ten feet she turned the pistol in her pocket, in position to fire through the material. She sucked in air and slipped the hammer back.

"Down!" She screamed the word and pulled the trigger. She never heard him fire back. The first warning he had was a slight sting, like an insect bite. It turned into a burning fire shooting from her thigh into her knee and her leg gave way. She fell to the hard floor.

Fifty feet away, Zelenin fell at the same time, moaning, holding his stomach with one hand. White powder showered his face and chest.

With great effort Miller pulled herself up onto her knees. White powder filled the air and her instincts kicked in. She held her breath, squinting into the semi-dark in front of her. If she was going to die here, she'd make sure she took the scumbag with her.

Versakos lay face up. She saw no movement. No sound came from him.

She tried to get to her feet and fell back as her right knee gave way. Pain shot up her thigh. She looked down. A pool of blood spread out about her foot.

She glanced behind her. Zelenin was on his feet. He looked like a clown, covered in white powder turned a garish orange in the light from the oven.

She crawled and clawed her way towards him.

He raised a white hand. "Stop! Get back! This is ricin all over me. There's no anecdote. If you don't get out now, you'll be dead in forty-eight hours!"

She pressed her head into her jacket, sucked in a breath and called out, "I can't leave you here!"

"I'm already dead! I inhaled too much." He coughed. "It's too late anyway. I'm bleeding out. Either way, I'm dead."

Huddling closer to the ground, she allowed herself a small breath and crawled, inching across the floor towards the door.

"Miller!" Zelenin coughed out her name. "Tell them I didn't mean to hurt anyone. I was trying to do some good!" His words slowed, the pauses longer. "My...one...chance to...be....a hero." The last words fell away, followed by silence.

She searched for the exit, clawing blindly at the floor. A minute later she ducked her head and took in a shallow breath, then raised her head and kept moving. Not towards the exit, but towards the still figure of Versakos. She needed to know.

Reaching across his inert body, she held two fingers in front of his mouth. Nothing. He twitched once, even in death threatening. Then lay still.

Now she began the slow crawl towards life. Cursing herself for her desire to live, she crept along, unable to stop the heaving struggle for air even as she refused to breath.

Zelenin. Versakos. Both dead.

Get out! *Get out!*

It was harder now. She clutched the gun still, jabbing it into her side to keep herself moving. The pain in her lungs matched the throbbing spread of pain up her leg into her buttock.

Grabbing hold of her jacket, she yanked it up over her head and scrambled on, heaving, gagging, wanting to push the dreaded ricin out of her lungs. Blindly she moved on towards the door and safety.

Desperate now, she fought to keep the cloth over her face, the pain in her knee agony.

"God!" The word erupted from her as though spoken by someone else. With hands outstretched, she fought forward.

The door. She had to reach the door. The world spun around her, one hand still clutching at her jacket, pushing it against her mouth and nose.

The door. As if by magic, it opened and a figure in black appeared, an apparition holding a weapon so large it dwarfed the hands that held it.

"Sparky!" Miller yelled. It came out a whisper. "Ricin. Don't come in."

Sparky hesitated only seconds. Miller felt a claw-like grip on her arm, pulling her.

Miller kept the jacket pressed to her nose. "Sparky! Keep your face covered. It's in the air." The muffled words drifted off.

"Hold on, Miller! I've got you."

The last few minutes of escape were the longest. Sparky pulling Miller forward with astounding strength.

Miller caught hold of Sparky's shirt and held tight with fingers slippery with blood. The pain in her leg made her gasp for air, her mind said not to breath. Her body fought the battle between instinct and thought, trembling with the effort.

Sparky wedged her body through the small space and pulled Miller out, both of them falling through as the door clanked shut behind them like the lid of a coffin.

They'd gone from hell to purgatory. The hallway was lit only by a thin stream coming from the low beam emergency lights. The exit lay one hundred yards further on.

"Sparky," Miller wheezed out the single word, unsure what she wanted.

"Hold on."

The sound of Sparky's voice grew faint as if it were miles away.

They edged down the dark hallway towards the watery light, Miller's legs had gone blessedly numb now and she crawled along with a force of her own will and Sparky's determination. They were three feet from the doorway to freedom when she fell forward, panting. Her body refused to move.

Her mind sorted thoughts in slow motion, drowning, reviewing their life. Ricin? Was she going to die? Versakos was dead and she wanted to live.

She slowed her breath, forcing herself to measure each inhalation to a ten count, inhale, exhale, inhale.

Sparky was yelling something now. Miller forced her eyes open and watched as a second dark shadow moved towards them, then heard voices speaking nearby. Someone else joined the group. A halo of light hung over them all, angels in the jaws of hell.

Suddenly she was outside where the night waited. Freedom. Life. The urge to live bubbled up, a tiny burst of desire that rushed through her mind and refused to acknowledge the tight fist that had a grip on her chest, fighting the poison demanding to have its way.

Life.

Darkness settled around her and she surrendered to it.

Chapter Twenty-eight

In every life we are the heroes of our stories

Friday After Midnight, July 22nd

Matisse drove slowly to his motel, the air as heavy as a ripe plum just fallen from the tree. The dread he felt had nothing to do with lyrical references to fruit. The day had turned out to be a bust. Aside from Sedlack's interrogation, he had nothing new. He paced the room, waiting, with a premonition that it was all about to end. When his phone rang, he reached for it on the night table and it fell hard to the linoleum floor.

He fumbled for it under the bed. "Matisse." A dead line. He switched on the bedside lamp. The caller ID read 'Miller Abel.' *Shit.*

He called her back quickly and waited. Instead of Miller's voice, he heard, "The number you dialed is not in service at this time." *Shit and double shit!*

He ran nervous fingers through his damp hair and forced himself to lie back. He still clutched the phone in his hand, waiting for her to call back. The motel room could hardly be rated much better than a dead space, impersonal and without any sense of humanity about it.

His phone rang again and he jumped this time and dropped it again. It landed on his chest, vibrating there like an artificial heart. Irrationally, his heart pounded like a gazelle on the run from a panther on the prowl.

"Matisse."

"This is Sparky, Matisse. I'm sitting outside North American Steel. Can you get here ASAP? Miller's inside and something's up." Her high-pitched voice telegraphed her fear better than her words.

Matisse only paused a second. "I'm on my way. I'll call when I'm on the road to get an update. You good for now?"

"Yup. 10-4."

Matisse smiled grimly as he threw on clothes, pulled on his shoulder holster, and dropped his phone in a pocket of his trousers. He reached for his keys and his jacket, not bothering to put it on.

He pressed redial when he hit the main highway.

"Sparky here."

"You still good?"

"Yeah."

"Give me a quick overview of what happened to-night and the layout of the entrance where you are."

"I followed Miller here about thirty minutes ago. She pulled up to the west entrance. The night guard, his name's Jerry, said he met her. He told her a guy who works at the place by the name of Greg something came over an hour ago and told the man to beat it. The guard, Jerry, got worried and called Miller. He said they were in Foundry Four. I'm at that entrance."

"It's not normal that this other guy turned up? Not just a normal night call for Miller?"

"Not according to the guard. And then I got really nervous when I saw Versakos pull up." There was a slight pause. "He's the guy who threatened Miller. He went inside."

Fear shot through Matisse like a fist punching a hole in his chest. "Shit. What the hell is he doing there?"

"Exactly. Matisse, I have a bad feeling about this. Get back-up here. I'm at the west entrance, sitting in my car."

He heard a muffled cry, then small sounds like fire-crackers.

"Damn. I'm going in, Matisse."

"Stay where you are. I'm five minutes away."

"I'm going in!"

The line went dead and Matisse cursed. He reached down and pulled out his bubble light, slamming it on top of his car. He pressed down on the accelerator and hit ninety in ten seconds.

As he drove he put in a call to Santos.

He took eight more minutes to reach the west side of North American Steel. Matisse pulled up with a squeal of brakes. He twisted off the ignition, flung open the driver's side door, and leaped out. He drew his Glock and headed for the door.

Miller. Miller. Zelenin. Miller. Sparky. Miller. Versakos. The names drummed over and over inside his head. It didn't matter since his body knew the drill. He ignored his fear and moved fast, ducking under the link barrier between the concrete girders.

Sirens screamed in the distance. *Thank God.*

The last fifty yards he took at a sprint.

He stopped just inside the dimly lit hallway, adjusting his vision in the dark. The passage ahead ran fifty yards, at the end of which he saw a small red sign that read Foundry Four. He flicked the safety off his Glock and moved to the wall, sliding along the pale tile towards the gun metal gray door. His automatic felt reassuring.

The door burst open and a dark figure burst out, crouched low, dragging a body.

"FBI. Put up your hands!" Matisse yelled.

"It's Sparky, Matisse! I've got Miller. We need a doctor!" Her voice echoed off the walls. "Ricin poisoning! She needs oxygen."

"Take the light." He pushed the flashlight into Sparky's hands and pushed her aside. He caught hold of Miller and pulled her against the far wall. He felt for her pulse. It was irregular but strong. He could see she had a faint white powder dusting her shoes. *Ricin.* Forty-eight hours before the full effects kicked in. No known cure.

"Who else is in there?" he yelled at Sparky.

"I didn't see anyone else. I just opened the door, found Miller inside, and grabbed her."

Matisse pulled out his cell. "Santos. Where the fuck are you? We need a medic in here."

"Outside. The EMS is just pulling up!"

"Get a Hazmat unit out here now. And some back-up. We've got possible ricin contamination." Matisse turned back to Miller, trying to pull out of his memory emergency procedures for breathing. He glanced up at Sparky. "You okay?"

"Yeah. I'm good."

He bent over Miller. With ricin, CPR had to be chest pressure only. He ran his hands over her body and encountered something sticky. "Shit! Blood. She's been shot."

Sparky knelt beside him. "Don't touch her feet, she said." She took off her jacket and pressed it against the oozing wound.

He nodded and began chest compression. "Miller," he called out. Press, release, call her name, press, release.

"We've got it now." An EMS nudged Matisse aside and took over the chest compressions.

"It's ricin poison. So chest compressions only. Don't breathe any of that white crap covering her feet. And watch her leg. She's been shot."

Large, round eyes meet Matisse's. "Sure it's ricin?"

"Sure enough to warn you to take precautions."

Another medic appeared and threw Matisse a questioning look.

"FBI," he told them.

They exchanged glances. "Get on with the chest compressions," one of the medics called out. "I'll grab the tank."

Seconds later, the man came back hauling oxygen. He slipped a mask around Miller's head and adjusted it, then began checking vitals.

Santos placed a hand on Matisse's shoulder. He took one look at Miller. "What the hell happened, Matisse?"

"Ricin. Stay out of Foundry Four. We need Hazmat now!"

"Jesus Christ! Anyone else inside?"

"Don't know. Sparky dragged Miller out. She only got a quick look, but says she heard more than one shot."

"How bad is Miller?"

"Looks like a flesh wound to the leg. The bigger problem is exposure to ricin. At least her vitals are stable," Matisse said. He didn't add she could be dead in forty-eight hours depending on how much she'd inhaled.

The med techs were starting an IV now, ignoring the two men and the woman standing over them.

"How far away is the Hazmat unit?"

Santos barked questions into his cell and turned back to Matisse. "They're outside. We need to get some lights in here."

The doors burst open and orange suites appeared wearing oxygen tanks. From then on, all hell broke loose. Lights flooded the hallway, with people rushing in carrying equipment. The hall filled up.

The EMS had Miller on a stretcher and moved her out of the chaos.

"So what the fuck happened here, Matisse?"

Matisse motioned Sparky forward "This is Special Agent Dougherty, Chief. Let's get out of here."

The three of them stepped outside and Matisse took the first deep breath he'd taken since he'd pulled into the lot. "Sparky, you sure you're okay?"

"Yeah, just adrenaline overload."

"Give Chief Santos a rundown of events tonight."

"Miller did a night run here to the mill around two and I followed her. The night watchman told me he called her because another employee by the name of Zelenin was acting peculiar." She went over the events she'd told Matisse.

When she got to Versakos' name, Santos stopped her. "Versakos? What's he got to do with any of this?"

The question hung in the air as they all watched the EMS load Miller into the back of the van.

"Fuck," Santos said.

The single word captured Matisse's feeling perfectly.

****

The next hour moved fast, too fast for Matisse to have much time to worry about Miller. He gave Santos everything Sparky had been passing to him in the past two days about Versakos, with Sparky adding her own comments.

Hazmat strung up spotlights that cast a cruel shadow on the scene. People swarmed everywhere, most of them in Hazmat gear. At the end of the hour, the team determined there were two bodies still inside Foundry Four, both without signs of life.

One of the Whiting cops brought the night watchman over to Santos and Matisse. "Miller going to be okay?" Jerry asked.

"We don't know, but she'd better fucking be okay." Santos said. He declared this like a threat to no one in particular. "You were here tonight when this whole thing started?"

"Yeah. Just me. I always work the night shift."

"What happened?" Santos asked.

"That guy, Zelenin, who does the EPA stuff, showed up here about two this morning. He ordered me to go home. The guy's not on the nighttime emergency call list, and he was acting sort of crazy. It just didn't feel right to me, so I called Miller." The man rubbed his face. "Jesus! I wished to God I never called her now. What happened in there?"

Santos ignored the question. "Call someone in to take your place here and get yourself home. And make sure you give one of my officers your contact information. We'll take down a statement tomorrow."

The guard nodded and left.

Fifty yards away EMS looked ready to close the door and move out.

"Hold it," Matisse called out. He motioned to Sparky to follow and jogged over to the door of the van. They both climbed inside.

Miller lay on her back with an oxygen mask snapped to her face. Her eyes were open. "Miller," he said, "Sparky will go with you to the hospital. You're going to be all right." She blinked once and shut her eyes.

Suddenly, the most important thing in his life was the survival of Miller Abel.

Matisse and Santos watched the ambulance pull away and stepped back as more Hazmat people pulled up, dragging out equipment.

"What the hell happens now with this ricin crap?" Santos asked.

Matisse shrugged. "Aside from one incident out in California last year, ricin hasn't been seen in this country for over ten years. Too dangerous to handle, even for terrorists. So there's no saying how this is gonna go. The first order of business is to isolate the room and make sure nothing, airborne or otherwise, gets out of that room."

Santos listened, nodded, and then intercepted one of the figures in orange. He flashed his badge at the man. "I need an update. We've got a crime scene we need to see and two bodies. How long is it gonna be before we can get inside?"

"We've got almost all the contamination contained to the one room, and we're in the process of starting cleanup. We'll let you know as soon as you can get to the bodies."

"Hell. If you're doing clean up, you'll destroy my crime scene."

"We'll be taking photos and do our best to keep things as intact as we can. Otherwise, you'll have a city-wide crime scene if we don't get the ricin contained."

Santos sighed and turned back to Matisse. "I assume those two bodies must be Zelenin and Versakos. What the hell does ricin have to do with Versakos? And how the crap did Miller get in the middle of all this?"

"Right now I can only guess. I'm assuming Zelenin was the one with the ricin and Versakos followed Miller here." Matisse said. "I've got the FBI's Hazardous Materials Response Unit on the way to work with your local unit. They'll be here by morning, along with an EPA investigating team."

"Yeah, okay." Santos looked gray in the fluorescent lights of the parking lot. "I got a feeling we're gonna need all the help we can get with this one."

"It's your crime scene for now." Matisse said.

****

By dawn, the local Hazmat team had the site secure around the foundry and began gaining limited access. They set up a camera to take a look inside Foundry Four. Everyone wore masks. All the exhaust systems from the foundries had been shut down, and Santos notified the owner that the plant was closed for the day. Emergency mill workers were let in to the other foundries to manage the furnaces and keep things static.

Matisse pushed his mask aside and wiped perspiration off his face. He glanced at his watch. Thank God the FBI team would be here soon. Ricin occurrences were so rare in the States, no small team could deal with this mess. The team had cordoned off the west side of the building, while reporters and North American employees wandered about in the east lot.

Santos, who looked as exhausted as Matisse felt, leaned against a wall, coffee in hand, chewing on a donut. He picked up another cup and held it out to Matisse. "Any word on Miller?"

Matisse sighed and took the cup from Santos. "They've got her stabilized in ICU." His stomach churned and the smell of the donut made it roil. "Sparky says she's resting, doing okay. They've got her on O2, taking saturation studies hourly." He stopped, not wanting to tell Santos the truth, that Miller had only a 50/50 chance she'd make it. Instead, Matisse told Santos, "They say she's got a 50/50 chance to come out of it without lung damage."

"Christ, Robert. She's gotta make it, I'm not gonna let her die too."

Matisse met his gaze and saw more pain than the man wanted him to see. He reached over and squeezed Santos' shoulder, knowing he'd hate any show of affection. The man didn't flinch, just nodded, and whispered something that sounded like 'thanks.'

"We've got the camera set up. Want to come over and take a look-see inside the scene with me?"

They moved into the building, heavy with hot, stale air, now that all circulation systems were turned off.

The camera was set up at the south entrance, as far as possible from the nearer west door where the contamination would be stronger. The first view showed a dim interior, hazy and distorted. Working the lens, the view moved into focus. On the floor lay the two prone figures. The infrared equipment detected no life in the room.

"Can you get it closer?" Santos asked the woman working the camera to move in for a close-up. The video made a quiet hum, capturing the scene for CSI.

Matisse inhaled sharply when he got his first look at the faces. Zelenin lay facing the camera, his face easily identifiable. The other body would be that of Dmitri Versakos, his glazed eyes staring into the camera in death.

Chapter Twenty-nine

A happy ending is dependent on where the story ends

Three days later, July 25th

A gray veil descended about Miller. Her world felt as remote as a dream too vague to remember the next morning. She was aware of people standing over her, talking in voices too low to hear. Matisse had turned up, too late, she thought, with a sad sense of loss. She didn't have the energy to stay alive.

By the third day, the voices drifted away and new figures appeared surrounded by light. Her mother, followed by her father, and later that night, Jacob stepped up to her bed. They said nothing.

Hallucinations, she reassured herself, more real than the nurses, more real than Matisse who stood by her bed or the window, peering silently at her. It was her family who she felt standing guard beside her bed. They continued to be silent but she knew what they said as if they'd spoken the words aloud. *Stay, Miller. Stay and complete this life. It's not time for you to leave. You still have a life to live.*

She'd first been wheeled down a hall and into an elevator, whisked into a room where the beeps and tubes multiplied. Her family followed her to the new room, hanging around until Matisse or Sparky or a nurse turned up, when they'd dissolve into the grey mist surrounding her bed.

Matisse, or his shadow, seemed to be present all the time now, speaking in some foreign tongue or some way where only his mouth moved and the sounds didn't reach Miller.

She was aware of the hospital staff only vaguely sensing them switch out IV bags, push O2 into her, adjust her mask. Time melted into a long tunnel with no beginning and no end, the light saturating and filling the world to overflowing, the glow blinding. Then suddenly, the glow began to subside as if someone had adjusted the light and moved it further and further from Miller.

Seventy-two hours after her exposure she'd survived the live or die cut-off point with ricin. At that point, the hospital moved her out of ICU. From then on the medical staff focus its attention on booting her out and freeing up the bed. The leg hurt like hell and bled a lot. In the end she needed nothing more than a few stitches for the wound. Her eyes suffered some minor ricin exposure and would need ointment for the next six weeks, and her lungs would require frequent monitoring. Soon it became clear there was no permanent damage. All in all, she'd done well. And now she was forced to confront a new future for herself with no revenge as a motive for living.

Sparky apparently stayed glued to the ICU, and when they moved Miller down to a med floor, the woman stood back as they wheeled Miller into the new room.

"Sparky," Miller whispered, her throat raw from the ventilator. "Sit down. You're making me nervous." Sparky turned from the window and came back to the bed.

"I'm sorry. I'm antsy. I need to be getting back to the scene."

"Please don't. No one's told me anything. I need to get some answers myself or I'll go crazy."

Sparky glanced around, found a chair, and pulled it over beside the bed. "I know. I probably shouldn't be doing this since you're still in serious condition. I'll do my best to update you as fast as I can before they catch us." She glanced up. "I can't give you a lot of answers right now, you know."

Miller nodded and shut her eyes. She felt strange, a ghost visiting the world, as if she wasn't a permanent fixture. She took some slow breaths and opened her eyes to see Sparky's watching her.

"Take it easy, Miller, okay? Let me do the talking. You're pretty sick."

"Yeah, I know."

"Ricin. You know the drill. Watch for signs and symptoms. So far, so good. Want some water?"

"Yes," she whispered.

"First off, I am Sparky Dougherty and I was a nun. Now don't get mad when I tell you I'm also Special Agent Sparky Dougherty."

It was Miller's turn to stare. She mentally shuffled through the past weeks, searching for some evidence of that statement.

"Why were you pretending?"

"Matisse's idea. To have a backup around to watch over you. And I'm from the Region, so it was a natural. Most of what I told you was true up to a point. I do like the apartment, though. I'm even thinking about staying there. Anyway, at first I was watching you. Matisse wasn't sure he could trust you, if you were involved in some way. And he promised Santos you'd be safe, if you worked with him. When things got crazy and he took the investigation away from you, he asked me to stick close."

Miller shut her eyes tight. What the hell? Matisse had hired a babysitter for her. She felt like a fool.

"Matisse is busy now working the case, so I'm here hanging over your bedside."

"Great. Well, tell him I'm fine. Please just go." She was too tired to care how harsh the words were.

Sparky shifted around, her frustration expressed in restless movements. "Okay, just let me finish. Matisse is at the scene. He's been by at least four times while you were in ICU. The EPA Hazmat arrived two days ago, and he's got his hands full juggling all the teams."

"What happened to Greg?" She knew the answer and still had to ask.

"Dead at the scene. Gunshot. Probably better in the end, since ricin was all over him. They're still trying to piece together the events."

Miller started to speak and Sparky held up a thin hand. "Don't, Miller. Save your strength. Since I started this, let me finish it. I'll be quick."'

Miller sank back, and listened to the rest of her litany.

"I followed you to the mill, watched you talk with the night watchman, and head in. When Dmitri Versakos pulled in five minutes later and headed inside also, I called Matisse." Sparky picked up Miller's water glass. "Water?"

Miller felt the touch of a straw on her lips and opened her eyes. Sparky held the straw close to her mouth. "Keep drinking. They want you to keep taking in fluids."

"And what does this ricin thing have to do with Versakos?"

"Nothing. Just a coincidence he turned up when Zelenin was getting ready to dump ricin into the waste water. Your dad found out his assistant, Henry Winston and the CEO of North American were conspiring by dumping illegally to save money. Jeffrey Owens found out, and he hired Joe Sedlack to kill him when Cornell threatened to expose the whole thing. Zelenin knew about the dumping from Wayne Cornell and kept stalling on doing something. When Cornell got killed, I'd guess Zelenin got scared and decided to go ahead with the ricin thing." Sparky stopped. "Should I stop or you want the rest?"

Miller waved a hand at Sparky. "Go on. I need to know this. In case I don't make it."

"Blast it, Miller! Don't say that. So, anyway, I found you inside the mill crawling across the floor of the foundry. And the rest is history."

Miller sighed. "I can't believe Greg was really going to dump the ricin. I think he thought he could, I can't believe he would have gone through with it. Except Versakos came along and the whole thing blew up on him."

"So Versakos came there to shoot you, right?"

Miller nodded, suddenly feeling too sick to respond.

"We've got the gun. Two rounds fired. One of the bullets got you. The other Zelenin. You shot Versakos?"

"Yes," she said. "He's dead?"

"Yup. You got 'um. The mill's been shut down until the EPA can clean it up. They're working to keep the ricin from contaminating the public water system. So far they believe the threat's contained."

Miller started to cry, silently without opening her eyes.

"Take it easy Miller. It's gonna be okay now. Oh, and Matisse called to say he'll stop by. Probably not today, tomorrow for sure."

Miller turned her head away.

****

On the fifth day, Miller stood at her window, her nose pressed against the pane. It was night and the lights danced across the lake. She heard a sound and turned. Matisse stood there, saying nothing.

"Matisse." That was all she could think of to say. She moved her fingers slightly, and he came across the room and caught her hand.

She stared up into his calm eyes. "Matisse," she tried again, louder this time. He bent forward and brushed his lips across her cracked ones. "How are you?"

"I'm not sure yet." She stepped around him and went back to her bed.

Watchful now, Matisse retreated. He leaned against the wall, watching her.

Then she smiled and he smiled back, releasing something that fluttered in her chest like a small white bird. She sighed. Alive. She was alive. She didn't want to die and she wasn't going to. And Matisse was here.

He tried again. Coming across the room to the bed, this time he caught her hand and bent over, kissing her knuckles. She studied his bent head, the military haircut with the gray growing around the sides. She reached out and touched the nape of his neck, feeling the prickle of the clipped hairs on her fingertips.

He raised his head. "Well?"

"Well, yourself, Matisse. How's your case?"

"Heading towards a wrap, I've just had Sunday dinner with my dad, and I've caught you smiling at me."

She laughed and the world did another tilt. "I'm happy to see you, Matisse. Can you believe that?"

He still held her hand and squeezed it. "You have no idea how happy I am to see you smile. I've spent the last four days looking at your eyelids, wondering if you'd ever smile again."

"I wondered that myself the last few days." She paused, weighing her words. "Actually, in the last few weeks. sometimes I was happy to be alive, Robert. After all the dark thoughts without a future I cared about, I find myself wanting to live."

"Good. That's the best news I've heard."

Her fingers trembled in his, but he didn't let go.

"Matisse, about Zelenin. I don't think he really planned to dump that stuff, just plant a little of it, and call in the Feds. He was desperate and afraid after Wayne Cornell's murder."

Matisse nodded. "I think you're probably right."

"Did he succeed in exposing North American Steel?"

"Probably. The EPA is definitely on to the whole business. Owens is definitely out on his ass. And the bank is searching for a way to recoup losses, so they may have a buyer lined up."

"I can't believe Jeffrey had Wayne Cornell killed. It seems impossible."

"Our friend, Joe Sedlack, turned out to be working for Owens, who paid him to make sure no one got close to uncovering the illegal activity at North American. And we're pretty sure Sedlack was the one who knocked you out and dumped you in the garbage bin the other night, since you were getting too close."

She sank back, avoiding the obvious subject. "And Versakos?"

"You ready to talk about him?"

"Yes. I need to."

"We've gotten your side of the story from Sparky," he said. "Bet that surprised you."

"Yeah, you got me there. How'd someone talk a woman like Sparky into joining the FBI?"

"Wasn't hard. She's a natural. Ditzy is a perfect cover." He let go of Miller's hand.

"What do you need to know about Dmitri from me?"

"We did a thorough search of his office, got into the shit pile of web sites he calls Patriot. And we've moved on to the bigger syndication who owns him, lock, stock, and all that crap. That's what made him desperate enough to commit murder, Miller. A hundred million dollar, world-wide, child pornography cartel, of which he's a very tiny, unimportant piece. Except he's responsible for the Chicago markets and he's a loose cannon. Either he covered his tracks, got himself clean of threats and evidence, or he'd be a dead man. Your family got in the way."

"I know." She sagged back, feeling as tired as she'd been in weeks. "My fault, Robert." She held up her hand. "I know. I was just a kid, yet all the dark things that happened because of my secret is unbearable to think about. If I'd told them twenty years ago, maybe, just maybe they'd have survived. Jacob wouldn't have found the picture of me on the Internet and he'd still be here."

"Miller. Don't hash that over. Not right now. Later, when you're feeling up to it, you can indulge in recriminations all you want. I'll be there to knock some sense into your head when you do. Right now, I can't justify knocking you around."

"Is that some sort of offer, Robert?"

"I guess it is. What do you say? Can I count on you to invite me in when I come calling once you're out of here?"

She smiled faintly, wanting so much. Needing. "Yes." The whisper held a promise.

Epilogue

The best future is invented

Miller knocked twice on the door, pressing Jacob tighter against her. He squirmed and reached for the ice cream cone, leaving a streak of chocolate on the white cotton.

"Darn. Watch it, Bub."

He grinned, his one small tooth making him look like a drunken old man. His hair, the exact color of Matisse's, curled around his chubby neck. It would be only a matter of time before Robert won out and gave the kid a buzz cut.

Lexie opened the front door, holding onto a little girl of six who was wearing a paper hat.

"Happy Birthday, Carrie!" Miller stepped inside and set her son down. At one, he had been walking three weeks. He toddled off toward a red balloon drifting into the dining room,

"Where's Matisse?" Lexie asked.

"He's meeting us here. He went out to breakfast with Lou Santos."

"When's that guy going to retire?"

"This year, he says, although I can't see him giving up his job. He loves this town too much."

Miller rubbed at the chocolate spot the size of a silver dollar decorating her right breast. "Ugh. I can barely manage one kid. How am I ever going to get the hang of two?"

"Miller. Hey, cool!" Lexie reached out and snared Miller in one-armed hug. "You're gonna be great! Who'd have thought two years ago you'd join the kiddie parade."

Miller hugged her back and smiled. The sadness felt gentle now, with brief moments of regret for what her parents and Jacob had missed. She kissed Lexie. "Well, we'll see how it goes. Robert's talking about four or five kids."

"Speaking of the fiend, here he comes now. Is it sex driving the kid bandwagon or does he really love living in chaos?"

"Hard to tell. He does like sex. I think he also wants to make up for lost time. He's on the down side of forty now, so maybe filling our house with kids is some sort of compensation."

She watched her husband climb out of his Corvette. He loved that car. Any excuse to drive alone, and he'd have it out of the garage.

"So you're moving back to Whiting? The deal's done?"

"We sign today."

"God, I'm excited, Miller. You'll be so close by. Our kids can be friends. It's the Cornell place, right?"

"Yes. Normally out of our price range, yet a steal with the housing market the way it is. I thought the realtor was going to kiss our feet."

Matisse did a quick tattoo on the screen door and stepped inside. "Hi, Lexie." He came over to Miller and slid an arm around her, dropping a quick kiss on her cheek.

Lexie punched him lightly on the arm. "So, big guy. I hear you're adding to the population again. Trying to catch up with me?"

He grinned and pulled Miller closer. "At least. You don't think I'm too old at forty-seven to be talking more kids, do you?"

"Hell, probably. But these days fifty is the new forty and all that bullshit."

"Well, at least Miller doesn't seem to mind my mid-life need to procreate." Matisse leaned around his wife, searching the room. "Where's Jacob?"

"I think he wandered off after a balloon," Lexie said. "Don't worry. Nothing's in his reach. And my oldest will herd him around. They're back in the family room."

"How's Lou?" Miller asked.

"He's good. Talking retirement as usual, but I don't think it'll happen this year. He's excited we're moving back to the Region. Already setting up ways to rope me into his poker club."

"How's Sparky managing our move?"

"She told me she's looking for a rental opening up at your old place in Whiting." He stared down at her chest. "What the heck did you get on you?"

"Ice cream. Jacob's work."

"He picked a great spot." He dabbed at the brown blob on her white tank top perfectly perched over her nipple.

"Yeah, well like father, like son."

He bent over and gave her another quick kiss. "You feeling okay?"

"Sure. I'm an old hand at this pregnancy thing. All I need is to figure out how to manage them once they come out."

"You'll manage. You're one tough engineer lady. That's one of the things I love about you."

The End

About the Author

Lynn Romaine has a Master's Degree in Information Science from Indiana University. She has worked in various writing and editing capacities for ten years, as well as having published four novels. This year she received the Midwest Writers Fellow for her current manuscript, Night Noise, published by Turquoise Morning Press.

In 2008 she created Red Pants for the World, a project encouraging young women in difficult circumstances to find their self-expression through words that inspire the world. Red Pants is currently working with Solidaire Provence Afghanistan to bring education to the women and children of the most remote villages of Afghanistan as well as working with various programs to support young girls discovering the power of writing. (www.redpantslegacy.blogspot.com)

www.lynnromaine.com
www.womenwritersunderground.blogspot.com

More books by Lynn Romaine

Leave No Trace, The Wild Rose Press
Long Run Home, The Wild Rose Press

Red Pants for the World—
An army of women living created lives out to alter the planet.

Red Pants is an organization committed to women finding their self expression and creating great lives. *Red Pants* sources writing groups for young girls, education for women in Afghanistan and various eco-lending projects through www.kiva.org

www.redpantslegacy.com

If you liked this *romantic suspense* novel by Lynn Romaine,
you might also like romantic suspense novels by these
Turquoise Morning Press authors:

Cheryl Norman—*Rebuild My Word*

Cat Shaffer—*No Safe Place*

Cat Shaffer—*Kentucky Blues*

Romantic Suspense
by Turquoise Morning Press
www.turquoisemorningpress.com

Thank you!

For purchasing this book from
Turquoise Morning Press.

We invite you to visit our Web site to learn more about
our
quality Trade Paperback and eBook selections.

www.turquoisemorningpress.com
www.sapphirenightsbooks.com

You can also find our books at many digital and print
retailers, including:
Amazon
Barnes and Noble
All Romance eBooks
OmniLit
Bookstrand
Diesel eBooks
Kobo
Sony Reader Store
Apple iBooks Store
Smashwords
Coffee Time Romance eBookstore
1PlaceForRomance
1EroticaEbooks
XinXii
Owjo

Turquoise Morning Press
Because every good beach deserves a book.
www.turquoisemorningpress.com

~~~~~

Sapphire Nights Books
Because sometimes the beach just isn't hot enough.
www.sapphirenightsbooks

Made in the USA
Charleston, SC
11 July 2011